SURVIVING UNION GRACE

JOURNEY SLOANE

A book is not something you do solo starting out. Without a good foundation, a house can't be built. Thank you to the women who made it possible for me to even have a Dedications page.

"Surviving Union Grace is an absolute blast of a ghost-hunting tale. A perfect, skin-crawling abandoned hospital setting, intriguing history, and kickass characters, Journey Sloane pulls no punches and plunges their readers into scares from the very beginning. An exciting new voice in horror—I'll read everything they write."

- **Laurel Hightower**, author of *CROSSROADS and THE DAY OF THE DOOR*

PROLOGUE

Surviving Union Grace

By Journey Sloane

If there was anything positive about the dead surrounding me, it was the way they drew heat from the air.

And you, too, can have your own personal, non-polluting, rechargeable air conditioner for the small price of rousing the dead! Unfortunately, side effects include killing the people you love. Still, in this heatwave, who's gonna blame you, really? The booming, playful commentator's voice in her head belonged to her best friend, Emerson. He'd been Jiminy Cricket to her Pinocchio since she was thirteen. Since...

Eventually, even the peaceful dead responded to Charlie Hawkins' unconscious call. The sheer predictability of it made her sigh even as the grande java chip frappe slid slug-like across the ancient oak study table. Thankfully, the spirit moving the drink was scooting it on the coaster she'd placed it on. Whomever it was, they weren't looking to make a mess. At least not right now. It gave her time to stop it. Stop this one just in time to go do the opposite at Cheswaithe.

Surrounded by dark tables peppered with a handful of

people reading and taking notes, she was leery of making a scene, but she couldn't ignore what was happening. When a spirit did something like this, they wanted attention. If she didn't give them what they wanted, there was a small chance they might escalate. Small, but not something she could ignore. If its activity escalated, people could get hurt. She knew that better than anyone. Keeping her head down, Charlie placed her open hand on the table and whispered, "Have mercy on my uncaffeinated soul, please?"

The drink stopped sliding, but the spirit lingered. She couldn't see it. It didn't even have enough presence yet to make the air ripple, but she could feel it. Both in the unnatural, but not unwelcome coolness that surrounded her and the way hair on her forearms lifted as if charged with electricity.

A thud from the aisle on the right side of the library, a book hitting the thin carpet. If they were lingering in a library, they'd likely either been a librarian, or this was a safe space for them. "I hope the book's okay. People should be more careful."

The spirit left, presumably to go check on the book. One of the nearby patrons shushed her. Charlie accepted the shushing with grace, relieved to have ended the encounter with her drink and peace intact. They wouldn't be able to do much of anything, being several feet away from her. At least for a few more hours. But her time here was up, and that made her sad. Libraries were one of the few places where she could be around people without worry, but even here she couldn't overstay her welcome.

She turned her attention back to her computer, sweat dampening her forehead as the air returned to a normal temperature. The spirit's continued presence would have wreaked havoc on her laptop battery if nothing else, but it also battled the oppressive heat the library's beleaguered air-conditioning struggled to defeat.

She bit down hard on the inside of her cheek, almost to the point of drawing blood. Reminding herself to focus, she hunched over her small screen to block out distractions. Cheswaithe Inn, per the anonymous source that had told her about more than a handful of places in the last few months, was an old farmhouse converted to a bed-and-breakfast in the mid-1900s. It had become very popular among certain circles once it got out that a few spirits occupied the inn. However, business had been declining for several years now as the spirits became increasingly less likely to show themselves.

Her source hinted that the old woman who owned the inn could end up losing it if something didn't change. Nobody should lose their home. She'd done her own research on Cheswaithe before heading out this way, but there was little to find outside of r tame paranormal experiences by a handful of folks. That meant she'd had to come closer. Search the local library and any records they had available to make sure it was safe.

As far as she could tell, it was. She was free to head out that way, if the owner was up for a visit. No one had turned her down yet. Why would they? It was a win-win situation for everyone. She slept in a comfy bed for a few days in a row without worrying about people freaking out if something happened. In return, they got a boost to their business for a while afterward. Another unseen benefit to her fucked-up curse.

She wanted to believe in some small way she was balancing the scales.

A little voice in the back of her head laughed, saying, *Don't act like you're doing this out of the goodness of your heart. Just because you get paid to sleep in a bed doesn't mean it's not a business transaction.*

That was her other inner voice, and it was a right bitch. Charlie sighed, and rubbed at the back of her neck, trying to ease the tension setting up in the muscles. Her short brown hair brushed the tops of her fingers, but it wasn't long enough yet to justify taking scissors to it, so she ignored it.

Business transaction or not, the older she got, the easier it was to convince herself most places deserved a visit. Her standards were getting a little slacker each year. It didn't matter that her camper bed was quite nice. It was still a bed in a camper. One she passed the hours of her life alone in. She was so damned lonely.

Charlie hated being alone, though it was safest for everyone. She didn't need a crowd around her. Just one person was enough, as life with her dad had proved. But once he'd died, things had gone all to hell, and she'd found herself trapped in this vicious cycle of having to feed her need for peopling as carefully as possible. Which was how she ended up in this situation. Traveling around the country, staying in places like Cheswaithe, trading off an ability that had taken the lives of people she loved for a few nights in a warm bed and people who thought it was cool when weird shit happened.

It weirded her out if she thought too hard about it. About other people being happy to have ghosts around them. Charlie supposed that was what it was like to be normal. Ghosts were exciting instead of ... terrifying.

Opening the side pocket on her backpack, she pulled out her phone. It took a couple minutes to power on, but then started pinging with notifications. As the surrounding library users shot her dirty looks, she fumbled to turn the sound down, mouthing apologies. She thought she'd put the damned thing on silent. As soon as it was usable, she put the number in her contacts. She didn't dial yet; instead, she slipped her phone in her pocket. Charlie packed away her laptop and miscellaneous items strewn on the table.

As she headed toward the library doors, a book on the receptionist's desk flipped open. The librarian, a younger woman with rainbow bright hair, gasped. "Oh my god, did you see that? Was that ... Edna?" But Charlie didn't let herself look, or even slow down, other than the brief second needed to toss the remains of her drink in the trash can.

Outside, she leaned against her truck and dialed the number. On the third ring, a frail but cheerful voice answered the phone. Charlie awkwardly introduced herself. She hated making initial contact, even if all she was technically doing was booking a room for a few nights. It was so much easier when she could just book through a website. The owner didn't seem phased by the way she stumbled over her words, though. Instead, she just reassured her that there were rooms available tonight and that she looked forward to seeing her.

Charlie hung up and pulled up the GPS. Once she was sure she had the directions memorized (thank God for one-stoplight towns where it was almost impossible to get lost), she turned her phone off and stuck it back in her backpack, then tossed the backpack in the larger Faraday cage taking up precious space in the back of her truck. The Faraday cage was an enclosure made to block electromagnetic fields. Using one seemed to extend the life of her devices. And while a Faraday inside of a Faraday felt like overkill, considering how much time the electronic devices spent in her proximity, she figured it couldn't hurt to be safe.

After closing the back, she opened the door to the 1973 Aqua and White Ford F250 Highboy which had been her constant companion since she turned eighteen. And, for the millionth time, she wished she could paint the damned thing some other color. Unfortunately, keeping it in mint condition made too much sense. Especially if she ever needed to sell it.

"Cheswaithe Inn, here we come," she muttered as the engine purred to life with a twist of the key. "May your ghosts be benevolent, your pillows be soft, and may there be absolutely no fucking spiders. So help me God, Apollo, Ganesha, and Jizo, Amen."

She put the truck in reverse and backed out of the library parking lot. Roughly forty minutes of driving past flat fields teeming with knee high corn stalks, she pulled up in front of Cheswaithe. It was a two-story building recently painted a gleaming white. Pots of pretty pink and purple flowers ringed the large wrap-around porch. Near the door, an old woman sat in a rocking chair. A massive Cadillac was the only other car in the parking lot.

She climbed down out of the truck, small puffs of dust rising from the impact of her shoes on the gravel and got her bag out of the back. The woman stood with a smoothness that surprised Charlie as she got closer. Her grip was firm and dry when Charlie extended her hand. "Charlie Hawkins. We spoke earlier."

"Margarite Cheswaithe, but you can call me Margie, dear." The woman assessed her with bright blue eyes. "I thought I recognized your name. I'm glad to have you visit the Cheswaithe. We do need your assistance. Things have been a bit too calm around here. Cheswaithe's ghosts need their chains rattled a bit."

Her consternation must have shown on her face because the woman gave her a small smile. "The dead only have the power we give them, dear."

Charlie envied her at that moment. That lack of fear meant she'd never witnessed what the dead could truly do. Charlie vowed she'd not stay any longer than she had to. She wouldn't risk powering up the Cheswaithe to the point the lady had anything to fear.

Instead of saying any of that, she smiled and faked a yawn before asking to be shown her room. Once inside, she collapsed face down on a paisley bed cover reeking of lavender.

CHAPTER ONE

"Leave me be." The static-laden demand came through the spirit box sitting on a table near Jacques. Though there were smaller, handheld versions available, this box was the size of a small boombox and outfitted with an LED display that simulated voice waves when in use.

Jacques de Molyneux sucked in a breath and looked into the camera held by Birdie, the tall, heavy-set, bearded main cameraman who had been with him for the past three years. Everyone else wore harnesses with dual mounts for GoPros and flashlights, but Birdie carried a rig that held a high-performance camcorder, a thermal camera, a microphone, and a few other small devices. "You heard that, right?"

It was impossible Birdie hadn't heard, but the viewers needed the theatrics, the confirmation they hadn't imagined what had just happened.

"Yeah," Birdie panned over the corner of the room Jacques sat in, "hard not to."

Resisting the urge to smirk, Jacques cleared his throat and responded. "Am I talking to Miriam Cheswaithe? Is it you, Miriam, who wants to be left alone?"

"Yes. Leave me be."

It was incredible how the voices coming through the spirit box could be so different—in gender, accent, et cetera, —and yet the overall feeling those on the team (and, presumably, the viewers) got was undeniably Southern woman. Jacques was aware of the widespread skepticism regarding the device's authenticity, but he believed in it. Many people assumed ghost hunters, including Banshee Investigations, manipulated the box to fake said the responses. It wasn't hard to do. But Banshee prided itself on never faking evidence. They enjoyed going into a "haunted" building and disproving what others had seen.

It had made them a few enemies, but he didn't care. Ghosts were real, and a respectable investigator either took the time to suss it out, or they didn't investigate at all. Making shit up was *mais c'est ridicule, meme pas pour mentionné*.

Birdie snapped his fingers. Jacques realized he'd been silent too long. "Miriam, are you the only spirit who inhabits the Cheswaithe?"

Silence, yet a chilling breeze encircled him from his left.

"Temperature drop. Ten degrees. Right on top of you," said Mackenzie Smith, their blonde-haired, golden-voiced investigator. Even as a gay man, he could admit she had a voice that could make the dictionary sound sexy. And that was before he paid her to take lessons. Taking the hard edge off her silky tone had been one hell of a business investment.

"I can feel it." He shifted in his chair to face the cold. "Miriam, are you standing beside me? Are you the only spirit in Cheswaithe?"

"No." The word boomed from the speakers on the box. A split second later, a small 5x7 picture that had been on the darkly stained oak mantle over the unlit fireplace rocketed across the room. It slammed into the opposite wall, so close to Jacques' face he could feel the air part with its passing.

The voice coming from the spirit box was different now. The words dipped in malice the way he dipped his sandwich into Au Jus. "Don't know what you think you're doin', walking around like you own the place. Ain't no room for ni-"

Jacques grabbed the box and switched it off, cutting the slur off on the first syllable.

He swallowed the familiar rage down, heat coursing through his body and begging him to rise to action. It was never a surprise when they ran into a spirit who spewed racist rhetoric, but that didn't mean he could control his body's instinctive reaction to it. He wiped damp palms over his khakis and tried to sound perky and upbeat. "Oh, look, old dead white people being racist. Whoever would have thought?"

Birdie snorted.

The hair on the back of Jacques' neck bristled. The spirit box screeched to life once more, scanner moving so rapidly that nothing more than incoherent syllables emerged. Jacques' next breath crystallized in front of him.

Mac stepped back, cursing.

Kiffer, their man in charge of equipment and assistant director for the episodes, backpedaled until he bumped into the wall behind him. His black-clad, extensively tattooed form looked laughable against the cabbage-rose wallpaper.

Clamping down hard on his emotions, Jacques held up a hand. "Stop," he shouted over the squeal of the spirit box. "Get yourself under control. We do not fear the dead."

It was one of the cardinal rules of doing what they did. Fear opened the door for other things. Gave the spirits something to draw from.

Kiffer straightened, squaring his shoulders. Heat flushed his face and neck, lending his olive skin a rosy hue.

Mac, long and lean and looking thoroughly pissed off now, nodded almost imperceptibly then flipped the box a defiant middle finger.

Birdie, who as far as Jacques could tell, hadn't moved an inch, said, 'Bout time we wrap up, boss. Good note to end on."

His words steadied the emotional ground they all stood on. It tempted Jacques to plant one on the man for it.

"Sounds like a plan." He lifted his chin at Kiffer. "Start gathering equipment. Mac, give him a hand. Bird, let's grab the newbie out of the van and do an exit interview with Ms. Cheswaithe."

Their host, a frail-looking woman with an incredibly large bun of blue-tinged hair ruthlessly pinned into submission on top of her head—waited for them in a gorgeous rocking chair that had been in her family since before her birth.

Jacques took the moment before she noticed him to take a deep, fortifying breath. Then she turned toward him, a friendly smile exposing denture-perfect teeth. Her cornflower blue eyes, still sharp even with her advanced age, swept over him, and the smile faltered. "You look a mite unsettled, Mr. Demolono."

The butchering of his last name gave him a tickle of amusement, steadied him further as he strolled toward her. Birdie thumped along behind him.

"A mite," he said, sitting down in a newer-looking (and plainer) rocking chair beside her. As previously discussed, neither acknowledged the cameraman as he moved to find the best angle for filming their conversation. "I was trying to have a pleasant talk with Miss Miriam when we were, ah, rudely interrupted by a gentleman who seemed rather displeased by my presence, *trou du cul.*"

"Ah, that'd be my grandpappy, I suppose," she said, filling a glass with sweet tea from a pitcher sitting on a tiny round table between them and handing it over. As he took a careful sip, she continued, "Racist sonuvabitch."

Jacques nearly spewed his tea at the language coming out of the woman's mouth. "Yes," he cleared his throat, "quite."

The rest of the interview was decidedly more mundane as they reassured her they had found evidence of at least two spirits haunting Cheswaithe Inn. They would mail her digital copies of film and audio once they'd reviewed everything. It was only at the end where things got interesting.

"Lucky you came by when you did," Ms. Cheswaithe said, rocking idly in her chair. "Things were awful quiet until a week or two ago."

He got the impression the woman wasn't ready for her company to go. Since a few more minutes didn't matter, he humored her. "What do you think set things off?"

"That young woman came to visit," she said. "Miss Charlie."

Jacques scowled.

CHAPTER TWO

Later, sitting cross-legged on his bed in a dingy hotel room while moisturizer soaked into his shamefully ashy skin, Jacques woke his computer up. Thankfully, the audio from the Digital Audio Recorder finally completed the transfer. He navigated to the DAR file, renamed it, and began the tedious process of listening to hours of ambient sounds to see if they had picked anything up. The spirit box was handy, but sometimes the DAR caught stuff it didn't. Thirty minutes in, he found their first electronic voice phenomenon. The EVP was a familiar voice, repeating a message it had been telling him for over a year now. "Be careful, Squirt."

Only one person ever called him Squirt. His sister, Ana. Thinking of her brought his mind back to the person he'd been trying not to think about since they'd left the Cheswaithe several hours ago: Charlie Hawkins.

The last time he'd seen her had been the joint funeral for his siblings, Emerson, and Ana. Pale and unable to quit crying, she'd clung to her father's side as they'd filed past the closed caskets topped with white roses. He'd wanted to say something to her then, and again when they came through the receiving line to pay their respects to the family, but he couldn't find the words. He wanted to scream at her. To yell that it was her fault his family was dead. Wanted to hug her and tell her he was sorry and it wasn't her fault. If they had just listened to him, listened like she had, they'd be alive.

He had been nine years old, and the storm of emotions

and thoughts had glued his mouth shut and numbed his surface. All he could do was squeeze her hand when the time came. Wave when he saw them getting into their Volvo to drive away. After that, there'd been a long stretch of time when he hated her. It had taken years of therapy to find peace. Not with what happened, but with everyone's role in it. Still, it was one thing to accept no one person had been to blame for the Event, another to forgive them for the part they played.

The thought ignited a familiar anger, so Jacques tabled it and spent the next few hours listening to the day's recording. He found two other EVPs. Both lower in quality than he liked, but audible, nonetheless. Since both EVPS belonged to Cheswaithe, he noted those. Both on the small, leather-bound notebook he took everywhere, and in the evidence file on his laptop.

He made it halfway through day four of the recordings before exhaustion set in. Carefully, he saved his files, put away the voice recorder, and finished getting ready for bed.

Sliding between the sheets, he loaded up his Banshee Investigations email. Part of his bedtime ritual was sorting through the multitude of suggestions they got from viewers or property owners on where to go next. He got through the first page of emails, mostly trash, before finding an email from a name he hadn't heard in a few years.

Frowning, wondering why Grant Erschon was reaching out to him via his business email, Jacques opened the correspondence.

JACQUES,

. . .

I HOPE YOU ARE WELL. It has been much too long; I believe since my graduation party, correct? We will have to schedule some time on the links in the near future. I owe you recompense from my last defeat.

Tell me, is it true your little ghost-hunting hobby has expanded into actually paying dividends? If this is true, I believe I have a mutually beneficial situation.

As I am sure you well know, there is an abandoned hospital that has been in my family's possession for generations. Unfortunately, it has not always had the most sterling of reputations. After the regrettable gas leak in the 1940s, the decision to distance ourselves from the facility was made. It is difficult to maintain our steadfast support to patient outcomes in the face of so much death. The 1960s were no kinder to us, what with the near constant accidents that plagued the facility. I know my father urged the rest of the family to sell our interests, but he was never able to gain the appropriate traction. Too many of them felt that abandonment of the facility would cause the public perception of the abandonment of our family's causes. You know how fickle public sentiment tends to be. The decision to instead close the facility was made in the late 70s and the building has remained vacant ever since.

Jacques, I wholeheartedly believe the facility is haunted. I have urged the family to investigate, but they continue to refuse out of fear of a public scandal if my theory was proved correct. Due to this, any potential arrangement will need to remain off the books, so to speak. But I have the utmost confidence this ability remains in your purview.

I look forward to speaking with you. Note my new contact details below. My last companion and I did not part mutually agreeable.

REGARDS, Grant Erschon

CHAPTER THREE

Emerson's charred and cracked face filled her vision; angry pink lines ran where the skin split. His beautiful brown eyes, lids missing, pained and desperate as he begged her to help him, seared into her soul. He needed her to rescue him from the cabin's inferno.

Charlie wanted to save him, but she couldn't get her feet to move. She was stuck in the thick circle of salt on the floor, heat baking her skin and smoke swirling around her, but safe. So unbelievably safe. Nearby, a window cracked from the heat, and oxygen slipped through the gap, sending the flames roaring higher.

Charlie couldn't take her eyes off Emerson. Couldn't reach out a hand to him because of the stove knobs filling her hands. She knew they didn't matter now, but still couldn't make herself let go of them. "I'm sorry," she said, tears coursing down her cheeks. "Em, I'm sorry. I'm sorry," she repeated, desperately wishing she could move out of the circle and be with her friend. Even if she couldn't save him, she could die with him. That's what she deserved. To die with her best friend.

"Charlie." His lips formed her name and for a moment, there was something like acceptance in his eyes before malice filled his expression as he sank to his knees. "Your fault. Your fault."

All she could do was keep her eyes on him. Watch as life fled his body, listen as the corpse screamed in a high, trilling beep that got louder and louder—

Charlie jolted awake, grabbing her phone and fumbling for the buttons on the side to turn off the alarm. Then she flopped back against the pillow, swiping angrily at the tears, and stared at the too-close ceiling of the camper. She and Jacques had screamed themselves hoarse, unable to get close to the too-still bodies, before the rapidly spreading flames had forced them to risk the spirits attacking them and flee the cabin.

She needed to believe that. They were already dead. The injuries they'd received ... and she'd screamed for him. Yelled for Emerson to wake up, to roll over and put the flames that seared his skin out. He hadn't moved. Not even a finger twitched. She had not left her best friend to die in the heat of the fire. But that didn't stop her brain from tormenting her with the what-ifs.

Her phone buzzed beside her. She frowned. It was a text from a number she didn't recognize. She almost dismissed it for being spam, but her filters were decent. Out of curiosity and a desperate need to distract herself from the nightmare, she expanded the text.

Charlie, my name is Grant Erschon—Erschon — Her mother's maiden name—*your first cousin once removed on Madeleine's side. I'd like to call you, if you'd be so kind? (Texting first because I know how I react to numbers I don't know! ;))*

She blinked disbelievingly, gaze going. Her mother hadn't sprung from a well, of course, but her mom's side of the family had never tried to contact her. They disowned her mother when she had married Charlie's father, and as far as Charlie knew, that was the end of the story. So why the hell was this Grant guy reaching out after all these years?

And more importantly, how had he gotten her phone number?

She got out of bed and grabbed a bottle of cold brew from

inside the small fridge she kept her perishables in. She indulged in several long drinks straight from the container, then snagged a package of wet wipes and scrubbed her face with one. After the shock of the cold helped her feel a little more alert, she texted him back with her permission to call.

CHAPTER FOUR

Grant Erschon rose and opened his arms to Charlie as the hostess escorted her to their table. He was on the shorter side, but his lean frame and tailored suit made him seem taller. So, it surprised her to find when she stepped into his embrace that her head came up to his shoulder. The hug thing was a bit weird, but she was desperate enough for human contact to hug a virtual stranger.

Grant had thick blond hair and a tan, orange enough she didn't think it was natural. He smelled of some sort of overpowering spice blend that made her eyes want to water, but as he released her, she noted a lingering note of something off. Unpleasant and unidentifiable. It made her uneasy, but she forced a smile and sat without comment after he held out a chair for her and glanced around the room.

She didn't often eat at this kind of restaurant. Where tablecloths didn't have a sheet of paper pulled over them, or fresh flowers on every table. She was keenly aware of the small stain on the hem of her green mid-calf dress and the scuff marks on her thrift-store heels.

A server in a crisp white shirt and black pants appeared before she and Grant said anything to each other beyond hello. She took the menu the woman offered and requested water to drink. Grant ordered a glass of wine older than she was. The menu had no prices on it, and she bit her lip while she studied it. It didn't bode well for her budget.

"It's my treat," Grant said, startling her.

She looked up, embarrassed he'd figured out what she was thinking. "No. I mean, it's fine. I can–I have–"

He pointed a finger at her, one corner of his mouth curling up into a self-assured smirk. "My treat. It's what I like to call ... a business expense. Order whatever you like."

That made her feel a little better even while it pinged home the point that she was way out of her depth having lunch here, with him. She thanked him and turned her attention back to the menu. It was a lot more interesting when she wasn't looking for the cheapest item.

Steak caught her eye, and it didn't take long to decide after that. Decision made, she put the menu aside and looked at her cousin.

Menu already on the table, Grant studied her while he played with a large jeweled ring on his right hand. "Let me guess: Steak. Medium rare. Roasted vegetables?"

Charlie blinked twice in disbelief. "How?"

He stopped playing with his ring and took a sip of water from a gold-rimmed glass. The lines around the corners of his mouth and eyes deepened a bit, making her think he was laughing at her internally. "It's what I would have ordered if someone else was paying. Never settle for less than the best."

The statement felt off somehow. Like he had meant to say more, but cut himself short. She considered asking him to finish his thought, but decided she didn't want to hear what he might say. Also, the familiarity was weird, considering they barely knew each other. "So, you said you had a business proposition?"

He tapped manicured fingernails on the tablecloth. She had cleaned under her nails, but her thumbnails' edges were still ragged. She put her hands on her lap. "I'm a firm believer that business before a meal affects the constitution. Let's set that aside until coffee and dessert. The sugar may help ... sweeten our potential deal."

She didn't want to talk pleasantries. She wanted to ask him about her mom. About why the Erschon family shunned them. Ask if anyone else in the family had special abilities, even if they weren't quite like hers. But all she said was, "Of course." She searched her blank mind for the proper pleasantries. "Uh, did you have a long drive?"

Grant's nostrils flared and he leaned back in his chair, boredom on his face. "I took my private jet and then my driver brought me the rest of the way. My schedule allows nothing so pedantic as driving time these days. In business, every second needs to ... count."

Nothing so pedantic as driving. What a dickhead, she thought. A twinge of wistfulness hit her. If things had worked out differently, her life might have been as easy as his was now.

They passed the next few minutes with small talk that he steered. It made Charlie want to pull her hair out. Luckily, the food came before she got to that point. She was quite happy to lapse into a silence punctuated only by the sounds of cutlery against plates as she dug into her steak. Her small yet tasty steak.

Neither of them talked much until they'd eaten about half their food. Then Grant said conversationally, "Psychic abilities are not unique to the women in our lineage, though, I grant you, your specific talents are peculiar.".

Charlie put her fork down. "Did ... Did my mom?"

"Indeed. One could say her specialty was precognitive dreams. Not as specific a gift as some, but enough to save your grandfather's life."

Her eyebrows went up. Her fork stayed down.

Grant pursed his lips and stared at her for a moment. She could feel his judgment grating against her skin. Finally, he spoke. "When she was just a child, your mother dreamed of your grandfather's demise while on a business trip across the pond. She became hysterical, so much so that your grandfather postponed his trip because of concerns for her health. Lo-and-behold, the plane he should have been on experienced mechanical failure, resulting in the deaths of all aboard. Your mother, Maddy, was only six years old, if you can believe it."

Wow. Her mom, *Maddy*, had saved her grandfather's life. Why couldn't she have a useful ability like that?

"That's amazing," she said and sighed.

Grant took a sip of his wine, lifting one shoulder in a blasé shrug. "Of course it is. But your specific talents are even more valuable."

That depended on your point of view, Charlie thought. And from hers, it was not. But it gave her a chance to ask another question high on her list. "How do you know what I can do? It's not something I go around advertising. And the Erschon family wasn't a part of my life growing up, obviously."

She didn't mean it to come out as bitter as it had. Over the years, Charlie thought she'd made her peace with the way her mom's family had abandoned them. The way her mom had abandoned her when she was three. Apparently, she was wrong.

Grant tapped his fingers on the table again. "We'll get to that first part soon. But to answer the second part of your statement: Your grandfather had very specific plans for your mother and the betterment of the family coffers. Madeleine was aware of those expectations and ignored them. While her ousting was, perhaps, regrettable, it was also understandable. Blood is thicker than water, as they say."

"That's not the actual saying," Charlie said, anger rising at Grant's words. She tried to remind herself that he wasn't responsible for her mother's excommunication from the family, but seriously? How could he talk about it like he was discussing the weather?

Grant arched a single eyebrow. "Enlighten me, then."

"The direct quote is 'The blood of the covenant is thicker than the water of the womb.' It means the opposite of the bastardization everyone flings around."

His lips thinned and his eyes darkened, just for a moment. But then Grant cleared his throat and said, "Well, perhaps that's the public-school interpretation. In other circles, we interpret it ... differently."

Charlie picked up her fork, wondering how much trouble she'd get in for maiming her cousin. She settled for stabbing a piece of steak. Public school interpretation? Pretentious prick. The longer she spent with him, the more she regretted answering his text. *Stab him,* Emerson told her. *Even if you get in trouble, it's worth it.* She ignored the thought, tempting as it was, and narrowed her eyes. "Yeah, I can see how people more concerned with bloodline than intelligence and accuracy would favor the other interpretation."

Grant patted her hand. "My dear, bloodline trumps all else in many cases. You'll learn soon enough." He sat back. "Now, you must try the tiramisu. It's to die for."

Without waiting for her response, or even acknowledging her still half-full plate, he waved the server over. "Two tiramisu and two cappuccinos."

He turned back to her and said, "I find the double-dose of caffeine most beneficial this late in the afternoon."

Charlie popped the bite of steak she'd stabbed into her mouth even as the server was removing her plate. She chewed slowly, hoping to give herself time to calm down. He'd called her there for a reason. One he'd assured her would be profitable. She needed to at least hear him out before she told him to fuck so far off he'd die of old age before making it back to where he sat now.

Her cousin–first cousin once removed, whatever that meant–seemed content to wait for dessert to arrive before he said anything else. Once the server brought the items out, Grant turned to business. "Earlier, you asked how I knew what your abilities are. With the right people, it's easy to find most things. And I *always* have the right people. They confirmed what your Erschon blood already alluded: you're very special."

A slow, shark-like grin spread across his face. "I've tested you several times since, and you've always exceeded my expectations."

Charlie gaped at him as the pieces fit together, linking him with her anonymous benefactor. "You're the one who has been sending me the emails?"

"Not me, precisely," he said, looking smug. "But, again, my people."

She thought about that while she took a bite of her tiramisu. She couldn't identify all the flavors, but she didn't need to. It was delicious. She closed her eyes as she took another bite so that she didn't have her cousin's face ruining the experience. So damned delicious. Too bad the rapidly rising anger upon finding out her cousin had been manipulating the hell out of her for his own purposes left a bad taste in her mouth even the tiramisu couldn't override.

When she opened her eyes again, a different darkness painted Grant's gaze. The kind that said he'd enjoyed her tiramisu experience, too. It made her uncomfortable and added a sharp edge to her growing anger. They were blood relatives, for Christ's sake. She started to lick her lips but grabbed the napkin from her lap to dab at her mouth instead. "So, rather than introduce yourself and work with me, you chose to move me around like a pawn on a chessboard. Why?"

One of his shoulders rose and fell in a careless shrug. "You might have said no."

She almost got up right then. The temptation to fling her cappuccino all over that expensive suit and shove the remains of her tiramisu in his pretty-boy face made her fingers itch. But she needed money, and a small part of her couldn't give up on the hope that somewhere deep inside, her cousin was a decent person.

Charlie took a long drink from her cup. "So, what do you want me to do?"

One corner of his mouth ticked up, and she added, "For the job."

Oh, he's a fucking pervert, her other bitchier internal voice added. *I agree with Em. Public maiming is acceptable in these circumstances.*

"There's a hospital in the Erschon portfolio that's been abandoned for quite some time. Terrible backstory. Filled with tragedy. Quite sad." He picked at an invisible piece of lint on his tie, then reached into his suit jacket to remove a small, painted case. Popping it open, with his thumbnail, he tilted the contents into his palm and downed them with a sip of his cappuccino. "It's rumored to be haunted. A rumor that I believe to be true. Unfortunately, a haunted building only adds to the price if you're selling to someone either too rich or too stupid to know better."

She picked up her cappuccino and watched him over the rim of the mug. "I fail to see why you want me there, considering I'll make the building *more* haunted."

"Mm," he held up a finger to pause the conversation and took a large bite of his own dessert before wiping his mouth with his napkin. "I need you to make it more haunted so that my people can make it *less* haunted."

Charlie raised her brows. "Riiight."

Grant sighed, and a line appeared between his eyebrows. "The building has been cleansed. Twice. The first attempt resulted in finding nothing to cleanse. That Union Grace was ghost-free." He scooped another bite of dessert and gestured with it. "The lead investigator then killed himself a week later." He popped the bite into his mouth, undisturbed.

"Perhaps nothing more than a simple coincidence, but I believe less in coincidence than most people believe in ghosts. So, I sent in a second team. That attempt resulted in declaring ghosts were present, but so faint they could do nothing about them. Whatever that means."

It wasn't exactly news. Without an active source of psychic energy, if enough time passed, ghosts went dormant. And not everyone had that psychic energy. That was why even places with regular inhabitants, like at Cheswaithe, eventually had issues. But at least it told her where he was going with this. She bit the inside of her cheek as she waited for him to get to the point.

"And that, my dear Cousin Charlotte, is why I'm coming to you in my hour of need. The building needs to be sold. Good land should not go to waste. But if the building is haunted, I cannot possibly go through with the sale. I can't predict what the buyers might do with the land, and I would feel forever responsible if the ghosts were ever to ... cause harm."

He leaned back in his chair and flashed her an admittedly charming, self-conscious smile. "So, I need your help to ensure the safety of, well, everyone."

Charlie sipped her cappuccino while her mind churned. While she didn't believe for a second that Grant Erschon gave a single fuck about anyone getting hurt, she did. She did, and he'd dangled an opportunity in front of her that was hard to resist. A chance to use her ability to do something truly *good* rather than just drumming up business for haunted B&Bs.

"As gauche as it is to talk money, do the job well and you'll receive $50,000."

She nearly choked on her cappuccino and ended up coughing hard for a few minutes before she could get her breathing under control.

After she finished coughing, Grant continued. "It is a business transaction, though, so there are certain expectations." He reached into an inner pocket of his suit jacket and pulled out an envelope. He laid it on the table between them. "Your little visits to those tourist traps typically last three days. Those buildings are small. Union Grace is not. Therefore, you are expected to remain on her premises for a minimum of four days to ensure proper ... saturation. After the four days are complete, if you feel she is not haunted or you feel ... no longer welcomed, you may leave. But, if the four-day minimum has not been completed, your pay will be prorated by 75%. On the other hand, each day in addition to the original four will earn you $5,000 to ensure her residents are ... well fed." She did the math in her head. Almost ten thousand just to show up for a day. And while she wouldn't stay a full seven days under any circumstances, even another day would put her at $55,000. It would be a blessing for her bank account for several years.

"And after I charge up the ghosts, I leave and you bring in exorcists to lay the spirits to rest?"

Grant took a sip of his cappuccino and patted his lips with a napkin. "The proper team is already in place. My people will join you the morning of the fourth day. At that point, you will familiarize them with the grounds and anything you have encountered thus far."

His people. Professionals. People trained to handle the nasty shit. At four days, the ghosts would be active, but not actively dangerous. They could cleanse the place before things got bad; they weren't innocent bystanders like Em, Ana, and Jacques. Professionals would be okay, right?

But what if they weren't?

Grant watched her with intense concentration, leaving her feeling like a bug under a microscope. Though he wasn't speaking now, she could feel the weight of his anticipation pinning her in place. She needed to get away from him and think about it for a bit.

Charlie tapped the envelope he'd laid between them. "Is this a contract?"

"It is."

"I assume you won't mind if I have my lawyer look it over?"

Her cousin smirked. "Of course. But mind the deadline stipulated within it. If you decline, Plan B will need to be mobilized."

"Why the hurry?" she asked, cocking her head to the side to study him. Was he wearing makeup? She wasn't a big fan of cosmetics, but she'd swear there was concealer beneath his eyes. More men were wearing makeup now, which was fine, but he didn't strike her as the type to wear it just because. "They're ghosts. Time doesn't matter to them."

"It matters to me," he said, but refused to go into further detail. Instead, he gestured for the bill and said, "I need to go. My schedule is very busy. You have my number. I expect to hear from you within the next two days."

After he signed the bill, he got to his feet and Charlie did the same. His hand was an unwelcome presence on the small of her back as he escorted her to the door.

Once they were outside, he turned to leave, then paused and looked over his shoulder. "And Charlotte? If you prove to me we can have a viable working relationship, I'll put you in touch with people that may help you control your ability. But only if you make this worth my time and money."

With that, he was ducking into the back seat of a black car that had pulled up to the curb.

Control her ability? Charlie watched the car pull away. She didn't want to control it. She wanted to fucking eliminate it.

CHAPTER FIVE

Twenty-four hours later, Charlie still hadn't decided. The lawyer thing had been a bluff to give her time to think, but the contract had looked okay from what she could tell. It was straightforward, and nothing he said seemed at odds with the contents of the letter.

She tried to justify taking the job. He wasn't asking for anything untoward. One extra day, given how big the building was, wasn't a strange request. It was abandoned, so it wasn't like there were others on the premises. At least not until the team came. And he'd said the team he'd call in were professionals. There was no reason to not do it.

No reason not to do something that would benefit everyone. But.

But...

Charlie no sooner arrived at her truck, fresh from a stop at the local coffee shop where she'd been trying to find out more about Union Grace online, when her phone rang. Already in a mood, the last thing she wanted to do was deal with someone else. But the caller ID told her it was a healthcare call. Scowling, and her stomach already letting her know she was going to regret the caffeine she'd just downed, she swiped her thumb across the screen to answer it. Putting it between her cheek and shoulder, she opened the door to her truck. "Hello?"

"Hi, this is Samar from Kings Neurology Center. Am I speaking with Charlie Hawkins?"

Wondering what the hell a surgery place was calling her for, Charlie verified her identity.

Samar said, "Ms. Hawkins, we received a referral for you to have the—"

Charlie tuned him out. Her doctor had been on her ass for a while, telling her it was a necessity at this point, but there were too many reasons it wasn't possible. Aware Samar had stopped talking, she said, "I understand what the doc ordered, but unless he's willing to cough up the money to pay for it, it's not going to happen."

There was a beat of silence on the other end. Then Samar said, "We have financial help available for qualifying patients."

Charlie sighed and rolled down her window. The truck was ridiculously hot. Stupid rich people with their fancy cars and top-of-the-line air conditioning still couldn't leave the shade for people who needed it. "I wish I qualified. But I won't."

"Ma'am, we've checked with your insurance and they'll cover 70% of the surgery cost once you've met your deductible. We can make a payment plan for the rest. I'm sure we can make this work."

"Look, Samar, right? I appreciate you trying to make this happen. But my insurance sucks and as this is a capitalist society, I'm sure it's ungodly expensive." She'd heard that some people somehow managed to find amazing insurance through the marketplace, but that wasn't her.

"Well, the cost depends on a variety of factors ..."

She pressed, asking for the most expensive version of things, because it was better to expect the worst. The number that he gave her made her throat dry out. Her deductible and twenty percent of that amount would wipe out a quarter of her remaining money. What was wrong with her was not life-threatening. Just extremely painful. And she'd dealt with it this long, so she'd just keep dealing with it. It wasn't like she had a choice.

"You do the job–do it right–and I'll pay you $50,000," Grant had said.

She wet her lips. The money he'd offered would cover the cost and replenish her dwindling bank account. Fifty thousand dollars for less than a week's worth of work. More if she stayed another day. That was the deal. He'd been clear that she didn't need to stay there longer than she thought was safe once the four days were up.

Fifty thousand dollars to live the rest of her life without near-crippling pain. She could give her liver a break and maybe go a couple places because she wanted to. Not because she was following a trail of beds.

"Miss Hawkins, are you still there?"

Snapping back to awareness, Charlie cleared her throat. "Yeah, sorry."

"So, can we get this scheduled for you?"

If it got too bad, too dangerous, she could leave. Keep them all safe. But they would be professionals. They could handle it. Right?

She blew out a puff of air. "Yeah," she said. "Yeah, you can."

Samar seemed happy to get her scheduled. Charlie fished her notebook from the glove compartment and jotted down the pertinent details. Then she went through her contact list and found Grant's name. She pressed the call button.

Grant answered on the first ring, and from the way he said her name, it was clear what he was expecting. "Yes, Charlotte?"

"I'll do it. Go stir up Union Grace." Her stomach churned with anxiety. She fished a half-gone bottle of antacids from the glove compartment and popped two into her mouth.

"Fantastic."

She asked, "You promise me the team you'll send is the best? That they'll be able to handle themselves if something goes wrong? And afterward, you'll introduce me to those people you mentioned? The ones who might be able to help?"

There was silence on the other end of the line for a moment, but then Grant said, "I'm a man of my word. The team has a solid reputation. I dare say they'll even surprise you. And yes, I will introduce you to the others after. The ones who can help you learn to control your ability —"

"I'd prefer to be able to shut it off completely."

Grant was silent for a long moment. Then, "Yes, well, we'll cross that bridge when we come to it."

Charlie ended the call after he gave her the address for Union Grace, leaning her head back against the headrest. After a moment, she flipped the visor down to shield her eyes. Her gaze went right to the picture tucked inside the visor band. Her father, light brown skin and thick black hair, had a three-year-old Charlie on his left hip while his right hand was around her mother's slim waist. Her mom's blonde hair trailed over one shoulder, reaching almost to her abdomen, and her light blue eyes gleamed like ice chips. All three were beaming at the camera.

For so long, her mother's disappearance had haunted both her and her father, although in different ways. Her father believed something had happened, causing Madeleine to run. He'd insisted that she would never leave them otherwise. As Charlie had aged, she'd stopped believing what her dad told her. That her mom had turned her back on them for more selfish reasons. Grant's words made her wonder if they were both right. What if her mom had seen what would happen when Charlie turned thirteen? What if she'd ran because her daughter's future actions had horrified her?

Charlie sighed, flicked the visor up with a quick wrist

movement, and started up the truck. She knew she should put her stuff in the back away from her, but she just didn't have the energy to care right now.

CHAPTER SIX

The scent of brewed dark roast mingling with the enticing aroma of freshly baked banana nut muffins greeted Jacques as he entered the small coffee shop. He stepped away from the door and closed his eyes for a moment, inhaling deeply. The stress of the phone call he'd just completed started to loosen the grip it had on his neck muscles.

That'll Do was hands down his favorite cafe, even though he couldn't stand the coffee itself. He glanced around the quaint shop, appreciating the dark red walls, mismatched yet cozy furniture, and small tables scattered around. Seeing his crew wasn't present yet—not surprising, Jacques was always early—he gave the barista a wave and headed to claim a cluster of seats.

Jacques slid his messenger bag off his shoulder and sat down in a black modern wingback. He pulled out the file he'd put together for Union Grace. He'd told his team in the group chat that a unique opportunity had fallen into their laps, but hadn't gone into details. They were going to lose their collective minds over the chance to investigate Union Grace. Like he should be. But he wasn't, and he didn't know why.

Ten minutes into his file review, the small bell above the thick wooden door of the coffee shop chimed. He looked up as his team entered. In the two weeks since he'd last seen them, Mac had streaked her platinum hair with dark green. Kiffer sported a bandage covering his upper arm. Likely another tattoo. Jacques didn't judge, but he wondered how old his friend was going to be before he ran out of usable space for ink. Birdie came in next, holding the door open for Rachelle, who was a half-sized twig next to the man.

Mac spotted him within seconds, and soon they surrounded him, collapsing into chairs. He let them all get situated and grinned. "Now that you're all here, abominably late as usual—"

Rachelle's eyes widened, and she sat up ramrod straight. "I thought the meeting was at 10:30?" She checked her smartphone. "It's 10:25. Did I read it wrong?"

From fine to high-strung in a half a second, and she still hadn't gotten a manual watch like they'd told her. Jacques resisted the urge to sigh.

"Chill, 'Chelle," Birdie said, patting her hand.

Jacques gave him a grateful look and put the copies of his data on Union Grace on the table. "Alright, everyone want their usual?"

They nodded. He headed off to place everyone's orders.

"Don't forget Mac's bumble nut muffin," Kiffer said with a smirk.

From her sprawled position on the club chair across from him, Mac stopped fidgeting with the rowan wood stake necklace she'd worn for as long as Jacques had known her long enough to give Kiffer a middle-finger salute. "One fucking time," she grumbled. "I forgot the word banana one fucking time."

Jacques snickered as he walked to the counter.

He was back less than five minutes later. They were a predictable lot, and the barista had started on their orders the moment the rest of the team came in. He passed out the heavily creamed and sugared plain black coffees first. Besides water, they were the safest drink to order. Next came the real reason the shop survived. The pastries. Banana nut muffin for

Mac. Chocolate chip scone for Kiffer. Cheese danish for Birdie. Banana bread for Rachelle. And for his own enjoyment, a chocolate eclair.

They took a few minutes to nibble their treats in silence. When everyone looked about half done, he set his aside on a small biodegradable plate and fastidiously cleaned off his fingers. "Alright, let's talk about Union Grace and whether we want to do this."

"I mean, do we have to?" Mac's copy rested on her lap. "Exclusive first foray into a hospital closed for fifty-ish years with some deliciously creepy history behind it? What's there to talk about?"

Kiffer was nodding before she'd finished speaking. He spoke up as soon as she went quiet. "We can do some teasers, drop some hints about the hospital's history without naming it. Get everyone primed for the experience. This could be the show that makes us, brother."

Jacques looked at Birdie.

"Do it," he said, around a mouthful of danish.

"Um, a question?" Rachelle frowned, clutching her copy. "Will anyone even be able to hear us?"

The question was so random his brain blue-screened like a computer on its last legs.

She clarified a second later. "I mean, it's got asbestos, right? So, we're going to have to wear masks. Will people even understand what we're saying?" She shifted in her seat. "Never mind. I'm probably just being an idiot."

"No," Birdie straightened in his chair. "It's a solid question. We haven't really had to deal with it before."

"Our benefactor is providing some equipment that'll help us out there." Jacques pulled another sheaf of papers from his messenger bag. He passed them out and explained. "Because this is a much bigger job than we're prepared to handle with current inventory, we'll be getting eight battery-powered

CCTVs, extra thermal imaging cameras, et cetera. We're also being provided with some high-end masks with a built-in communication system that will broadcast our voices from the in-mask mic to the group. The camera should have no problem picking it up."

"What about using our radios? There could be some feedback issues." He could count on Kiffer to bring up possible technical complications.

"Possibly," he said. Grant had reassured problems should be minimal, but one never knew.

"Equipment boy can figure it out," Mac said into the silence.

Kiffer glared at her. "Do not call me that."

She smiled, pure angel on the surface but with a devilish gleam lurking in her green eyes. "You up to the challenge, sound geek?"

"Of course," he said.

Mac opened her mouth to say something, but Jacques cut her off. "I'll need you all to sign waivers. The owner insists. If we get hurt while in the building, or god forbid develop cancer from exposure to asbestos twenty years down the road, we each waive the ability to hold them responsible."

He leaned forward in his seat, meeting each of their eyes. "I need you to understand. Union Grace is dangerous. They have left it alone for fifty years. Many people died because of a gas leak there. It could still be dangerous, even without factoring in the asbestos that's bound to be there. Also, it's likely a signal dead zone. If something goes wrong, we're fucked. I can't guarantee I can keep you safe."

To their credit, the Banshee Investigations crew were quiet for a whole ten seconds. Then, talking over each other, they all said the same thing: Let's do it.

Jacques stifled a sigh and got the waivers from his messenger bag, but then realized he hadn't told them about

Charlie. A glimmer of hope shone. Maybe, if luck was on his side, they'd rebel at doing the investigation with an unknown person on board. "One last thing ..."

Mac groaned, and he pointed a finger at her. She clasped her hands in prayer style and batted her lashes at him. He rolled his eyes and took off his glasses to clean the lenses while he talked. "Our benefactor—Grant Erschon, in case you didn't see that in the notes—has a special request. One tied directly into whether we do this mission. He wants us to bring a ... medium. Charlie Hawkins."

Birdie frowned, tilting his head.

Mac scowled. "We don't work with mediums."

"Then we don't do this mission," he said, coating his words with a light dusting of *aww shucks*.

"We are not turning down this opportunity just because this Erschon fellow wants us to use a medium," Kiffer sat up straight. "We give him a minimum of screen time, pay just enough attention to their input that they can't whine we didn't use them, and do our jobs. Also, that name sounds familiar."

Mac pursed her lips. "Actually, yeah, it does."

Kiffer's expression cleared as recognition dawned. "A couple of our clients have mentioned them. Including the Cheswaithe house. Nobody's said much about them other than Charlie brings good luck. Dunno what the hell that means, but it doesn't make them sound like a drama queen, at least."

Birdie, a pondering look on his face, said only, "Kiff's right."

"If he's annoying, I'll knock him out and claim that, like, a piece of ceiling tile fell on him or something. But yeah, Kiff's right," Mac agreed, and flashed the group a brilliant smile.

He knew he needed to tell them about the relationship between the two of them, but he shoved the thought down.

He'd pull Charlie aside when they first met up and get her to agree to keep everything between them. They could be professionals.

He passed around the waivers. After they returned with signatures, the planning phase of the mission began.

ABOUT AN HOUR LATER, walking toward their respective vehicles, Birdie clapped a large hand onto Jacques' shoulder. "If you wrap everyone in cotton wool, they might live a long time, but they will not have a very fun life. We're all adults. If something bad happens, it ain't on you, you know that, right?"

Birdie knew the real reason behind his brother's and sister's death, so he knew why his friend was trying to reassure him. But it was one he struggled to accept. Grown or not, they were still his people. That meant he was directly responsible for them.

CHAPTER SEVEN

Union Grace hospital crouched behind a high wire fence overtaken by creeping vines. The life-signaling greenery contrasted with the large sign on the gate declaring the building was a health hazard. Another sign announced Erschon Realty was not responsible for any bodily harm suffered within the grounds. The *No Trespassing* sign was almost small in comparison.

Charlie gawked at the warning through the windshield, wondering what she was getting herself into. She still wasn't sure accepting the job was a good idea. She avoided hospitals like the plague. For too many people, it was a place where they came to die. Often with a lot of traumas associated with those deaths. Traumatized ghosts didn't tend to be the friendly sort. There was no telling what she would awaken. But she needed the money.

God bless the American healthcare system, where one could pay for insurance every month and still end up facing a financially decimating bill. Especially when they couldn't hold a steady job, or stay in one location, and had a finite and ever-shrinking trust fund to pay most of their daily expenses.

Charlie groaned, leaning her forehead against the steering wheel. The Ford's AC struggled to keep up with the heat baking in through the windows. Life sucked. She wondered why she even bothered. It wasn't like she was a contributing member of society. Or that she could ever settle down with a husband or wife, a dog, and handle the expense of having a snot-nosed ankle biter of her own or anything. But giving up was not something she could do.

Still. Accepting this job? She barely even knew Grant. Her best searches hadn't turned up anything too bad about him, but he had the money to keep his skeletons deep in the closet.

A sharp knock on the truck door startled her. She jerked her head up and looked out the window. Brown eyes stared at her from a wizened face framed by an unruly mop of white curls springing in all directions. Charlie blanked for a few seconds before remembering she was supposed to meet a caretaker here to get the keys.

She plastered a smile on her face, rolling down the window. The eau de ashtray of a long-time smoker invaded her senses, tempting her to roll the window back up. "Ms. Elwood, I presume?"

White brows with sharp arches raised high, causing a cascade of wrinkles to slink up the woman's forehead. "How'd you know my name?"

Oh, yay. The woman was either small-town suspicious of everyone or senile. Or both. "Grant—uh—Mr. Erschon told me to meet you here. That you'd be waiting with the keys?"

Thin lips pursing, the caretaker shook her head. "Mr. Erschon told me I was to meet a Charlie Hawkins here. You don't look like no Charlie I've ever seen. Get on out of here before I call the police."

Small-town suspicious then. And a cantankerous bitch, to boot. "Appearances can be deceiving," she countered with a cheery chirp. "My name's Charlotte but I've gone by Charlie since I was old enough to talk. If you want to just hand over the keys, I'll be happy to go head inside and get out of your hair."

"You one of them non-binary people? Think being a girl ain't good enough for you?"

Pressure built in the center of Charlie's forehead as a headache set up camp. She was going to have to detail her interior after this just to get the woman's smell to go away. Honestly, who even smoked anymore? It was disgusting.

She was lucky Charlie needed this job, otherwise she'd tell her to go to hell. "No, ma'am. I'm comfortably AFAB. I just prefer Charlie, that's all. About those keys?"

"AFAB?"

She did not come all the way out to the middle of God's nowhere to educate some woman on today's acronyms and how to not be a bigot. She almost rolled her eyes, but knew from experience if she offended the groundskeeper, it'd just be more difficult to get what she needed. "Assigned female at birth. It just means I'm comfortable with the fact that I'm a woman."

The caretaker stepped back; her gaze darted over Charlie's truck. "You sure about that?"

Charlie did not need the woman reporting to Grant that she'd been an asshole. She would not jeopardize either her money or her chance of help. She repeated that to herself a few times, keeping the pleasant smile plastered on her face. "Yes, ma'am." She let a dollop of Southern drawl slink into her voice. "This was my daddy's truck. I promised him I'd take good care of it. He taught me how to drive in it, you know?"

A damned lie, of course. She'd learned to drive in a dinky electric blue Volvo named Snoopy. But it served its purpose. The suspicion eased in the woman's eyes, the furrows around her mouth lessening.

"I can appreciate a woman who honors her family," the caretaker said, and went to the rust-eaten Chevy Charlie had not heard pull up. The door screeched as the woman opened it and retrieved a manila envelope and a somewhat bulky package wrapped in plastic. She came back over and thrust the stuff at Charlie.

Charlie laid the package beside her and opened the envelope, pulling out a set of keys. She didn't want to push her luck, but she had to ask. "Thank you. Anything I should know about the hospital? Like that hazardous warning?"

Ms. Elwood cleared her throat. "Mostly because of the asbestos. But that's only in the bad parts of the building, and Grace has held up pretty well for her years." She paused, then added, "But if you want my advice, I'd get your business done as soon as you can."

"Oh, I intend on it," Charlie assured her, and for a moment, the woman looked flummoxed. Charlie flipped the script on how this part of the encounter was supposed to go.

"It's dangerous," she said. "You go in that building and you can feel something ain't right."

"I know," Charlie said in agreement. "Places that have seen a lot of death are never right." The dead always left their mark, even after their energy dissipated and they'd moved on to whatever awaited them.

Ms. Elwood frowned. "You go in there, you might not come back out. You should be afraid of it."

Now that was a delightful piece of common-sense reasoning Charlie could appreciate. She gave the woman a small smile. "I am afraid," she said. "But that doesn't mean I'm not going to do it anyway." She shrugged. "Need the money."

The caretaker stared at her for a moment, then stepped back. "I'll unlock the gate for you with my set."

'Preciated." Charlie rolled her window back up and fished a bit of vanilla-scented body spray out of the glove box of the truck while she waited. She made sure the caretaker wasn't looking back at her and spritzed the cab several times.

A minute or two later, the ivy-laced gate swung open. Charlie eased her truck onto the grounds and got her first look at Union Grace.

CHAPTER EIGHT

Union Grace was an ugly bitch. Three squat stories of gray stone weathered black in places greeted Charlie as she rolled through the gate. Small windows, which lacked shutters but were remarkably intact, reminded her of the archer-slits in castles. She half expected to see the long, thin arrow shafts arching through the air as she got closer. Or at least slivers of faces peeking through, watching her every move.

Charlie parked on the broken asphalt pull-through, which was devoid of grass as if not even the vegetation wanted to get too close to the hospital. She grabbed her knife from its holster underneath the dash and used it to tear into the plastic-wrapped package Elwood had sent her. A heavy-duty black mask with thick elastic straps slid out, followed by a sheet of instructions.

Charlie pursed her lips and dropped the mask to the seat so she could open the manila envelope. As predicted, a set of keys lay heavy in the bottom; however, there was a single sheet of paper included as well.

She pulled the note out and scanned it.

Charlotte,

Thank you again for your services in regards to Union Grace. I have complete faith in your skills and judgment. If the hospital is verified as psychically active, I give you my word again that I will do everything in my power to neutralize any threats and lay the spirits to rest.

As a token of my appreciation, another two thousand has been wired to your account. Think of it as the culmination of all the missing birthday gifts you should have received from the family.

Sincerely,

Grant Erschon.

The wording was weird. A mix of formal and friendly, like he didn't know what tone to go for; or maybe it was just because of the stick wedged up his ass. Still, it was a pleasant note, and the extra money was very welcome. And it meant she'd feel extra guilty about backing out. Fuck.

Charlie folded up the letter and stuck it in her glove box, then tilted the envelope. The keys fell into her hand, clinking together. One had a head painted bright red. She assumed it was for the main doors, which looked constructed of wire-reinforced glass.

Charlie frowned. Grant had been clear that the hospital had not served as an asylum, so why would it have reinforced doors? It made little sense, with what she knew from her brief experiences with hospitals. Shrugging off the thought, she glanced at the mask on the seat beside her.

The caretaker said the asbestos was only an issue in the bad parts of the building, so she'd probably be fine without it. Besides, she was only going to be there for a few days, so she didn't think she had anything to worry about.

She tucked it beneath the seat, slipped her knife into her pocket, and then got out of the truck and went around to the back to get the gear bag she'd put together. She'd already put her cell phone's case onto a belt, which she slipped through the loops of her jeans and fastened it, then double-checked the contents of the bag. A full-sized old-fashioned Maglite, and three extra sets of batteries for it, a box of granola bars, and a multi-tool.

She also included a few thick pieces of neon-colored side-walk chalk for path marking purposes, a value-sized bottle of painkillers, and a bottle of water. She put a piece of chalk into the front pocket of her jeans. As someone who could lose their way in an empty field with a three-story sign reading EXIT at one end, she wasn't crazy about her chances of not getting lost and dying of thirst before the other people Grant hired arrived. Toilet paper for the port-a-potty to the left of the doors went in her bag as well. That was good. She had a black water tank for her truck camper, but avoided using it if she could.

The lobby of Union Grace revealed two things. One: The caretaker for the hospital grounds didn't consider the interior their duty. Only the tracks in the dust coating the floor, and the dust-mop beside told her the woman had even set foot in the door. Two: The hospital hadn't gracefully shut down, but instead evacuated and never returned to. It left Charlie with the impression that with a single breath Union Grace could return to a life cut abruptly short.

She frowned, then went back out to the truck to retrieve the military-looking mask. Maybe she wasn't concerned about catching cancer in the next few days, but dust could make her life miserable.

Once she re-entered the hospital, she flicked on the flashlight and took the chalk from her pocket. By the time the exorcism crew got there, she planned to be able to walk this building with her eyes closed. Or dead of thirst and hunger.

CHAPTER NINE

Jacques pulled the RV up to the gate of Union Grace. An old woman leaning against a beat-up rust bucket of a car scowled at them. Then she put out her cigarette against the sole of her boot and dropped the butt into a pocket on her baggy overalls. He grimaced. She must have seen it, because she squared up as she approached.

"May need your help, Mac." Having a white woman on his team had been a blessing on more than one occasion.

Mac scurried up from where she'd been sitting on the fold-down bench and plopped down in the passenger bucket seat as the woman approached the RV. He rolled the window down, pasting on his most charming smile. "You must be the caretaker, Ms. Elwood. My name is Jacques De Molyneux, and I am—"

"Think you're better than me? I seen the look on your face when you saw me."

"Ma'am, I assure you—"

Beady eyes studied him from beneath thick eyebrows. "Bad enough I had t'let that young woman in here a few days ago, disturbing the hospital. Stirring up what ought to be left alone. Now you show up." She sneered at him. "Would have thought Mr. Erschon had better taste. We don't need your kind around here."

Wow. She wasted no time, did she? Fine. She was about to see that a lot had changed since she was a child. He did not need to kowtow to the white lady. "What kind would that be, Ms. Elwood? The Black kind or the ghost-hunting kind?"

"I don't give a flying fuck about the color of your skin. I voted Obama," she said, visibly bristling. "What I care about y'all coming in and messing with things best left alone. I don't get paid enough to clean up after a bunch of young'uns lackin' the common sense to fill a thimble."

He believed her. The indignation of her face rang too true. "Ma'am, I assure you we will do everything we can to not unduly stir up the spirits haunting Union Grace."

"That's what your kind do," she said. "I've got Netflix. I've seen the shows. You come through and get things all stirred up for the sake of ratings." She leaned back a little to take in the name on the side of the RV. "Haven't heard of this one before though. You new?"

"We have a show on YouTube," he told her, longing for the day when he could say they were with an actual network.

"Oh, amateur bullshit then." Her tone changed, becoming dismissive as she stepped back. She pulled a key ring from her pocket. "I'm sure y'all will come screaming out of here the first time a door creaks. If you break something for shits and giggles, I'll make sure Mr. Erschon charges you for it."

"Amateur bullshit?" Mac swore under her breath. "I'll show that miserable cunt amateur bullshit."

Jacques ignored her. "I understand. We'll just be out of your way then. If you'd open the gate ... please."

She ambled in that direction. It was the spiteful sort of move Jacques had seen a hundred times. He waited it out, and when they passed through, called out a saccharine-sweet thanks for her wonderful help.

A couple minutes later, he parked the RV on the side of the drive opposite a well-maintained but old Ford sitting high off the ground. It was an interesting choice, one that fed the idle flames of curiosity he'd had regarding Charlie. Birdie pulled up in the van right behind him.

"Compensating for something," Mac muttered.

"Not what you think," Jacques said with a wry grin. He unbuckled and exited the RV, Mac on his heels. He'd rounded the front, wondering if he'd have to holler into the hospital, when a female figure emerged from the shadowy interior. She stopped under the overhang as soon as she spotted him.

Jacques stopped and stared back. A lot had changed in the 13 years since he'd seen Charlie, but she was still recognizable. Big brown eyes, bold brows, and a round face under a mop of choppy dark brown hair that screamed self-cut. Where he'd grown several inches and now came in at just under six feet, she'd stopped growing at around 5'2", max. And she was clearly not the constant dieter type.

Looking at her brought back memories of her and Em's shenanigans, and he smiled as he stepped forward, extending his hands. "Charlie."

She shuffled back, crossing her arms over her midsection. Voice rising in pitch, she said, "Jacques? What the fuck are you doing here?"

Jacques frowned. "I own Banshee Investigations. Grant hired us. Same as you."

Charlie shook her head. "No, he said he'd hired professionals to come in and help deal with the ghosts."

"We are the professionals." He might only be twenty-two, but he was still a professional. Losing his brother and sister, watching it destroy his family, and years of therapy along with the determination to keep the dead from hurting anyone ever again made him feel like he was closer to forty-five than twenty-five. But that experience also gave him a clue as to what was happening. That bastard Erschon hadn't told Charlie who she'd been working with. Had sprung this reunion on her. "We don't do the heavier cleansings ourselves, but we can help identify what's going on and bring in other professionals if it's something we don't think we can handle."

"Why the hell would you do this? How could you put

yourself in danger after–" Charlie's eyes were wide and wet as she spoke.

He cut her off, not wanting to rehash what happened with the others present. Things were already going off the rails. "Because it's the right thing to do. If we can bring peace to the spirits, it keeps everyone safe."

"Do you think Ana would want this? Want you to–"

"Ana's dead!" He tried to suppress his frustration. It wasn't her fault. He had time to process meeting up with her again. She hadn't. He gave her a small, tight smile, jaw aching. "I've spent years mastering how to do this. How to keep us *safe*. And now people listen to me when I tell them what to do."

Mac stepped between the two of them, holding her palms out. "Okay, obviously you two know each other." She glanced between the two of them, as if searching for answers. "Mind cluing the rest of us in, fearless leader?"

Jacques removed his glasses and pinched the bridge of his nose. "Charlie was a friend of the family when I was growing up," he said, choosing his words with care. They didn't need to know about Charlie's involvement in the event which had changed their lives. Not yet. "Before Ana and Emerson passed."

Mac was silent for a second, but then: "This is one of those things you should have mentioned, boss."

"It wasn't your business," Jacques said.

Mac stepped into his space, staring up at him with green eyes alight with anger. "But it had the potential to affect *our* business. You've said it yourself. We need to know all the facts possible when we go into a situation that might affect the outcome."

"Charlie and I knowing each other won't affect the outcome," he snapped, his cheeks flushing with heat. "We haven't even seen each other since I was nine. Get out of my face, Mac."

"Yeah, and there's obviously no unresolved issues between the two of you," Mac said, and snorted. She didn't step back, but he hadn't expected her to. Not really. She had a white woman's confidence. One of these days that was going to bite her in the ass.

"Our unresolved issues aren't your problem," he said, voice filled with ice. "We're here to do a job. Charlie is here to do hers. End of conversation."

Mac narrowed her eyes, then whirled around to face Charlie. "How long have you been here?" There was an angry heat to her voice. He knew why. Jacques had pissed her off, perhaps understandably, and then he hadn't given her the fight she was spoiling for.

"This is day four." Charlie flicked a glance at her as she answered, but then went back to staring at Jacques.

"Mediums aren't supposed to have prior knowledge of a location. It can influence how they react. You should know that."

Charlie lifted her chin, giving him a challenging look. Telling him it was his problem to handle.

He sighed. "If you want to be pissed, Mac, that's fine. But be pissed at me. And remember what our original plans were. We don't rely on mediums for information. We never have, and we never will. Erschon wanted her here, she's here. How she does her job doesn't matter as long as he's satisfied with the results."

Charlie's nostrils flared, but she didn't correct him. Instead, she looked at Mac. "If you're going to keep standing this close to me, the least you could do is introduce yourself."

The two women locked gazes for a long moment, the air thick between them. Just when Jacques was wondering if he needed to separate them before claws started flying, Mac surprised him by extending a hand to her. "Mackenzie Smith. Mac if you want to stay on my good side."

"Oh, good. I was afraid I was on your bad side." Charlie shook her hand. "Charlotte Hawkins. Charlie, if you want to, stay on mine. Chuck if you want slapped."

"Hm. What if I wanted spanked?" Mac asked huskily.

Jacques' eyes widened, and he had to bite back a laugh as Birdie and Kiffer came up behind them.

"Slapping is free. I charge for spanking," Charlie sassed, not missing a beat. She gave Mac a quick once over. "Might give you a discount, though. You're cute."

Even though he'd never caught Charlie and Em kissing, Jacques assumed Charlie was straight. Either he was wrong, or she'd changed as she'd grown up.

Kiffer laughed. Charlie's gaze darted to him. Her cheeks pinked, and she clapped a hand to her mouth as her shoulders shook with a suppressed giggle.

"Charlie, meet the rest of Banshee Investigations." Jacques turned, gesturing to Kiffer and Birdie. "Kiffer is our equipment tech and show runner. Birdie is our primary camera man and assists Kiffer with putting everything together."

"And Mac?"

Jacques relaxed a bit. The tension had dissipated, and he'd do anything to keep things chill for a bit. They'd all have to talk later, but right now they needed to get set up if they wanted to get the equipment set up and get their baseline readings before nightfall. "Grunt work," he said, smirking at Mac.

Mac glared.

He gave her an innocent look and then clapped his hands together. "Alright, let's get the genny set up and go from there. Daylight's wasting, Banshee."

"Oo-rah," Birdie said.

Mac gave Jacques a look that let him know he had a chewing out coming his way later, and went to help unload the van.

After she walked off, Charlie stepped closer and whispered, "I wouldn't have taken this job if I'd known it was you."

Jacques nodded. "I'm guessing Erschon at least suspected that. I can't think of a better reason for him not to tell you who you would be working with."

"He told you?"

He nodded again, then put a hand on her shoulder. "We'll talk later, okay? It's good to see you again, Charlie. I mean that."

To his surprise, it was true.

CHAPTER TEN

Banshee Investigations made camp with military efficiency. Charlie watched them work from where she sat on the bumper of the Ford. Generators hauled out, gassed up, and running was the first step. Then Jacques worked with the one he'd called Birdie (God, she hoped that was a nickname) on pulling out and setting up a couple two-person tents while Mac—who had a delightful ass for a white woman—and Kiffer ferried equipment out of the van to lay it in front of the main door. She wondered why there were only two tents, but they were adults and it wasn't her business.

With camp setup completed, Kiffer went to the back of the van and called the crew over for a "rig-out." Each person got a shoulder harness with a GoPro fastened to one side and a flashlight clipped to the other. They clipped belts around their waist featuring an array of equipment stuck on them. Some of it Charlie recognized, some she didn't.

Masks—like the one she wore pulled down beneath her chin—but with additional cables and pieces attached to them apparently completed the gear. She wasn't sure what the mask attachments did, or what half the equipment was, but they were outside and safe, so that was okay. She was content to watch and try to suss things out.

Kiffer must have sensed her puzzlement, because he beckoned her over with a smile. When she was beside him, he shoved a hand through his shoulder-length black hair and said, "We've got a harness and radio setup for you, too. The radio hooks into your mask and lets us communicate safely and clearly. I'll get you hooked up and show you how to use it once we get everything settled."

It was interesting observing the whole process. It seemed like they took their job seriously, which reassured Charlie. She spent little time on the net, or watching television, but she'd seen enough ghost hunting shows to realize people loved to be stupid and dramatic for attention. The professional rigging helped reassure her that Jacques wasn't nine any more.

She told herself he wasn't a little boy with a frying pan and a thing of salt. He could do this. And no matter how much she repeated that, she still wanted to escort them all to the gate and refuse to continue until Grant sent someone else.

She wondered how his team would react once things got active inside the hospital. If they did. The first couple of days, Union Grace had been quiet. Too quiet. Dealing with this type of atmosphere in places where the dead had faded to nothingness was her norm. By the start of her third day there, it was only the oppressive weight that settled on her chest whenever she entered the building that kept her from writing it off as uninhabited. It made her hopeful that this would be easy. That it was just a few lost spirits that Jacques and his team could help pass with no trouble.

But she knew nothing was ever that easy. As the minutes ticked by that morning, her fourth and their first, it wasn't just seeing Jacques for the first time in thirteen years making her stomach twist. She had a feeling Union Grace was going to show its ass spectacularly once it woke up.

She wanted to leave. Pack up now and get out before any more of her energy could leech into the hospital. But she couldn't. Not until Grace's inhabitants showed themselves.

Not until tomorrow morning if she wanted to afford the surgery scheduled three weeks from now.

Maybe she'd get lucky for once. Maybe Grace would stay quiet and they could all go to Grant knowing they'd done the best they could, and now he could get rid of the building. And maybe pigs would fly.

A hand on her shoulder brought her back to reality with a violent start. Kiffer stepped back, hands raised. "Sorry. You just looked ... intense. Everything okay?"

Pulse jack hammering in her throat, Charlie swallowed hard and nodded. "Just thinking." She looked around, surprised to see everyone else gone.

"They went inside just a second ago," Kiffer explained. "I need to record baseline readings. Want to join me?"

It was a reason to stay out of the building, granting those inside a little more peace. Charlie smiled. "Sure."

He beckoned her to the RV, explaining, "Birdie has his own small set-up in the van for editing work, but generally the van is for equipment storage while this is where all the action happens." He stepped up into the RV and turned around to offer her a hand. "It's pretty cool."

Suddenly, it wasn't Kiffer's hand Charlie saw.

From her position halfway up the ladder, Charlie stared at the long-fingered, broad-palmed hand, with the dark dot in the meat right between his first two finger knuckles. A buried piece of pencil lead. She still felt guilty about it, but he laughed it off whenever she brought it up. Told her not to worry. That it was a memento of their friendship.

The fingers wiggled. "Come on, you won't notice once you're up here." He knew her thing for heights. Never teased her about it, but was always pushing her to overcome it when possible.

Trusting him, Charlie took his hand, and he steadied her as she walked up the stairs. It was something he'd picked up from her dad, and it made her feel all warm and squishy inside. A bright shaft of sunlight streaming through a stop sign-shaped window lit most the room. Stacks of boxes hid almost every inch of the walls and ate into floor space as well.

"Most of the stuff is pretty boring," Em told her, voice just above a whisper. "But I found this box ..." Still holding her hand, he led her over to one of the darkest corners of the attic, where a small chest, old even to her inexperienced eyes, sat. Laying open on top of it was a black heart-shaped lock.

"You didn't," she whispered. He'd started learning to pick locks a few months ago and that became some weird personal challenge to open anything he could get his hands on.

"I had to," he said, grinning. "I've never seen a lock like that. Anyways, you won't believe what I found inside. I'm not even sure what they are!"

"Charlie?" The memory fled. The hand she'd been looking at was suddenly much lighter, though the fingers were similarly skinny. Kiffer started to withdraw it, but she took hold of it and let him help her into the RV, too curious to bitch about not being that damned short.

"Sorry," she said, glancing around the space. "I'm an astronaut today."

The RV had an incredible amount of space in it. Jealousy pinged. The camper on her truck was nice—an investment to make up for her lack of stationary living space—but didn't even compare. It had eaten a solid quarter of her trust fund, and she hadn't truly regretted it until this point. Looking around at what she could have gotten if electronics didn't go so wonky around her.

Speaking of electronics, the RV bristled with them. Fastened to one wall were three large monitors . Another two mounted onto the slim desk underneath them. There was space for two people to sit in rotating bucket seats attached to the floor, but computer towers and other bits and bobs with a lot of blinking lights cluttered the space on either side. It was not a space she could spend too much time in.

Kiffer slid onto one seat, gesturing for her to take the other. When her ass contacted a piece of heaven in the form of a cushion, she groaned in delight. Her dark-haired companion grinned. "Jacques said that as much time as we were going to be in one of these, it made little sense to be any less than as comfortable as possible."

She smiled tightly and murmured her agreement before turning on her seat to face the monitors. Only the center of the top three was on. Four squares divided the images on screen. The top two and the bottom two showed similar scenes of light bouncing off now familiar hospital walls. "So, you watch them from out here? You don't go in?"

"I'll go inside if need be," Kiffer said. "Mostly I'm in there helping to set up and calibrate the equipment, and to troubleshoot when need be. My primary job during an investigation, though, is to watch these screens. Both what the cameras are seeing and what the sensors will pick up. This center screen will always show the footage from the team's cameras, but the others will show a variety of other feeds. When something happens, or they think something has happened, I'll roll back the footage and verify. If it's real, I'll make a clip of it and save it, as well as note down the details such as what the temperature readings—"

His voice got much more animated as he talked. He obviously loved his job. Charlie tried to focus, but when he got into the technical jargon, it went over her head. His voice trailed off after a moment, and he shifted awkwardly in his chair. "Sorry," he said. "I tend to geek out a bit."

It was cute. When she told him as much, heat rose in his cheeks. That was downright adorable. He was adorable, really. She smiled when he turned away to fiddle with a large walkie-talkie looking thing on the desk. A second later, Jacques' voice filled the air.

"-pond please? Mic check. Respond please, Kiffer."

Kiffer pulled the walkie from its base and pushed a button on the side. "Sorry, Jacques. Had some—ah—technical difficulties, but they're resolved now." His green eyes sparkled with humor as he looked at Charlie.

After a moment of silence, Jacques came back with, "Alright, as long as everything's good now. Let's keep going."

A second later, Mac's voice came over the radio, and then the rest of the crew in succession. Charlie sat quietly beside him as they watched the rest of the crew move through the building. They were almost done when the screens flickered.

That was her cue to leave. She stood up as he fussed with wires. "It's me," she said. "They'll straighten up after I leave."

He paused with one hand inches away from one monitor. "Um ... what?"

"I don't play with electronics. Something about my body chemistry."

"That's—"

"Weird, yeah." She shrugged at him and then opened the door to the RV and headed to her truck. She didn't think he'd follow her, but before she could even disappear inside her camper, he was beside her.

"Hey," he said, "weirdness or not, we still need to get you set up, okay?"

Charlie smiled. "I have my own stuff, you know?" She turned partway around to show off the waterproof black backpack she wore.

Kiffer eyed it, asking, "What do you carry?"

"Maglite, extra batteries, protein bars, water, pain killer. That type of thing."

His brows tried to crawl up his forehead. "What about protection?"

He was nosy, but it felt like he cared. She was coming to understand how desperate she was for that, and didn't like it. "That's why I carry a full-size Maglite," she told him. "They're made of some sort of metal and use D batteries, so you can really deliver a thumping if you need to."

He blinked. "Er ... I meant for protection against paranormal entities."

"Oh." Oh, hell. What did mediums carry for protection? She wasn't religious, so carrying a cross or other religious symbol never made sense to her. Mostly dealing with the dead consisted of staying far away from potentially dangerous hot spots and getting the hell out of Dodge before things hit the tipping point when she stayed elsewhere. But if she told him that, it'd blow Jacques's story all to hell.

"I, uh ..." Suddenly she remembered the pretty purple rock she'd found a few weeks ago. She'd tucked it into a side pocket of her bag, but as far as she could recall, hadn't taken it out. Mediums did crystals and rocks and stuff, right? "I have a rock!"

"A rock," he said, looking at her suspiciously.

"Yep." She reached backwards and unzipped one of the side pockets, fishing around until her fingers touched the quarter-sized stone. She pulled it out and showed it to him. The crystalline purple caught the light and shimmered.

"Ah, lepidolite," he said at once. "I can see that. It's supposed to help bring inner peace and harmony. Maybe not quite the protection I thought, but if it works for you ..."

Saved by the random grab of a pretty rock, she thought. She shrugged and slipped it back into the side pocket. "Anyway, you mentioned gear?"

He nodded, then held up a finger and jogged back to the RV. He was back seconds later, hands full of equipment. "This is a shoulder harness," he said. "Like you saw the rest of the team put on. You can wear it underneath your backpack without a problem."

He handed it to her, and she took off her backpack long enough to put it on. He attached the rest of the gear for her, standing close enough she could feel his body heat.

She watched his mouth as he talked through what she was doing. It was times like these that made Charlie grateful to be a bisexual. She really did get the best of both worlds. Then she noticed he'd stopped talking and was standing there with his hands resting lightly on the harness straps.

His eyes dipped to her lips, then back up. Attraction fissioned in the air between them. And for a moment—just a small one—Charlie considered leaning in and pressing her lips to his. But even she knew it would be poor form. Bringing hormones into everything was stupid and dangerous and how people died in horror movies. That didn't mean she could make herself back away from him, though.

The radio crackled with Jacques' voice from the RV. Kiffer stepped back. He gave her a regretful half-smile before going back to the RV. Charlie watched him walk away and then made herself go inside her camper. Even though she liked him, there was no way in hell she was going to be present for setting up their equipment.

What she had picked up from Kiffer's spiel was that the equipment was very sensitive and likely expensive. Her luck, she'd touch the infrared kilometer thing and it would explode or something. So, nope. She'd nap while they set up everything to play Record-A-Spook. Nap or maybe indulge in a light bit of fantasizing.

Anything to distract her from the upcoming hours.

CHAPTER ELEVEN

[CCTV camera #4 - Location: 1st Floor, Original Structure - View: Left side of main lobby, showing emergency room exterior through to cafeteria entrance]

An empty lobby—faded chairs gathered round circular tables. In the feed, colors were indistinguishable, reduced to shades of gray. Orbs occasionally drift in front of the camera, but these are not worth paying attention to. It is merely dust knocked loose by the movement of fresh blood within the building.

The quality of the footage is crisp. Though Union Grace resists the sunlight, enough creeps through its grimy windows to let the camera do its job. It reveals a walkway abandoned without notice. The smears of graffiti infected wounds on the aging hospital's dignity.

At first there is nothing to see but the slow rot of potential and the death of an area once intended solely for healing. But then, toward the back of the area, a smudge of white flickers into existence. It is small. So small that if it had not been mid-summer, one could have mistaken it as a lone traveler's icy breath.

But there is no one, and no easy way to account for the smudge as it disappears and then reappears again a little larger, a little closer to the camera.

The progression toward the camera is slow. More than once the smudge, now close enough that it looks like a threadbare towel once spun of graveyard fog, does not advance, but twists in place. It is easy to imagine a figure there, looking for something familiar only to find itself in an alien world.

But that is just imagination. There is not enough detail to give any credence to the human need to see patterns, to see shapes, where none exists.

It is now parallel to the internal entrance to the emergency room. For the first time it deviates from its rectilinear path, turning tightly before dissolving into nothingness against—or maybe through—the door.

CHAPTER TWELVE

Jacques normally enjoyed the quiet time of the initial set-up for an investigation. The dead needed time or a certain combination of factors before they could start showing out, so these first few hours brimmed with a heady mix equal parts anticipation and excitement.

Today was a little different. More nervous anticipation than excitement. He still didn't have a good feeling about this job; though his teammate's infectious energy had started affecting him. Union Grace was going to be big. They all felt it. As long as he could keep everyone safe, the views would be through the roof.

After the first sweep, they'd gotten baseline readings. Then the four of them had gone back outside to load up on the equipment they'd spread throughout the hospital. Kiffer waited for them next to the RV. Charlie did not show. He told himself it was a good thing. They needed to discuss several things, including the exact role she'd play here, but that could wait until they'd set everything up.

The first equipment he grabbed was a larger version of the safety kit he insisted they have at all investigations. His team considered it an eccentricity, but they'd never seen exactly how deadly spirits could be. While Birdie and Kiffer hauled the first round of cameras into place, he gathered a bunch of neon green bags and headed back into Union Grace.

The green was an eyesore, but it was also highly visible. He put the first one on the ground floor right in front of the reception desk. Another went on top of the nurse's station in the Emergency Room to the left. He deposited the third and fourth in the middle of the hallways separating the various rooms on the right half of the level.

Once he'd repeated the process three more times, he helped place the other equipment. Working together with Mac and Rachelle, they distributed sensors throughout the building. It took them until nearly noon, but eventually they had thermometers and mics set up in every location that was a potential hot spot. They could always move things around later if needed.

Occasionally, they ran into Kiffer and Birdie, who were taking care of the cams. They were going to monitor Grace via several infrared motion detector cams and a few traditional ones. He didn't expect to get much use of the traditional cameras. Even though Union Grace had a fair amount of windows, unless they were practically right beside one of them, the light inside the hospital was more akin to dusk falling.

Once done with deployment, they broke for lunch. He hoped Charlie would join them, but she stayed in her truck camper. He was semi-amused by the fact both Mac and Kiffer gave the truck pondering glances. Especially as much as Mac had bitched off-radio while they did their sweep about Charlie having days ahead of them to set things up.

He'd placated her again, reminding her that Charlie's involvement ultimately didn't matter. That her being on the grounds was part of the contract, but there was no obligation to use her extensively in the show's final product. As far as he was concerned, her mere presence was fulfilling the requirement Grant Erschon had insisted upon.

That appeased the blonde, and it hadn't taken long until she'd asked, "Probably a flake, but cute though. Got a vibe that she'd swing my way. Confirm or was she just being a flirt?"

He rolled his eyes. "We're here to investigate, not get you laid."

"Ah," Mac said, "that's right. I forgot you were a man for a second. Multitasking just doesn't compute with your brain."

LUNCH OVER, he hung his digital audio recorder around his neck, snagged his leather-bound journal from his messenger bag and headed inside to do the first official non-baseline EVP and temperature readings taken. While Kiffer could and would take his own notes inside the RV, this was standard practice. Electronic equipment could fail. A fresh pen and a journal could not. Meanwhile, Birdie and Rachelle started on the top floor, where the administrative offices were, getting B-roll and recording some of their impressions of the hospital.

His self-assigned job took him back to his earliest forays into ghost hunting. Days when he would traipse around with a voice recorder hung around his neck. As now, he used a pen to record quick sketches and initial impressions of the area he was investigating. He had little equipment then, but he made up for it with a lot of enthusiasm. Enough to annoy the hell out of his mom and dad. And Ana too, or so he had thought. Even though she was the one who had given him the notebook.

His pen came to rest against the lined paper as he remembered that birthday. His ninth, and the last he'd have with his siblings.

IT WAS HIS NINTH BIRTHDAY, and Jacques had been bouncing off the walls all day, waiting for time to open presents. His parents had always been awesome about getting him what he wanted for his birthday, so he was looking forward to getting a load of ghost-hunting equipment. He especially wanted an EMF and a good handheld camera. One with night vision.

His parents had rented out a room at the local country club for his birthday, which he'd tried hard not to roll his eyes at. His entire class was at the party, even James, the class bully. The jerk who always made fun of him because he didn't like to play rough and get dirty. A bunch of his parents' friends came too, which was ridiculous because they didn't even know him, but "appearances and connections are important", whatever that meant.

Finally, after everyone had taken forever to eat, a waiter wheeled a large cart of presents over. His mother gave him the okay to open them, but accompanied it with the Look. The one which said "don't be common." Which meant no tearing into presents like it was Christmas morning.

Most of the gifts were stuff he wasn't interested in, but he smiled, politely thanking each giver before he handed the gift over to a waiting attendant packing everything away for him. The only thing he'd gotten before getting to the presents from his family that could really be useful was a nice Nikon camera. It was a few steps up from the hand-me-down his sister had given him last year. He could take pictures and look for ghost orbs and stuff.

Finally, it was time to open the presents from his family, and anticipation had him grinning even as he opened the first box from his parents. He pushed aside the tissue paper. The box was too small for the camcorder, but maybe it was the EMF? He opened the box to reveal something bright yellow and soft. He lifted it from the box, holding it up. A signed jersey from his dad's favorite football team. Identical to the one framed and on his wall since he was five.

He forced a smile and thanked his parents, then handed the jersey off and went to the next box. One precisely the right size for the slim camcorder he'd requested. It was an iPad, with some headphones and stuff in the box with it. By the time he got to their last present, he'd given up hope of getting anything on his list from them. It was a new type of disappointment from normally attentive parents.

The box contained a new iPhone, and he could feel tears threatening. He struggled to keep his expression happy and moved on to Emerson's present. It took him a second to recognize the slim silver device, but after it clicked, he gave his brother a brilliant smile.

Emerson winked at him, but then darted a meaningful glance in his parent's direction. He said, "I know you like to, uh, talk stuff out aloud with your, uh, homework and stuff. Thought that would help."

"It's perfect!" Jacques admired the digital voice recorder for a minute longer before passing it over to the assistant.

Ana's gift was last. She was a superb gift giver. Sometimes she got him stuff he didn't think he'd like but he always ended up loving. However, she acted so annoyed by his obsession with ghosts he didn't expect to get anything on his list from her.

The package wasn't wrapped as nicely as some others. Her handwriting was on the tag. That made him smile. Everyone else let the store wrap theirs. Ana had done hers by hand.

He opened the silver wrapping paper to find a book inside—The Hound of The Baskervilles by Arthur Conan Doyle. A slip of paper stuck from between the pages. He opened it and saw a note. It read: "Sherlock Holmes is the most famous investigator of all time, and he didn't have the fancy equipment they do on your ghost-hunting shows. Take a page out of his book. You might get better results. -A"

Underneath the Sherlock Holmes book there was a soft brown leather book with his name stamped on the front of it. She'd taped a nice pen to the spine. He opened it to see lined but empty cream colored pages. There was a note inside it, too. It read "Now stop leaving your little bitty crappy notebooks everywhere. -A"

When he looked up from it, Ana arched a brow at him, giving him a snooty look like she was daring him to act a fool. He gave her a posh and abrupt thank you in French. She rolled her eyes at him before turning her attention to the window, but he could see by the way her lips twitched that she was trying not to smile.

THE RADIO CRACKLING in his ear brought him back to the present. It was just a normal check-in, so he moved onto the next room to repeat his process. His mind lingered on Ana as he did. Before her death, his sister had been everything to him. Emerson tolerated him good-naturedly, and they'd had a few shared interests, but his sister *got* him. She gave him hell and had been annoying but, out of everyone, she was his friend. His confidante.

When his dad told him to man up, Ana stood up for him. When she'd caught wind that bullies were harassing him, she'd handled it. She'd skipped class, came to his school during recess, and asked him to point out the assholes. He refused, knowing it would just make the teasing worse because he'd look like a wimp for getting his sister involved. Ana had given him a friendly pat before saying: "Don't worry. Bullies have a type. I've got this." Sure enough, she'd gone straight for the group of boys who had been making his life hell.

He watched from the corner of his eye, not knowing what to expect. Ana leaned close to James, who was openly eyeballing her boobs, and said something. A few seconds later they were all nodding like bobble-heads. Ana left without another word, headed back to class. He hadn't dealt with those assholes again until his sister had been gone for a couple of years.

She had been so good to him. He wanted to return the favor. His big sister needed to let go of this world—to stop watching over him—and move on. He just needed to figure out how to make that happen.

CHAPTER THIRTEEN

"It is four p.m. on June 24th, our first official day of investigation into Union Grace hospital. If it's not been on your radar before now, it will be after this. Full details later, Union Grace is a hospital closed not once but twice. Both times due to tragedy. Built in 1933, the hospital closed its doors for the first time on June 6th, 1944 after the first tragedy. One that resulted in an enormous loss of life. One would think this would make headlines; however, something of national importance dominated the news that week."

He paused for a long moment. It would give Kiffer an opportunity to put up an on-screen graphic about the significance of that date. He'd done a poll on social media asking who—without looking it up—knew why the date was significant, and few people responded with certainty. He couldn't blame them, he honestly hadn't either. D-Day was, like, his great-grandfather's time. There'd been a lot of wars and stuff since then.

"It sat neglected, the small village that had sprung up around the hospital swiftly dying, until trustees reopened the building in the late sixties. They did this to help deal with the influx of soldiers returning from the Vietnam war. It closed again just a few years later due to 'multiple health and safety concerns.' Quite disturbing ones."

Grant had not fully disclosed the reasons for the hospital closing in the paperwork given to him. A former flame with a talent for traditional investigation and a love for spooky shit had filled in the blanks.

"Shortly thereafter, the hospital fell under the ownership of Gerald Erschon, who allowed no one to investigate the premises for reasons unknown. After his death, his son, Grant, inherited the property and granted Banshee Investigations an exclusive foray into Union Grace.

"What we know is normal for Union Grace hospital now is: Though there are minor variations in temperature throughout the building, allowed for because heat rises, amongst other practical considerations, the ambient averages around seventy-five degrees. That's oddly cool for the end of June, Jacques, I hear you thinking. Especially when an old building like this likely has no air conditioning. It should be warmer. Well, mes amis, that's because of the asbestos."

He rotated the handheld Sony Handycam FDR-AX53 4k Ultra so that it was facing him and gave the (later) viewers a finger-waggle. His GoPro was on and always running so they wouldn't miss anything; the Handycam produced quality footage. "That's right, Grace is filled with the stuff. Unfortunately, to keep my crew safe, I'm afraid you'll only be seeing our lovely smiles when we're out of the hospital or in areas where asbestos is a minimal risk."

He turned the camera back around, slowly sweeping the main lobby of the hospital. There was a semi-circular laminate receptionist's desk in the middle of the room. Two mustard-yellow chairs sat behind it, molding and leaning in different directions.

There were rows of similarly colored basic waiting room chairs scattered throughout the open area, some gathered around low-lying circular tables. Some enterprising young artistic soul had snuck in once upon a time and painted large flowers upon the tables. Another young soul, this time obviously an asshole hooligan, had come in later and partially obscured the flowers with thick streaks of red spray paint forming the never edgy pentagram. Similar paint marred the peeling once-white walls of the lobby with phrases such as "Satin Rulez" and "Jo H. is a slut."

Overall, though, as he slowly walked viewers through the lobby, the general atmosphere the hospital gave off was one of abrupt abandonment. As far as he could tell, the owners hadn't even bothered to remove equipment after the hospital had closed. The only things missing were the medicines, and from the way someone had forced open the medical carts and storage bins, obviously that had not been under the purview of the owners.

"Now, Union Grace has not gone unnoticed by nocturnal young citizens with too much time on their hands, as evidenced by the graffiti you see. However, there is something worth noting. Look." He pushed through the doors leading into the Emergency Room and panned the camera around. It showed walls free of graffiti. Pulling back out of the room, not saying a word, he crossed to the other side, and went a few feet down one hallway that broke off into various treatment or diagnostic rooms. The hallway walls were similarly free of artistic license.

He dropped his voice into a stage whisper. "Why does the graffiti extend no further than the lobby? Security does not patrol the hospital. The caretaker does not come on the property after dark. But yet no one has taken advantage of the ripe opportunities to leave their mark on the hospital. And you cannot tell me it is the single basic fence surrounding the property stopping them."

As soon as he spoke the words, the hair on the back of his neck prickled. He went to thumb the Push to Talk button that was affixed to his harness a few inches below his GoPro, but paused first to tell the viewers, "I'm about to speak to the team over radio. The EMF is going to go off. It's not ghosts, mes amis, not always. Not even often."

He pressed the button, and, as predicted, the EMF reader

beeped annoyingly at him for a few seconds. He spoke over it. "Anything yet, Banshees?"

"Not unless you count Birdie setting off every sound detector we had placed within the Imaging and Radiology lab with what has to be one of the loudest farts I've ever heard," Kiffer said, voice filled with awed disgust.

"Told you that Mexican place was a bad idea," Birdie said after his Scooby-Doo-like laughter died down.

Jacques should have known better than to take them to a restaurant which did Mexican-inspired Appalachian food. But, Jesus Christ, after several days on the road, he needed something other than McDonalds or lunch meat.

He shook his head and released the button, turning his attention back to narrating for the camera. Time to drop a few creepy facts to lean harder into the spook. "On the surface, this quaint little hospital, two steps above a charming band aid station, was your typical, run-of-the-mill rural hospital." He paused, let the word linger in the air, and dropped his voice a notch before repeating the word. "But Union Grace hospital was the point of care for the locals," he used that term loosely because in rural areas, what was 'local' varied widely, "prison, and we know plenty of unsavory characters were kept there. So, is it any wonder that as we walk the abandoned halls of Union Grace, our minds drift to the possibilities? How many inmates were brought here, suffering violence inflicted trauma from attacks? How many died here, after decades spent locked in tiny cells, with only those of violent and deadly histories surrounding them? Does, even now, the spirit of a mass murderer stalk these very—"

"Houston, we have activity," Mac said in satisfaction, her breathing heavy enough to tell him she'd probably just gotten the shit scared out of her.

He keyed his radio. "Report?"

"Heading into third floor swing ward A on my rounds, and

the blasted door swung open a few inches before I could touch it."

"Breeze? Those doors swing easy."

"All windows in the surrounding area are intact, and I closed the hallway door as I entered, per protocol," she told him, not the slightest bit ruffled by his questioning.

"Anything on cams?" he asked Kiffer, monitoring all their feeds from the RV.

"Rolling back. Hold, please." A few seconds later he said, "Confirmed. Both sides of the door clear from human intervention. It opened inward a few seconds at 4:04 p.m."

"Mark—paranormal activity, third floor, Ward A. Small-scale object movement. Initial witness: Mackenzie Smith. Confirmed via infrared cam as happening at 4:04 p.m." He carefully turned the camera back to face him, and intoned gravely, "Ladies and gentlemen, Union Grace is waking up. Let's hope she's a morning person, shall we?"

Charlie spoke over the radio for the first time. Her words sent a shiver down his spine. "She's not."

He swallowed, and then brightly said, "A reminder for viewers: Those dulcet tones you just heard belong to Charlie, a first-time guest on Banshee Investigations. Whilst we normally shy away from mediums, Charlie has proven herself proficient with ... getting the dead to interact. We are honored to have her working with us at Union—"

The sound of EMFs screeching and other equipment going nuts interrupted him.

CHAPTER FOURTEEN

Charlie had never felt a building wake up the way Union Grace did. Normally, once she'd leaked enough power into the environment, manifestations of paranormal energy followed a pattern. They started off small, growing in power the longer she stayed in the area. Not here. Everything had been fine, then it wasn't.

A shift in the air heralded the oncoming of a rolling, languid wave of necrotic energy. One which swept through the area, almost taking her mental feet out from under her. Her stomach churned as it washed over her, the questing probes brushing her skin, her soul, looking for a way in.

"No!" She widened her stance, bending her knees and consciously pushing against the energy trying to violate her. She couldn't explain how she knew to do it. She didn't even know if it would work.

There was a pause, then. Surprise, maybe? She wasn't sure. But one second it was hovering, considering, and the next it was gone as the wave swept through the rest of the building. She took in one careful breath, and then another, hardly registering the conversation that was going on over the radio.

Her stomach still roiling, Charlie looked around the ward that she barely remembered entering. Mindless walking was a trademark for her. She'd even set a few of the hospital's garish chairs in the middle of the hall leading to the maternity and pediatrics ward. She hoped it would keep her from wandering into the area when she wasn't paying attention.

The surgery area was small. A single OR, recovery room,

and surgery waiting area all crammed into one corner of the floor. She'd never had much of a reason to be inside a surgery ward, thankfully, but it looked close to what she'd seen on medical drama shows. A multitude of blocky overhead lights, a single table, bare of sheets, came near to the bottom of her rib cage. She recognized some items surrounding the bed. A hook to hang IVs on. A table with a metal tray on it where surgical instruments would have lain. Another with a pile of bloody gauze heaped upon it.

She frowned. Something about the scene wasn't right, but she couldn't place what. That was when Jacques' voice finally registered, and she heard him saying something about Union Grace waking up. His tone was so melodramatic. He had no idea what they'd just gotten themselves into. None of them did.

Charlie fumbled with the button on the radio pack, and said, "She's not." She couldn't say more, not right then.

She and Jacques had saved each other thirteen years ago, but that had seemed like pure luck and happenstance. What were the chances that they could do it again? Would he want to save her again after how things happened? Also, what in the hell did they not know about this damned hospital?

Her legs threatened to buckle. She took an unsteady step toward the gauze-covered table and grabbed the edge. The thin threads of material, tacky with blood, clung to her fingertips. She then recognized what was so off about the sight. The hospital was clean. She had been through the Surgery Ward at least three times this morning, not to mention the countless circuits she had made on previous days. The gauze had never been there.

Movement caught in the corner of her eye, a flicker of pale blue sheet there and gone again.

Charlie slammed her lids shut, squeezing the edge of the metal cart hard enough that she felt like she was going to leave the impressions of her fingers in it. It was too soon for manifestations with this much substance. There were rules to this. Hell, she'd made a chart at one point because the activity level was so damned predictable. Union Grace had said fuck her chart.

Somewhere nearby, maybe in the overnight stay area, a piece of equipment beeped loudly. The sound made her pulse race. In the next second, there was cursing and the sounds of that thing Jacques called an EMF started making a hellacious noise. The sudden cacophony slammed into her senses, going after her temples with an ice pick. "Shut up," she whispered. "Shut up, shut up, shut up!"

And then, as abruptly as it had begun, the hospital snapped back to normal. The sudden shift had her opening her eyes in surprise, head whipping around the room. When she saw nothing, she looked at the cart again. It was empty now. She swallowed. Even the bed was now bare of its pale blue sheet.

Silence held long enough for her to take several unsteady breaths before chaos erupted from the radio as the team attempted to talk over each other. It took a piercing whistle from someone—she guessed Jacques—before everyone quieted down.

"Whose EMF went off?" Yeah, it had to have been Jacques.

"Mine." It was the fifth member of the team, the skinny one, though she couldn't think of the woman's name.

"Give your location, the level that the EMF registered at, and what happened, Rachelle," Jacques said, his voice firm but kind.

"Um ... L&D. Orange, I think. One of those machines, you know, the ones that monitor your heart rate and stuff? It just kind of," her voice went up an octave, "came on? It scared the fuck out of me. Pardon my Fre—uh, language."

"Kiffer?" Jacques again.

"Confirming on cams now."

The way they all snapped into business mode jarred her. Almost as much as the shift the hospital made to fucking scary and back again. Charlie shook her head and started toward the stairs. This wasn't business as usual. If they couldn't understand that, she'd have to make them. Starting with Jacques.

CHAPTER FIFTEEN

Charlie shot out of the surgery ward and down the stairs. She hit the door heading into the lobby of the ground floor with both hands, expecting it to fly open. Pain rocketed up from the palm of her hands, through her wrists, and into her forearms as the door resisted her. She took a step backwards, clutching her arms to her chest. "Crap!"

She waited for the pain to subside and tried again. The door sprung open with no resistance, knocking against the doorstop with a thud. Charlie scowled. *And the evil door has met its defeat! Next step, the evil within! Or, you know, death. That'll work, too.* Sometimes she couldn't tell the difference between her friendly inner voice and her bitchy one.

But she did know the last thing they needed was for stuck doors to trap them in the building. Unease traced a cold trail down her spine. If she couldn't get Jacques to leave, at the least she was going to WD-40 the hell out of all the doors.

Stepping through the doorway, she spotted Jacques heading down the right wing's hallway. "Jacques!"

He stopped, turning to look over his shoulder. She hurried to his side. He frowned, asking, "What's up?"

"We need to leave."

Turning to face her fully, he said, "We just got here."

"Didn't you feel that? That's not normal!" Frustration edged her voice with a sharpness she didn't intend.

"A display like that this early, when it's not even fully dark outside, is a little weird," he said. "But nothing to be concerned about. Nobody got hurt." His gaze searched her face, and he tilted his head. "You witnessed something too, didn't you?"

Charlie bit her lip. When Jacques was little, his instinct was to run toward weird or scary shit, not away from it. Had that changed? Would telling him what she'd experienced convince him they needed to leave, or make him more determined to stay?

"Charlie?" He pointed his camera in her direction. "What happened?"

She froze, her attention going to the round dark eye of the camcorder leering into her soul. Charlie didn't deny what she could do. It was a part of her life, but it was one that went unspoken, unacknowledged as much as possible. Admitting she was some sort of freak on camera? Charlie swallowed hard.

"We run a show," Jacques said. "Occasionally, you're going to be on camera."

"I'm not comfortable with this." The lens of the camera seemed to grow larger the more she looked at it. "I try to avoid attention, not feed into it. Could you turn that off so we can talk?"

"If you were trying to avoid attention, why have you spent the last several years staying in all the haunted inns, then?" There was an edge to his voice as well. He didn't turn the camera off.

She wondered briefly how he knew what she'd been up to before realizing Grant must have told him. She tore her gaze from the camera. "I," she paused, swallowed hard. Her reasons made sense to her, but admitting them to someone else made her insides twist. "They don't hurt anyone. The spirits at the places I stay. Pests sometimes, yeah, but for the most part they're fine."

He snorted, then pulled his mask down under his chin. "Tell that to Cheswaithe."

She frowned. "What about Cheswaithe?"

"One of the spirits nearly clobbered me with a picture frame when we were investigating it. Got quite rude through the spirit box. Not too fond of a black man messing about on his property."

Charlie recoiled, shame sweeping through her. "Oh my god," she whispered. "I had no clue. I'm so sorry. Jacques, I'm sorry. I would never have–I do my research. I saw nothing showing the ghosts were dangerous. Shit. I'm sorry. I didn't even stay that long. It should have been okay. Shit. Shit."

He raised a palm, and she fell silent. He touched something on the side of the camera in his hand. The red light went off. Over the radio, he said, "Need a moment," and then fussed with his GoPro, turning it off. He pointed at hers. She stood stiff, frozen with horror at the fact she'd inadvertently almost gotten him hurt *again*, while he deactivated it.

Once free from monitoring, he said, "I turned the cameras off because the team doesn't know exactly what you do. For both of our sakes, I want to keep it that way. Okay?"

She nodded.

"Regarding Cheswaithe, it wasn't a big deal. And it's not important. Tell me what scared you to the point you came running to tell me we needed to leave?"

And they were back to square one. Would admitting what she'd experience help or hinder her efforts? "The details don't matter, do they? It scared me, Jacques. Union Grace shouldn't be acting up this powerfully. Not yet. It's not time. You should go. Please. Before anyone gets hurt."

He ignored her pleas. "What do you mean it's not time? They're spirits, Charlie. They only obey schedules in–"

She cut him off. "When I'm involved, they do! It takes about three days to charge up dormant spirits. On day four, small stuff happens, and it builds from there. It's a pattern, Jacques. We saw it that week."

The words weighed heavy between them. Charlie tried to fight the memories from swamping her again. She didn't need to spiral right now. She needed to get Jacques and his crew out of the building. "Look, can you just trust me? Please? If Union Grace is going to come out swinging like that, I can't predict what will happen, Jacques. If I can't predict it, I can't keep you safe."

A door creaked somewhere nearby. The air felt charged, heavy.

His perfectly groomed eyebrows drew together. He studied her with an intensity which made her want to squirm. Finally, slowly, he said, "The obvious solution would be for you to leave. Things can't get any stronger if you're not here, right?"

Charlie scowled. "I'm planning on it. I just can't leave until tomorrow afternoon."

"Why not? If it's dangerous enough that you're telling me I need to get my crew out of here asap, then why are you staying until tomorrow?"

Now she squirmed. "It's in my contract."

"And it's in our contract that we'll investigate and do our best to exorcise any spirits here."

"Yes but–"

"But what?" His voice got harder. "I wasn't eager to be here either, but now that we're here, we're going to make the best of it unless I think things are getting too dangerous. This is what we do, Charlie. We train to handle dangerous paranormal situations. Do you know how to do anything but cause them?"

The question rocked her back on her heels. She reeled, but before she could find the words to say, he scrubbed a hand across his face. "I didn't mean it like that," he said, taking a deep breath. A muscle in his jaw twitched. "I mean, not the way it came out. Do you have any practical experience in defending yourself in paranormal situations? Besides *that* time?"

She thought about it for a moment and then shook her head. Her defense was mostly staying on the move and not going to places she knew were dangerous.

He nodded. "Okay, then we're not going anywhere. Not yet. Just because you're scared that we can't handle something doesn't mean it's true. I'm not nine anymore, Charlie. We have tools available to us now that we didn't before. I'm not convinced we're in over our heads. At least not yet."

How could he be so calm about this? Only stupid people willingly put themselves in the line of fire unless they were trying to be a big damn hero. This wasn't a big damn hero situation. "But what if something happens like it—"

"Of the two of us, I'm the one who lost half of my family that night, Charlotte. I know just how dangerous spirits can be." He exhaled noisily, and when he spoke again, his voice was gentler. "It's a hospital. Lots of people died here, so naturally it's going to be more intense than you're used to."

"Jacques ..."

Wheels squeaked as a derelict gurney covered in cracked, thin padding shifted an inch or so. He seemed oblivious to it.

"Enough," he snapped. "We're both working here together, but you aren't part of Banshee Investigations, Charlie. You're certainly not the boss. I'll take what you said under advisement, but I make the call on whether my team pulls out. Not you."

Embarrassment and anger heated Charlie's cheeks. He was right, but she didn't have to like it. Her pulse hammering in her ears, she turned to leave.

He caught her arm. "Hey, wait." His voice was gentle. "I stocked the hospital with some basic defensive tools. Salt, cold iron, et cetera. There are bags of equipment on every floor. Did you see them?"

"Those neon bags?"

He offered a small, sad smile. "A better kit than a cast-iron skillet and salt. My team knows how to use everything in the bags. Let's grab one and I'll run you through the basics, okay?"

She nodded, unsure of how to handle his sudden change of tack.

"Okay. Before we go any further, let's talk about the role you'll play in front of the cameras. Because you will have to be in front of them sometimes. Do you know what a medium is?"

"Yeah, I'm not completely ignorant." There was nothing to read in his tone. His question hadn't been rude. But she was too damned on edge. In her peripheral vision, a sheet of paper slid along the floor like a breeze had picked it up. "They claim they can communicate with the dead. Give details about them."

"Right. Can you do that? Em never went into detail about what you could do when we were younger, so I'm not sure exactly how wide a range you have."

His explanation helped calm her a bit. She licked her lips. "Kind of. I can't see them, but I can sense them."

"Okay, then we go with that. On camera, you only talk about feeling their presence and if they feel good or bad or whatever. Okay?"

Charlie tentatively nodded. She'd seen enough of this type of thing, sometimes even in person if a medium was on location when she was there. Before they could say anything more, Kiffer's voice came over the radio. "Showing a temperature drop in the morgue. It dropped five degrees in the last minute."

"I'll go look," he said, pulling his mask back up. He raised his eyebrows at Charlie, cocking his head toward the stairs.

"Jacques, did you hear me?" Kiffer's voice came through again, static worse than usual.

Rolling his eyes, Jacques repeated himself. He looked at Charlie questioningly. She gave him a small smile and nodded to show she'd be fine tagging along. She wanted that run through.

CHAPTER SIXTEEN

Charlie's emotions were still raw as she trailed Jacques across the cracked and dull linoleum floor towards the stairs. She made herself focus on her surroundings. The hair on the back of her neck prickled as their boots clomped down the bare concrete stairs in a slow and steady rhythm. The only light source in the stairwell was their battery-operated harness lights, creating sharp and twisting shadows.

Stairways were some of the creepiest places to her mind. This wasn't something unique to Union Grace. Something about them made her feel like if she didn't concentrate hard on where she was going, she might end up somewhere else. Or bring someone out with her who wasn't there when she went in. With Union Grace, though, it wasn't just one stairwell. It was all of them.

The only area that gave the stairs any actual competition was the morgue. Though she was almost sure that was because it was somewhere they stored dead people on slabs. Ergo, even completely absent of spirits, a morgue would never not be creepy as hell.

A few steps from the bottom, she heard the sharp tapping of high heels coming down the stairs. Far faster than she would have ever been capable of managing. Instinctively, she hugged the railing, making sure whomever was in such a hurry had plenty of room. Jacques did the same, and the woman swept past them, perfume trailing behind her. She was down the stairs and through the door leading into the basement floor before both even registered that once again, an EMF was raising hell.

This time it was the EMF attached to Jacques' belt.

He turned slowly, looking slightly up at Charlie because of where she was on the stairs. She looked past him to the door, which had made no sound as it closed behind the woman. "Did you see her?"

Charlie shook her head. "Sensed her. Smelled her perfume, but that was it. You?"

Jacques' brows drew together. "Nothing I trust. The way these lights bounce as we step down makes visuals entirely unreliable. Hold on a sec." He activated his radio and went through the now familiar process of confirming and time stamping the activity.

This time Kiffer had nothing to tell them. There had been a slight temperature drop in the stairwell, but nothing dramatic. No evidence of the basement door opening on the infrared camera, either. It had been a purely visual and olfactory manifestation. He yelled at them to turn their cameras back on, though.

Jacques acknowledged it and activated both of their cameras. Once his handheld was on, he rotated the LCD screen toward him and said, "Union Grace isn't a lady who needs three cups of coffee before she's ready to face the day. Just now, Charlie and I were on our way down to the morgue to investigate a drop in temperature and we both heard this woman in heels running down the stairs behind us. We moved over, as one does, and she zipped past us to head into the bottom floor. It was only after she'd passed that our brains finally caught up, and we realized it had to have been a ghostly encounter. Because while fashion might be fun, none of my team is wearing heels here."

He winked at the camera, and Charlie turned away, rolling her eyes. "We could even smell her perfume. So now it's time to go see if our ghostly visitor was going anywhere in particular ... and check out anything that might be bumping around in the morgue. You'll be with us for this leg of the experience!" With that, he flipped the camera back around and held it in one hand as he stepped down the last couple of stairs.

At the doorway, he looked pointedly at her and inclined his head toward the door. Resisting the urge to roll her eyes because she really did not want to be on camera any more than was necessary, Charlie slipped by him. Unlike the ground floor door, this door didn't have the push bar. She grabbed the large metal handle there instead and pulled. As with the other, it resisted her initial attempt. She growled.

"You okay?"

"These fucking doors," she said, and tried again.

"Is it locked?"

The sheer stupidity of the question had her turning to him and saying, "I'm pretty sure locking the exit to a fire escape route was probably illegal even back in the ... whenever."

"Well, maybe they installed a lock after it closed down? To keep people from snooping?"

"Jacques?"

"What?"

Stepping aside, she gestured at the door. "In order for the door to be locked, there would have to be a lock." Without waiting for his acknowledgment, she put both hands on the handle and yanked.

At first, there was only resistance. Her mind conjured up someone on the other side, pulling as hard as she was in the opposite direction, doing their best to make sure that the door to this level stayed closed. Like whomever it was didn't want her going into the basement. But then, with an audible pop, the door gave in to the pressure. The sudden release took her by surprise, and she almost landed on her ass.

"I don't think Grace wants us poking around her bottom," Jacques drawled as he walked past her onto the bottom floor.

Charlie didn't dignify the comment with a direct response. Instead, she swerved around him and strode toward the morgue. Soonest begun, soonest done. "I swear, if one drawer rattles ..." she mumbled.

"I'll race you to the exit," Jacques said in agreement, coming up on her heels.

CHAPTER SEVENTEEN

The morgue's cold raised goose-flesh on Jacques' skin. As the metal doors swung silently shut behind them, they looked around the room.

On the far wall, close to where body storage began, the bright red digital numbers of a thermometer ticked slowly downward. Jacques brought his camera up and panned the room, looking for visible signs of paranormal activity. The room felt too large for the small hospital. It, combined with the on-site crematorium, took up about one fourth of the basement.

It looked much like the morgues he saw in new television shows. A little surprising, but he guessed if the original design wasn't broken, there would be no need to fix it. Cold stainless steel lined one wall, with several thick, hinged doors set only a few inches apart. Dominating the center of the room, two autopsy stations stood. Large light stands loomed over metal tables with rust-colored lines running down them. Equipment trays—one full, one empty—stood silent sentinel.

Scales perched at the feet of the tables, and Jacques was suddenly positive that if he tipped the hanging basket down, he "would see the thick, red, decaying muscle of a heart lying in congealed blood, struggling to provide for a circulatory system long gone, as it–"

"Seriously? Lay off the horror movie voice over, Jacques," Charlie groused beside him. Jacques startled, unaware he'd been narrating his thoughts out loud.

"Sorry. Force of habit when I have a camera in my hands."

He subtly turned the cam in her direction, hoping she wouldn't see it in the darkness. The GoPro footage would be grainy and dim, but his baby should be able to use the light from their flashlights. Unable to resist poking at her a bit—spooking each other was part of the fun of ghost hunting, especially if you were a little pissed at the other person—he said, "Creep you out?"

"We're in a morgue," she said, giving him a look that said he was mentally deficient. "A place where they brought dead people and cut them open and ... Yes, you did, alright?" She rolled her shoulders and shuddered. "What are we doing down here? I mean, we confirmed the temperature drop because it's obviously cold as fuck, so now what?"

"Now we take EMF readings and ask a few questions with the DAR to see if we get any answers."

She cocked her head at him. "DAR?"

Jacques picked up the DAR from where it hung on a lanyard against his chest and waggled it at her. "Digital audio recorder," he said. "Sometimes referred to as a DVR, but that can get confusing—"

"Oh, my dad used one of those to take notes on the fly so he could type them up later." She bobbed her head in understanding. "And if the activity is high, you probably can't use your smartphone, right?"

He looked at her in surprise, and she shrugged, saying, "I have to limit my time around electronics. They start to go haywire after a few hours. I gotta keep them turned off and in a Faraday cage when I'm not using them or I end up replacing them, like, every year."

"Huh." He knew some people couldn't wear watches because they stopped for no apparent reason. Were they like her? Maybe just not as powerful? It was the sort of thought which stoked anew the deep-rooted curiosity he'd had about her since Em barged into his room when he was seven, talking about his new friend and swearing him to secrecy.

He made a mental note to look into it later. But for now, they had work to do. Turning the recorder on, he said, "My name is Jacques, and I'm here with Charlie. It is June 24th, and approximately," he turned his wrist to get a look at his analogue watch, "five p.m. Are there any spirits present?" He paused for about twenty seconds, then continued. "Could you tell me your name?"

Jacques took his time with the questions while Charlie wandered around the room. He tracked her movements with the camera, watching as she inspected things, hands clasped behind her in a childlike posture. He got the feeling from the way she examined things she hadn't spent a lot of time down here before they came. Not that he could blame her.

He pulled himself back to the task at hand. It was time for them to move on. He thanked the spirits for talking with them. After he turned off the DAR, he radioed Kiffer to let him know it had been dead. If anything had happened, it had finished before they'd arrived.

Since they were already down there, he figured they could cover the other rooms in the basement. See if they got any bites. He doubted the viewers knew how much time they spent talking to the air and hoping for glimpses of things. The beauty of editing made everything seem much more intense than it normally was.

He got Charlie's attention, saying, "Come on. I owe you a review session with the safety bag and I'd rather not do it in the morgue."

Nodding like she was cosplaying a bobblehead, Charlie beat him through the doors and up the stairs.

CHAPTER EIGHTEEN

Rachelle took her job seriously, and Birdie was determined to make Jacques realize it. Even though she'd only been on a few small-scale investigations with them, Jacques had confided he regretted the decision. He didn't feel like she was coming up to standards quick enough, and he was thinking about letting her go depending on how this investigation went. So, after he gave her directions to do a sweep with her digital voice recorder, he mostly kept his rig trained on her after giving the nursery they were entering a few casual sweeps. And she did a great job. Even though her breathing was quick with excitement and her head kept snapping around like she expected some creature to appear from the shadows, her voice was calm and the hand holding the recorder did not tremble.

He envied her. Just a little. The fact that they were in a nursery didn't seem to bother her at all, while this section gave him the creeps more than any other area they'd been in. Even though all their preliminary rounds showed this was—pardon the pun—a dead area. There was something about the juxtaposition of the silent stillness of abandonment against what should have been happening. Fussy cries, gurgles, snuffling babies, and bustling nurses should have filled the room. Even the equipment showing zero activity added to the unnatural atmosphere in the room. But, he thought, he'd rather deal with too much silence here than the alternative. Ghosts were ghosts, but some were worse than the others. Disembodied baby cries would send him running—well, considering it at least—right the fuck out the door.

He swallowed and realized he was thirsty. Not wanting to fumble with his water bottle right now, he held the rig steady with one hand while he retrieved a tin of mints from his pants pocket. He fumbled trying to open it with one hand, and the tin slipped from his grasp and fell to the floor with a clang that seemed too loud in the silence.

Rachelle jumped and screeched, whirling around to find the noise.

He laughed, just a little. He couldn't help it. She was damned cute when she was all jumpy. "That was me, sorry. Tried to get my mints but dropped the tin." He pointed to his feet, where small, round white mints lay scattered across the floor.

He hadn't meant to drop the mints. Hadn't meant to laugh at her, either. But her cheeks flushed above the mask, and the way her eyes darkened, he knew she thought he'd done it to get a reaction out of her. Jacques? Yeah. Mac? Of course. None of them were above playing tricks on each other for giggles. But they hadn't hit that point with her yet. He heard her huff as she turned away from him. Shit. He needed to make nice. He knew Rachelle's reaction to the EMF going off embarrassed her. He was a little ashamed of the chuckle he'd given at her reaction. Especially since she'd gone pink-cheeked and refused to look at him for a few minutes after.

And now he'd went and made things worse, and he felt like a heel for it. In the relatively short amount of time they'd known each other, Rachelle had carved out a small place for herself in his heart. She loved what they did and exhibited an unbridled enthusiasm for the work that brought fresh energy to the job. The downside to this was sometimes she acted first and thought later, and she talked way too much—something that drove all of them nuts—but she meant no harm by it. And she was trainable. She'd already picked up so much. But there was a strong possibility that trainability alone would not be enough.

But Birdie thought she'd be good for the team overall. The comments about introducing "fresh meat" to the team, both on their videos and sent through their website, were positive. Since Rachelle startled easily, it made for some great clips. But also—and to him it was just as important as the numbers—she was good people. The world needed to value those types more. Even if she did occasionally make him want to duct tape her mouth shut.

He stepped over to her and put a hand on her shoulder. "It really was an accident, 'Chelle. My mouth was dry, but I didn't want to jostle the rig while I got a drink of water, so I figured I'd suck on a mint for a bit. Then I butterfingered the tin. That's all."

She went rigid under his touch, but didn't pull away. "I've been studying," she whispered, "and practicing. Been going out to cemeteries and stuff by myself." She looked over her shoulder at him, her eyes troubled. "I know I'm not performing like anyone wanted. That I'm not good enough for the show. But I'm trying. I just—"

He squeezed her shoulder. "Jacques been doing this stuff since he was little. Mac's shaped her whole persona around being the logical, non-excitable teammate that always looks for the fake first. If we'd brought on a clone of either of them, we'd run smoother, but it wouldn't be nearly as interesting. The numbers are good, 'Chelle. It'll be fine."

Birdie meant it. He'd stick to her like glue for the duration of the investigation. He didn't get as involved in the meat of things as others did, but it wasn't for lack of knowing what to do. Birdie was happy letting others be the face of things. He was happiest behind the camera.

Rachelle's expression slowly lightened. She turned and wrapped her arms around him, giving him a squeeze that made him grunt in surprise. She was strong for such a tiny thing.

"You're awesome," she said as she drew away.

"Yep."

She snickered, and he smiled.

"Hey," he said, "We've done all we can in this area. Why don't we head over to the peds area and look around?"

"Because peds is so much less creepy than the nursery," she said, rolling her eyes.

He grinned. "And here I thought I was the only one creeped out by being in the nursery."

This time they laughed together, and a little tension left his shoulders.

CHAPTER NINETEEN

It was after seven when they broke for dinner and headed out to the vehicles. This late in June, they had some gorgeous golden hour lighting going on. Jacques met Birdie's eyes and arched his brows.

Birdie gave him a chin lift in acknowledgment and came over. "What's doin'?"

"Thinking exterior shots with the drone, and ..." he cut a glance at Charlie's truck, where she'd disappeared as soon as they set foot outside.

"Yeah, look weird if we didn't," Bird told him.

His words reminded Jacques how much he appreciated the man. They might disagree occasionally, but Birdie's mind synced with his for the show.

'Chelle's good with the drone."

Rachelle was one of their areas of disagreement, but if he said she was good with a drone, Jacques believed him. He needed to give the girl a fair shake. Besides, he could always have Kiffer take new footage tomorrow evening if necessary. "Alright, get her set on that and I'll go drag Charlie out. Time to film her introduction."

Rachelle's excited squeak grated on his ears as he knocked on the door to Charlie's camper a half minute later. When the brunette opened it, giving him a wary look, he said, "We need to get an intro filmed for you."

Her shoulders slumped. She sighed. "Now?"

"Now," he said, smirking. "Take a minute to freshen up.

Maybe rub some of the mask lines out of your face a bit. Then meet us beside the van. Won't take long."

Charlie gave an Eeyore like "Okay" and headed for her wet wipes.

"It'll be painless, I swear," he reassured her before walking away from the open door.

CHARLIE FROZE the instant Birdie pointed the camera in her direction, brown eyes comically large. Jacques barely resisted the urge to bury his face in his hands. It had been funny the first time, but they were on their fourth take and no matter what he told her, how natural he instructed her to act, she gave the same startled, deer-in-the-headlights look.

Pinching the bridge of his nose, he motioned to Birdie to give them a minute. Bird nodded and went over to Rachelle, who was making another loop around the hospital with the drone. Quite competently from the looks Jacques had snuck.

Jacques turned back to Charlie. An idea struck. He was reluctant to bring up his brother, but at this point, he'd do whatever it took just to get the intro done. "When Em pointed a camera at you, you'd ham it up," he said, keeping his tone as light as possible.

"We were thirteen and not posting things on YouTube for half the world to see," she said, a whine edging her voice.

"Cherie, I'm honored you think the show is so popular, but I assure you, half the world will not see your lovely face." The numbers weren't paltry, but if playing down their base made Charlie comfortable enough to shoot this, then that's what he'd do. "And besides, people will not be focusing on you. Their attention will be on Union Grace and Banshee doing its thing, okay?"

She chewed on her lower lip, then nodded.

"Ready?"

She raised her eyebrows and gave a quick, definitive headshake. "But let's get it over with."

"Thattagirl," he said, grinning. He called for Birdie.

The big man came over and raised the fancier handheld cam into position once again. Charlie froze, but then she breathed out slowly and he saw her shoulders relax a bit. The way she was standing—arms crossed and fists hidden—made it clear she was uncomfortable, but she didn't look like she was staring down the barrel of a gun anymore. Hopefully, in time, she'd relax more ... but if not, he had a feeling they'd be getting enough kick-ass footage from Union Grace that nobody would pay too much attention to the little medium with stage fright.

His cameraman counted down from three on huge fingers. When he hit one, Jacques smiled into the camera and said, "Bonjour, mes amis, it's Jacques with Banshee Investigations! We are standing outside Union Grace hospital, where we've gotten exclusive permission to film an investigation. More on that later, of course, but for now, as a special bonus, we wanted to introduce you to someone who will join us for the upcoming investigation."

"Now, loyal fans of the show know we shy away from using mediums, preferring to gather our evidence with scientific tools so that we have measurable, exact data. However, sometimes you need to bend your own rules a bit!"

He turned, angling his body toward Charlie. "I've witnessed Charlie's ability to ... coax the dead to communicate, and I'm confident she will help us illustrate exactly how haunted Union Grace hospital is, won't you, Charlie?"

Charlie's eyes flicked in Birdie's direction, but then returned to him. She cleared her throat. "Yeah. I'm sure Grace will show out for us."

It wasn't the best answer, but at least it had more than one syllable.

Rather than push her any further and potentially have to reshoot the entire thing, he turned his attention back to the camera and said, "We'll be running a poll in the comment section for this video. Please let us know, have you ever heard of Union Grace hospital? Also, please remember to like and subscribe if you haven't already done so. Trust me, folks, you do not want to miss this."

Birdie nodded, signaling they were good, and lowered the camera. Jacques gave Charlie a bright smile. "Not so bad, was it?"

Brown eyes narrowed, she said, "I'll stick with the ghosts, thanks." Without another word, she strode in Mac's direction.

"Let's review that and get it put up on the website after dinner," he told Birdie. The area was almost a complete dead zone, but they'd found a small area with a weak signal they could use for slow as hell uploads with their Wi-Fi booster. "Use it as another teaser for the upcoming investigation."

Fifteen minutes, Birdie was calling for him through a mouth full of cold cuts as he worked with the footage.

Jacques hopped up into the back of the van and looked over Birdie's shoulder. They could have moved his station to the RV, but the bearded man enjoyed having his own space. Something Jacques could appreciate. "What am I looking at?"

His interview with Charlie was on the screen, but paused in a rather unflattering frame where his mouth was half open.

"This," Birdie said, and hit play.

"What the hell?"

"My thoughts exactly," the larger man said. "You're clear as day, so it's not an issue with the feed. But your little ghost whisperer ..."

"The fans are fucking going to love this," Jacques whispered.

"Yeah. The rest of us would like an explanation, though. I've never seen a *medium* display like this on film."

Jacques clapped a hand to his shoulder. "Soon, my friend. Soon."

CHAPTER TWENTY

After the crew demolished their fine dinner cuisine of sandwiches, fruit cups, and Gatorade, and bagged up the trash bagged, Kiffer ordered everyone to do another equipment check before the light faded, and they went back inside. The likelihood of anything having a problem at this point was low, but they still needed to check batteries if nothing else. Quickly draining batteries were a sign of paranormal activity by themselves. Well, a possible sign. It could just be the batteries going bad.

Mac groaned but got to work. Jacques nodded to signal he'd heard Kiffer, but then stepped around the other side of the RV to take a call. Birdie started helping Rachelle with her gear. Charlie looked around at the crew that had moved into swift action and then back to Kiffer, raising her eyebrows.

He beckoned her over, figuring it was a good time to learn a bit more about her. Maybe get some details on how she and Jacques knew each other. The air was heavy with tension when she and Jacques spent more than a couple minutes together, and he'd never seen his boss turn off all his comms in the middle of an investigation. Those two had a history beyond what they were telling people. And, from the looks of things, it wasn't a good one.

Also, the technology remark from earlier still intrigued him. It had taken no time once she left for the screens to go back to normal. Paranormal activity could mess with the screens, but there had been no activity in the van. Just the two of them. As far as he knew, a medium's mere presence didn't screw with shit like that.

Charlie came over willingly enough. He smiled. "Just need to check the battery in your harness flashlight and radio since you aren't carrying anything else. Oh, and the GoPro. Thought I'd walk you through it."

She nodded her agreement, and he got to work. It didn't take him long to realize that something was weird. He frowned, calling to Mac, "How's your batteries looking?"

Not looking up from what she was doing, Mac told him her stuff was good. On track for replacement at the end of the night like normal. What went unsaid was the batteries she had shoved in a pouch on her waist. They always carried backups.

Birdie gave the same answer for both his and Rachelle's equipment. He was still frowning when he looked back at Charlie. "There's no way that all three of your batteries are that low by sheer coincidence."

Charlie shrugged. "Told you electronics didn't like me."

He shook his head. "Alright, let me get these changed out."

He grabbed the replacements, and started with a casual question, "So, what do you think of Union Grace? You've had a lot more time to get acquainted with the old girl than we have."

"I think we need to get the job done as fast as we can and get out of here," Charlie said.

He was silent for a moment, wondering how much of his own misgivings to share with her. He decided not to feed into it after a moment. If she was a medium, he didn't need to taint her perceptions with his own. The idea was for them to interact with the environment as free of influence as possible.

"Why do you say that?"

"Because it's dangerous."

"Ah," he unscrewed the back of the radio to change that pack out, "we've been through worse. Don't worry, Jacques knows what he's doing. We all do."

"That's what I'm banking on," Charlie whispered.

"Sorry?"

She waved a hand, dismissing his question. "Never mind. Just a little keyed up." Her tone of voice let him know further questions weren't welcome. A second later, though, she said, "So, catch anything on those security camera things you guys were talking about earlier? Or just the stuff they told you about over the radio?"

His inner nerd perked up. "We did. While you and Jacques were down in the basement, there was an apparition on the third floor." While the hospital had four floors counting the basement, they'd all agreed to call them basement, ground, third and fourth.

"What'd you see?" Mac asked, suddenly beside them.

He jumped, and Mac laughed before telling Charlie, "He's a pussy."

"I am not," he shot back, as heat hit his cheeks. He was just easy to startle. Not the same thing as being a pussy.

"Yeah, sure." There was a bite to her voice that wasn't usually there. Mac headed to the RV. They followed her. In the door, she extended a hand to Charlie. "Come on. Can't see the footage he's going to show us for shit from there."

Charlie scowled. "I can manage. You've seen my truck."

"Yeah," Mac said, "but humor me anyway." She wiggled her eyebrows.

Charlie snorted and took her hand. Mac pulled her up into the RV with unnecessary force, bringing them into proximity.

"Hi," Mac said, using the voice Jacques loved for the camera.

Kiffer rolled his eyes at the theatrics. Mac wouldn't

understand subtlety if it bit her in the ass. Unfortunately, those theatrics worked a disgusting amount of time. "And she's the one who didn't want you to come."

"Oh, I want her to come," Mac said without skipping a beat, not turning her face away from Charlie's. "I just didn't think we needed a medium on this trip."

It took a second for Mac's innuendo to process. When it did, he groaned. She was worse than any of the men on the team. And Charlie was eating it up. "Can you please just ... not? And move so I can get in here, please."

Charlie snorted, but moved to stand as far away from the screens as she could get.

Mac grinned at him as she stepped aside. "I think that's the lady's choice, don't you?"

He shook his head in disbelief.

Charlie giggled, and he felt a pang of sadness It was a unique situation. He'd never imagined finding someone both he and Mac would be interested in. Their tastes were miles apart most of the time. He shrugged the thought off. They needed to concentrate on work. "Alright, you two. Let me focus."

He sat down at the computers and pulled up the clip from earlier. "So, first floor, right at the where the right hallway joins with the primary structure. This happened about thirty minutes ago."

He pressed play as the two gathered behind him and they all watched in fascinated silence. He'd played the footage countless times and still felt a zing of excitement.

When the incident finished, Kiffer tapped the space bar to halt it. He turned on the swivel seat and grinned at Mac. "Now, because I know you love me, I'll go ahead and tell you that prior to the 60s renovation of Union Grace, that door was not there. It was several feet further down the hallway. So whatever ghost we're dealing with ..."

"Is not an old one," Mac said, matching his grin with her own. "That is an excellent piece of footage, tech boy."

He laced his hands behind his head, hooking his feet under the circular footrest of the stool and faking a pose of utter confidence. "Your nickname bothers me not, for it is indeed the tech boy which has gotten the first evidence lasting longer than a sloth fart."

"Sloths don't fart," Charlie said.

He cut his eyes at the brunette, a childish spark of glee dancing in his chest. "How do you know?"

"Libraries are my friend," she said. "And Does It Fart was a perfect way to pass a cold winter day."

"A girl that also reads books about farts," he straightened and clasped a hand to his chest. He was still riding the high that came with sharing amazing footage, and he wanted to prove he could make her laugh, too. "We must marry. It's clearly meant to be."

She tried to hold a straight face, but the corners of her mouth twitched, and her eyes shone with amusement. Finally, the dam broke, and the laughter spilled out. "You need your future wife to like gas? Telling on yourself?"

He blinked, considered what he'd said for a moment, and groaned once more. Not his smoothest move.

Charlie was still laughing as she left the RV.

CHAPTER TWENTY-ONE

Jacques' phone buzzed in his hand. Grant Erschon's name popped up on display, hiding the upper half of the selfie he'd taken with Union Grace in the background. Brows raised, he gestured to Kiffer to give him a moment as he stepped around the side of the RV. "Jacques speaking," he said, half expecting the call to drop any second. His phone was showing one bar, and the line was as clear as graveyard fog.

"Jacques! It's Grant. I got your text earlier today. How are things going? Any excitement?"

Erschon sounded strange, voice imbued with an enthusiasm not present any other time they discussed Union Grace. "It's been ... interesting," Jacques said, choosing his words with care. He wanted to rail at Erschon for hiding who she'd be working with from Charlie, but it could wait until after they finished the job. "It's too early to tell how things are going to go, of course. We've not even spent our first night inside her."

Grant made a sound that sounded like a suppressed snort, and Jacques rolled his eyes. He tried to cut the conversation short. "I need to go get things ready for us to head back inside for the night, Grant. Was there something in particular you needed?"

Silence on the other end of the line. Long enough to make Jacques curious. Either the call dropped or Erschon was about to drop a bomb. Acting on the hunch, Jacques brought up the voice recorder function on his phone and started recording the conversation. Two seconds later, Grant spoke. "Actually, it occurred to me I'd forgotten to tell you something about the hospital. Nothing heinous, of course. But a bit of history to make things spicier for your little show."

Jacques pressed his lips together, nostrils flaring at the dig. "Oh? What's that?" Even if Grant wouldn't be professional about their business interaction, he had no excuse not to be.

"My grandfather, before his death, swore that a demon caused the hospital's demise. And after they committed him there—shortly before he died—he said that Union Grace wouldn't see peace until we could rectify the mistake that we'd made."

Dammit. This had drama written all over it, and he'd never been able to resist that. He was so damned glad he'd recorded the convo. "What mistake was that? Who is 'we'?"

"Well, that's the question, isn't it?" Grant said, voice too jovial. "Maybe you'll figure it out while you're investigating the hospital. Let me know if you find evidence of blood sacrifice or anything truly naughty, so we can get it handled, can you? Can't have anything sullying our name."

Jacques blinked in disbelief, then shrugged it off. Jacques had been the one in acting classes, but Grant had always been a dramatic sonuvabitch. "Will do." He pulled the phone away from his ear and found the airplane mode on the display. "I think we—" he said, and hit the button, "-need to end this conversation." He almost put the phone away, then reconsidered and went back to the selfie.

A quick filter gave the dilapidated building and his presence a more foreboding air. He loaded up a quick caption of: *Part of the joy of doing paranormal investigations in buildings built before the 90s - asbestos is everywhere. But, hey, it gives us an excuse to wear these sweet post-apocalyptic punk masks, right? #ByeAsbestos #GhostHunting #ParanormalInvestigations #BansheeInvestigations.* He paused, added a few more tags as an afterthought, and then saved it to his drafts before pocketing the device.

Digital addiction was definitely a thing. While he understood eliminating sources of electromagnetic interference, he hated having his phone off. Damned if he didn't crave the ability to pull up social media and get a quick hit of interaction whenever he had a spare minute. Right now, though, he needed to get his equipment checked, otherwise Kiffer would have his ass.

As Charlie bounded out, laughing, he peeked his head in. "What did I miss?"

"Oh, nothing," Kiffer said, groaning. "Just embarrassing myself, that's all."

"So, nothing new then," he declared.

Kiffer scowled while Mac cackled, and Jacques went to check his equipment.

CHAPTER TWENTY-TWO

E.R. to E.R. waiting room, then cross the open reception area. Spend a few moments lingering amongst the small in-house pharmacy area before peeking into the almost as small physical and occupational therapies area, and then Charlie'd make the trek through the old cafeteria. Last hit was imaging before she went for the stairs and up to the third floor.

It was a path Charlie could probably walk blindfolded and not one she wanted to be walking at all. Still, it gave her something to do while she let her mind wander. The interaction with Jacques earlier weighed on her. She didn't regret seeing him again but doing it under circumstances like these was less than ideal. Even the laughter (and the sparks) she'd shared with Mac and Kiffer only pushed the Anxiety Elephant off her chest for a little while. Also, the peopling. The team seemed nice enough, but Charlie had difficulty socializing with people she didn't know. The craving to be around people increased, but she didn't always want to interact with them. Life on the road had only emphasized her introvert's personality. People like Mac and Jacques particularly were a lot.

Watching the team's easy interactions with each other (apart from Rachelle, who was clearly New Girl) made her feel some sort of way, too. Knowing if Em was still alive, she'd have that easy camaraderie. Someone she could speak to in half-sentences and inside jokes that would leave them cracking up while others gave them the side-eye.

They'd have completed basic college by now. Both going towards getting their masters. Emerson wanted to be an astronaut. Charlie lacked the desire to strap her ass to a rocket hurtling her into space, but she'd thought being the geek on the ground keeping him safe sounded cool. And then when Em got married, she'd be his best woman, and when she met a person who she wanted to spend the rest of her life with, he'd be her best man.

Even their kids would have been friends, she thought, muttering an absent thank you to whichever spirit opened the pharmacy door for her. She went into the PT area and plopped down on one of the thickly cushioned mats she'd drug down from its hook on the wall. The plastic cover encasing the material crackled with age, but it was still soft enough to beat sitting on one of the hospital chairs.

She drew her legs in crisscross applesauce and let the air around her settle. Of all the rooms in the hospital, this one was one of the safest to her. Everywhere else was for the sick, but this room? This was one where people worked on getting stronger, not just healthy. There was a spirit, maybe belonging to a therapist who had worked in the room. She couldn't see it being a patient. It was so focused and calm. Like they had found their peace right here and had no desire to move on.

They did that sometimes, the spirits. Decided to stay and keep doing something rather than move on just because. She understood the desire to stay if it had been a life cut short or something, but sometimes spirits kept hanging around the places they'd felt happiest, whether it was the same as it had been or not.

She concentrated on that sense of peace in the corner for a few moments before reluctantly getting to her feet and heading for the door of the unit. She would, she thought, make a few more rounds before she noped out for the night.

The Banshee team seemed quite good with their nocturnal schedule, but her body was screaming at her to sleep.

Right before her hand closed around the metal pull bar of the PT room, the same malignant energy she sensed in the surgery ward earlier flickered across her senses. Charlie frowned and closed her eyes. It wasn't like it had been before. The wave that had almost overpowered her. This was more ... focused. She forced herself to visualize the hallway on the other side of the door, with its large square orange tiles and hallway walls flaking with paint. Of the eight fluorescent lights spaced evenly down the hallway, three were hanging loose from their moorings. One had a tube missing completely. On the opposite side of the hall were two small gender-separated restrooms. She had only gone into those once, because nobody needed bathroom ghosts or that smell.

It was fine. It was normal. She'd open the door and that was all she'd see. Taking a deep breath, she pulled open the door and stared into dead space.

At least that's how her brain interpreted the blackness. Like she'd opened the door to the Tardis mid-flight, only to find all the stars wiped from existence. The beam from her harness light was a futile hand trying to push the dark back as the inky blackness extended to fill the doorway opening.

Charlie swayed as vertigo overtook her, her body sure she was falling forward into a nothingness that would swallow her whole. But it would not be the nothingness of death, but an abyss that would trap her indefinitely, alive and screaming.

The distant sound of metal rasping against stone cut through the black, sent shivers racing down her back. It came again, closer. The next space between sounds closer still. Something was coming.

Her harness light flickered and then went black. In the complete absence of light, Charlie's mind raced to fill in the gaps. To identify who or what was coming down the hallway.

But the closest it could get was the sound of a knife against a whetstone. The promise of a deadly edge.

Taking a shallow breath, she slid one foot backwards. The plastic of the mat crinkled under her foot, and she froze.

The sound coming from the hallway stopped, arrested mid-stride. She wanted to freeze, to pretend if she could not see, she could not be seen. But staying in place was stupid. Her mouth as dry as the Sahara, pulse racing, Charlie took another step back, and then another. After each, she listened. Each time expecting to hear steps rushing toward her, an animalistic growl as it revealed itself before her world ended in teeth and pain and blood.

On the third step, her back came up against something firm and warm. Arms wrapped around her in a familiar embrace. *Hey, Chuck.* The unexpected sensation, the word murmured into her brain, shattered the flimsy wall of restraint keeping her voice in check, and Charlie screamed.

As she screamed and whirled around, the lights in the Physical Therapy room surged to eye-searing life long enough for her to see that no one was behind her before cutting out. Charlie fell to her ass on the mat and crab walked backward in the dark until her back and shoulders met with the reassuringly hard corner of the room.

She pulled her legs tight against her chest and wrapped her arms around them. She tried to get more air into her lungs, to calm herself down, but the mask was restricting her airflow, forcing her to take breaths that weren't enough. Suddenly she was unable to handle it touching her, suffocating her a second more. Charlie ripped it off her face and tossed it aside.

CHAPTER TWENTY-THREE

It happened like dominoes falling.

One moment the thermometer read seventy-three degrees, the next their breath crystallized in the air.

From below came the muffled but unmistakable sound of terrified screaming.

Then overhead lights flared into sudden, blinding brilliance as EMFs shrilled.

Darkness followed, returning with a nearly tangible pop. Their equipment quieted a heartbeat later. Jacques looked at his crew, counting them off, heart rabbiting in his chest. "What the hell was that?"

Mac rubbed her eyes, cursing.

Charlie. She was the only one not accounted for. Charlie screamed. Forgoing the radio attached to his belt, Jacques turned to his right and slammed through the door to the stairwell. He bounded down the stairs two at a time, hitting the door to the bottom floor at a run as Charlie's screams cut off. "Shit," he paused, trying to figure out where she was.

Unlike the rest of the crew who used the buddy system, Charlie wandered around alone and often in the opposite direction of where everyone else was going. He wasn't super happy about it, but she wasn't one of his crew he could command to buddy up. Besides, the less time they spent around her, the longer he could pretend she was just a medium.

"PT Room." Kiffer's voice fought through the heavy

static, broken but triumphant. Jacques hurried across the open reception area, stopping by the receptionist desk to scoop up a long iron poker from a neon bag. Then, gripping it like a baseball bat, he ran toward the PT room.

The sight of a single fluorescent light flickering right above the door to the physical therapy room had him slowing to a halt, heart pounding. He switched the radio to hands free and whispered, "You seeing this, Kif?"

"Yeah," his van camper replied. "How the hell is that light still on?"

It wasn't unusual for spirits to turn on lights, but generally there had to be power running to the building for that to happen. In Union Grace, there was no electrical power. All their equipment operated on rechargeable batteries for that very reason.

"I don't know," he said, struggling to catch his breath even though he kept himself in good shape. "What's the temp reading?"

"Couldn't tell you, boss," Kiffer replied, voice still so wrapped in static that Jacques understood him only through hours of experience with the radios. "I barely have visual as it is. All of our equipment is going nuts. Can you check with the handheld?"

He reached for the laser thermometer, but his conscience niggled. He asked, "Visual on Charlie?"

He recognized the heavy steps of Birdie coming up behind him and held up a hand to signal the man should come no further.

"Can't confirm. The camera in that room is nothing but static."

"Fuck," Jacques swore, shifting anxiously. She was one of the team, even if it was just this once, and he had to make sure she was okay. But he didn't know what sort of situation he was going to be walking into either. Scowling, he pulled the thermometer from his belt and took readings of the surrounding areas. The temperature rose from freezing to somewhere just below normal as he watched. Meanwhile, the light coming from overhead tapered to darkness.

He found his next breath came easily. The event was over. He took a moment, filling his lungs with air. Then, Birdie now so close on his heels he could feel the big man's heat, he edged open the door to the PT room.

Tucked into a corner at the back of the room, Charlie sat with her legs drawn up and her arms locked around them. Her respirator lay on the floor beside her, and she pressed her forehead against her knees.

"Hey," he said, approaching her like she was an injured animal he'd found on the road. "You okay?"

"I need," Charlie said, each word sharp and clear even though she didn't lift her head up, "a fucking whiskey."

Jacques winced. They didn't allow intoxicating substances during investigations. "Sorry, Charlie. We don't bring alcohol on site."

She lifted her head. There was a red mark around her cheeks where the mask had pressed against her face. She gave him a look spelling out how unhappy she was with the current situation and then said, "Maybe you don't. I don't have that problem."

She tried to rise to her feet, but then wobbled and sat back down hard. Birdie stepped around him and offered her a hand. Charlie stared at it for a second, then took it. Birdie kept hold of her hand until she was standing and steady. She thanked him, then pointed a finger at Jacques. "I'm going to go have a drink. Don't you say a damned word."

Jacques pressed his lips together, then pointed at the mask near her feet.

Charlie frowned, looking where he pointed. "Oh, for fuck's sake," she breathed, and scooped the offending item up. Rather than fitting it over her head with the straps, she held it to her face and stalked out of the room.

Jacques radioed to let everyone know he was heading outside with Charlie and followed her out.

CHAPTER TWENTY-FOUR

Outside the hospital, Charlie made a beeline for the back of her truck. Jacques barely got there in time to keep her from slamming the door closed. "Hey, talk to me," he said, then groaned and pulled the mask from his head, hooking it over the water bottle clipped to his belt so it hung at his side. He turned off his GoPro as he spoke. "What happened in there?"

Charlie scowled. "What do you think happened, Jacques? The ghost wanted to play chess?"

"I don't know what happened," he said, frowning. "I heard you scream; the lights went nuts. Bird and I came downstairs, and you were in the corner looking scared out of your wits. I need details, Charlie!"

"I don't know," she snapped, and sucked in a deep breath.

He saw her body tremble on the inhale and realized this wasn't just normal being shaken up after having the shit scared out of you. Something had really gotten to her. He braced a hand on the door to the camper and hauled himself into her space as she stepped back. Immediately, he felt a kinship with Gandalf. He could imagine how the wizard must have felt entering any of the houses in the Shire. Her camper was too fucking tiny. How did she live like this?

Up close, and in decent light, he could see red rimming her eyes and a pale cast to her skin. "Sit down," he said, looking pointedly at a small folding stool beside a tiny table.

She sat without protest, propping her elbows on the Formica and rubbing her temples.

"You mentioned whiskey?"

"Fridge."

He cringed at the liquor faux pas but grabbed the bottle of cinnamon whiskey out of the dorm-room sized fridge without a word. Rummaging found a cup with a flower-wreath wearing sloth and he filled it halfway up with whiskey before putting it on the table in front of Charlie.

Murmuring thanks, she grabbed the mug and downed the contents in a couple of swallows. Putting the cup back on the table, she beckoned for the bottle.

"You might wanna let that hit first, cherie."

"My whiskey. My camper. My rules," Charlie growled at him.

He filled the cup halfway up again and passed it over. She immediately lifted the cup to her lips again, but this time he was relieved to see roughly half of it remained. Setting the bottle on the counter, he took the second folding stool from its hook on the wall and sat down across from her.

"What happened?"

She told him in a rush of words, slowing down only when she got to where the arms had grabbed her. There, she took another drink of whiskey from the mug. Her next words were so quiet he could barely hear her. "It felt like Em. I swear it felt like Emerson."

He felt a little bolt of jealousy zing into his chest, followed by sadness. Ana had spoken to him, but never Emerson. Rather than sadden, it comforted him. The idea his big brother had moved on and wasn't still stuck here in the afterlife the way Ana was.

"Have you ... heard from him ... since?"

Charlie shook her head, and when she blinked, tears slipped down her cheeks. "The way the cabin burnt ... not hearing from him ... I thought they'd moved on. Have you heard from Ana?" Her face creased with pain, her eyes begged him to tell her no.

Hating to do it, he nodded. "Not until recently, but yeah. She keeps warning me about something. Telling me to be careful."

"Then they're both still here. Stuck here."

He nodded again, and Charlie buried her hands in her face. "Fuck!"

Disregarding his own rule about no alcohol during an investigation, Jacques twisted around to grab the bottle. He filled her cup back up again and then took a slug from the bottle.

He played with the edge of the label on the whiskey bottle, turning things over in his mind. Finally, he said, "We've got to help them. Like we couldn't before."

Without looking at him, Charlie drained her cup again. "Yeah," she said. "But how?"

He had a few ideas, but Charlie's eyes were already glazing over. She would not be useful tonight. "Let's think about it," he said, and rose to his feet. "But right now, you–"

An idea occurred to him, and he stopped. She was drunk. If there was a time to get an honest answer out of her, it was now. "Hey, Charlie?"

"Yeah?"

"What happened that night ... Nothing like that had ever happened to you before, right?"

She traced curlicues on the Formica with a finger. "Before that night, it had been all small shit. I knew that not all the surrounding spirits were friendly, but they'd done nothing more than pull my hair or hide things."

"What made things different? What changed?" He took another drink from the bottle, watching her over it. Charlie had never shown maliciousness in the time she'd been friends with Emerson. Recognizing that was one reason he could absolve her of blame.

Charlie continued tracing curlicues. She was silent for so long he thought she'd forgotten he was there. But then she said, "At first, I thought it was just a one off. Something specific to that location. Because it had never happened before, it couldn't have possibly been just my presence that triggered things. But after I'd been home for a couple of days, activity around the house intensified. Far beyond anything we'd experienced before."

She raised her cup to her lips, then scowled. "S'empty," she said, words slurring, and pushed the cup toward him.

"Why don't you drink some water instead?"

"Y'want me to finish this story or not?"

He poured about an inch of whiskey and handed the cup back.

She took a sip, grimaced, and continued. "It didn't get evil. Like at the cabin. But it got intense. Within just a couple of days, we couldn't even get our electricity to stay on. Dad was Dad, you know? He wasn't scared. He was fascinated by it, even though I was terrified the cabin was going to happen all over again."

"But then he woke me up early in the morning. Already had suitcases packed. He bundled me into the Volvo and told me we had to go. That if we didn't, things were just going to get worse."

Her words fascinated Jacques. He wanted to turn his camera back on, but if she noticed him doing it, he knew it'd be game over. So instead, he just concentrated on what she was saying, determined to memorize as much as he could.

Charlie scrubbed her eyes. "He was crying while we loaded everything up. I'd never seen him cry like that. And he didn't explain. Not for hours. Just drove. It wasn't until we stopped for lunch that day that he said much of anything."

She went silent again, hand stilling. Jacques gave her as long as he could, waiting for her to go on. When she didn't seem inclined to, he asked, "What did he say?"

She startled like she'd forgotten he was there. "Uh, that my mom had come to him in a dream. He didn't tell me the specifics, but she'd told him we had to be careful. Things were different now that I was a woman. My power was dangerous if it was allowed to pool. And so we just started staying on the road."

"Now that you were a woman?"

Charlie gave him a rueful smile. "Puberty's a real bitch for my family, apparently." She yawned, finished the shot in her cup, and pushed it back in his direction. "More."

He shook his head. He couldn't let her keep drinking. When she groused, he said, "My job site, my rules. I don't need you getting alcohol poisoning, or being so hungover you can't function tomorrow. Got it?"

She rolled her eyes but waved a hand at the door. "Whatever. Go 'way."

When he hopped down from the back of the truck, he heard a soft, "Be careful, Jacques."

"Always," he said, and eased the door shut. He took a minute, leaning his head against the metal of the camper before heading back into the building.

CHAPTER TWENTY-FIVE

Kiffer Kupu was an easy-going guy by nature, though he'd had to work hard to regain that equilibrium once upon a time. As long as he had enough money to pay his bills, make his monthly donations and have a little fun on the side, he was content. Cyber contracting work paid the bills and let him play with Banshee Investigations. It was a near-perfect set up.

Near-perfect except for the idiots who made it their mission to dispute every bit of paranormal evidence in existence. Especially when assholes with editing programs and too much time on their hands replicated their footage to prove that it wasn't real. Good fakes were one reason proof of the paranormal had never been accepted. Doubters doing it was one thing, but grifters playing to people's beliefs were the worst. They gave real paranormal investigators a bad name.

One day, though, someone—even if it wasn't them—would find evidence people couldn't refute. At least people who weren't so close-minded oxygen molecules had to fight their way in. Hopefully, it was them. And if any building was ripe to deliver incontrovertible proof of the paranormal, it was Union Grace. Contrary to Mac's teasing, while Kiffer admittedly was a tad jumpy, he was rarely afraid of playing active roles in investigations. He just was better on the technical side than the investigative side. But Grace? Grace gave him a feeling he'd only experienced one other time in his life.

Before he joined up with Banshee Investigations, he'd

been places so steeped in spirits they'd taken on a life of their own. Places like Aokigahara, the Suicide Forest. Walking through the dense growth there, canopy so thick the place existed in close to perpetual twilight, he had wondered about the traditional representation of demons. If darkness cloaked the forest because a demon had possessed the forest itself. The forest spoke—to him and to anyone who listened. Not in words the human ear could hear—or the DVR—but in a sort of emotional beckoning saying it was okay to give up. That things never would get better. That the best they could do was bring a merciful end to the life they were wasting.

Kiffer did not believe in suicide. While he would shame no one, it was not the route for him. He would work through his problems to overcome them. However, on that day, in a certain stretch of forest deep within Aokigahara where death sat heavy upon the air, he looked up at the sturdiest limbs and contemplated unthinkable things. It had taken him several days to recover his mental balance after exiting the forest. In the end, it involved a visit to a temple for a ritual cleansing and hours indulging in things good, charitable, and happy before he'd been able to cast aside the shadow.

He still didn't believe in suicide, but after that trip he believed in demons. And though Grace did not tempt him to harm himself as Aokigahara did, the heavy darkness was the same. With each step he'd taken deeper within the bowels of the hospital, busying himself with setting up the cameras, thermometers, and sound sensors, he'd fought the urge to hold his breath, expecting the linoleum to give way beneath his foot. For the shadows to gain substance and light to disappear. It was a creature holding its breath for the moment when their backs turned. For that moment, it could leap out of the shadows with a shriek.

Part of him wanted to tell his friends to leave. That they

needed to get away before it was too late. But—and maybe it was here that he was the pussy—he couldn't. Banshee Investigations might never get a chance like this again and he couldn't walk away ... or ask them to either.

The computer beeped, snatching him away from his thoughts. One mic in the basement had picked up activity. He checked the cameras for his team (and Charlie), but they were all where they were supposed to be. They'd reported the sound of disembodied voices down there, but the mic had picked nothing up. An excited tingle zipped up his spine. Reservations aside, he would always lose his shit in the best way over these moments. He tapped a few buttons, singled out the feed, and lifted his headset. He pressed one speaker to his ear, keeping the other free uncovered in case any of the team needed him, and listened.

It took his brain a second to parse that he was hearing at least three different voices. A bit longer for him to figure out that they were talking about him. Speaking of a past he'd left behind in high-pitched giggles cut with mean-girl shock. And then they were talking to him. Telling him, in vivid language, what they would do if he came to them. Taunting him to leave the RV and join them down in the dark.

Their promises sucked the moisture from his mouth and throat. Kiffer forced himself to put down the headphones and watch the feed until the oscillating lines disappeared completely. And then he isolated that section of the recording and overlaid it with dead silence.

Finally, he picked up his radio. Forcing the fear from his voice, he sang into it, "On the first day of hunting, my true love gave me disembodied voices ..." but then went on more seriously, "but unfortunately it was nonsense no matter how I filtered it. Sorry, team. Might need to check that mic later."

He hooked a thumb under the slim silver chain he wore, and lifted it until the small, worn medallion featuring St.

Michael appeared from beneath his green tee. He rarely alluded to his religious leanings amongst the group, but alone in the RV there was nothing to stop him from pressing the medallion against his lips and uttering a soft prayer for protection. Both for himself and for the rest of Banshee Investigations.

CHAPTER TWENTY-SIX

[CCTV camera #4 - Location: 1st Floor, Original Structure - View: Left side of main lobby, showing emergency room exterior through to cafeteria entrance]

THE HOSPITAL LOBBY IS UNCHANGED. Same chairs gathered around the same tables. Some pushed in, some pulled out like someone had left the table in a hurry. Through the gray-scale lens of the camera's eye, one might think perhaps the chairs are a touch darker, or notice there are not as many motes of dust floating through the air as there was the last time they paid attention to this camera. But this could be attributed to other things. It is, in fact, full dark and therefore the room is not as washed out as it was before, with the sprinkle of light that fought its way through Grace's windows.

There are other changes, of course, ones not caused by the light or lack thereof. But most of these are too small to notice. Minor changes, such as the wheelchair in the corner which has been moving back and forth a handful of inches for the last few hours, are not enough to get excited about. Especially not when Grace has shown them she is capable of so much more.

But it's still something to note. The wheelchair. The tray stands open now when they were closed. Open and ready for new diners to grab so they can eat their phantom scraps of hospital food. It is not the activity to expect, or catch, and it is not activity worthy of the avid adoration of amateur ghost hunters, but it is a sign of life. Possibly the most benevolent this section of the hospital has seen in quite some time.

But it is something to pay attention to. For as seen previously, and on a time scale that is subtly decreasing, a wisp of nebulous white has formed at the back of the camera's range. No longer a mere solitary breath in appearance, the apparition is an exhalation of smoke into freezing air.

Its movements are akin to those seen before. It does not deviate in its slow approach which guides it in a straight line toward the camera's watchful eye. But there is one obvious difference. Whereas before the suggestion of form could be played off as the human eye's need to see patterns in everything, now it is clear. Where the rest of the ghosts that haunt the halls of Union Grace are still half-imagined mists, faint presences lost to time, to heaven, to the life they once had, this figure is now exactly that. A figure, with broad shoulders and a narrow waist. With long legs and arms. There is no definition beyond that, but the promise of more is there.

It is something to wonder at. How, out of all the presences in Union Grace, has this one drawn such strength from the energy permeating the hospital now? What makes this presence so different?

It is intriguing. But not quite as intriguing as the fact that now, our ghost, whomever it might have been, has added an extra step to their movements. For as it draws parallel to the internal entrance of the emergency room, there is a fleeting moment where it hesitates before turning. Hesitates, as though it has caught notice of the blinking red eye of the camera.

Hesitates as though it is cataloging this change. But then it is turning tightly, continuing its ascribed path, disappearing into nothingness into the wall.

It is impossible, of course. The very definition of this type of ghost is that they repeat the same moments without variance.

They never break the cycle.

CHAPTER TWENTY-SEVEN

Goblins with ice picks set to mining inside Charlie's skull as she woke up the next morning. Groaning, she reached for the bottle of lukewarm water she'd stashed beside her bed before falling into drunken oblivion. It was mana from heaven to her parched body, and she had to stop herself from draining the whole thing in one go. She knew from experience that'd lead to it coming right back up.

Getting moving was painful, but one of the nice things about being on her own schedule was she could take her time with it. At least, that's what she thought until someone pounded on her camper door. She moved faster than she should have to get to the door before they could knock again and stared down at Kiffer with eyes squinted almost shut against the bright sunlight. "Whyyy?"

Kiffer raked his gaze down her body, then cleared his throat. His lips twitched. "Clothes, maybe."

Charlie scowled, looking down the length of her body. She was wearing ... not much, actually. Damn. Normally, she at least slept in fuzzy jammy pants and a t-shirt. At least she wore a bra and unders. Albeit mismatched and bought for comfort over style.

A couple of smart remarks flashed through her mind, but her head hurt too damned bad to be a smart-ass. She raised a hand to shield her eyes. "Oh no. You've seen my boobs. The horror. What do you want?"

"I bring a gift from the gods," Kiffer said, gesturing with a cup. There was a small packet of something clutched between his fingers. "Coffee and Midol for even more caffeine with your pain killer."

The gesture was a small one, but it damned near brought tears to her eyes. She took the items he offered and stepped back away from the evil light of day. She put the items on her tiny table and got dressed in yesterday's clothes as quickly as she dared.

Kiffer stood in the doorway until she'd gotten dressed, head averted. As soon as she'd downed the pills and taken the first sip of coffee, he cleared his throat. "Mind if I come in? Something I'd like to ask you in private."

She didn't have a clue what he wanted, but she didn't think he was up to no good, either. And, even if he was, the others were less than a hundred feet away. It would be fine.

"You brought coffee and Midol. You could do anything short of ravish me right now."

"What gets me ravishing rights?" He stepped into the camper and spent a few seconds looking around the small space. "I ... would go nuts spending too long here, I think."

Charlie patted one of the camper walls. "There, there, baby. Don't listen to him. You're the perfect size for me." She gave him a glare that was only half in jest. "Talking bad about my baby definitely won't get you ravishing rights. My truck is like a plant. If you don't talk nice to it, it doesn't do well. Be kind."

His lips twitched, but he gently patted the nearby counter and said, "Sorry. I didn't mean it. You're the perfect size for a Hobbit like Charlie."

Her mouth dropped open. "I am *not* that short!"

His grin was wicked. "Personally, I'd have denied the hairy feet before the height."

She didn't know whether to punch him or kiss him. She settled for rolling her eyes and asking, "Did you really invade my space just to insult me and my truck?"

He shook his head. As his expression sobered, he ran his fingers through his hair. "Um, this is a little awkward but... just bear with me, alright?"

Charlie chewed on her lower lip for a second before nodding.

"I'm pretty sure we were feeling each other. But then, all of the sudden, you just seemed to back off from me and turn to Mac. I'm not the jealous sort, so, like, no worries about me getting all weird and stalkery. I was just wondering if it was something I did?"

Yeah, it was a little awkward. But Charlie'd dealt with anxiety of her own, so she understood how evil the mind could be about stuff. Still, this wasn't going to be a fun conversation, and she could only hope he didn't get weird afterward. She nervously licked her lips. "You're a good guy—" She shushed him when he groaned. "No, listen. I'm not giving you the friends speech. I don't know you well enough for us to even really be friends. Okay?"

He nodded, expression going carefully neutral.

"As I was saying, you're a good guy. You strike me as the kind that's not interested in one-night stands and gossamer string connections. You know?"

She could have been wrong. She wasn't exactly top-notch at reading people. But she didn't think she was way off in this case, and he confirmed it with a quick dip of his chin a second later. "I'm a wanderer," she told him. "I don't stay in one place for more than a few days. The *only* thing I can do is one-night stands. I'd love to be the person who gets into long-term commitment and looking for happy-ever-after but that's... not something that's on the table for me. Not now and probably never."

Admitting it made her heart hurt a little. She'd told him the absolute truth. Charlie wanted that happy-ever-after. The chance to spend years in bed with the same person, sharing a house together. Having babies. A dog. An iguana. Anything. But that wasn't a life she was going to get. Not unless something drastic changed.

He studied her face for a moment, then gave a rueful smile. "Mac can do the no connections thing."

Charlie nodded and immediately regretted the action. "I'm not looking to hook up with her," she said. "We have our hands full with Union Grace, and I have seen enough horror movies to know that sex in scary places never works out well. But I can have fun with her without having to worry about her missing me when I'm gone."

He stepped into her space, hand coming up to cup her cheek. She leaned into his touch, but kept her eyes on his. "I noticed you didn't say that you wouldn't have to worry about missing her, either."

She pressed her lips together and dropped eye contact.

He slipped his thumb under her chin and nudged it upward. When she looked at him, he dipped his head and pressed his lips to hers.

The kiss was slow and sweet. He didn't attempt to pull her closer. She didn't move toward him. The contact between the soft skin of their lips and his hand on her face seemed even more precious for it.

Eventually, he dropped his hand and took his lips from hers. The look that they shared afterward felt more intimate than the kiss had been.

She whispered, "You're going to make someone a damned good forever, sir."

He opened his mouth to say something, his gaze tender, but then closed it. He leaned in once more to press a quick kiss to her temple, then did an about face and exited the camper.

Charlie sighed as the door closed.

CHAPTER TWENTY-EIGHT

The aroma of burnt toast, hot sauce, and strong coffee greeted Jacques as he drifted through the thick fog of poor sleep and half-remembered nightmares the next morning. Well, morning for them. Afternoon for the rest of the world.

Birdie was that morning's chef. The man always did the same breakfast, and always badly. No one said a word, though. Those who bitched were those who volunteered their services for meals, and none of them enjoyed cooking. At least not in camping conditions.

Besides, Birdie's coffee was strong enough to guarantee they'd be running full steam ahead halfway through the first cup.

Jacques took his time stretching out, pointing his toes up toward his knees when the cramp in his left calf reared its ugly head. Outside the bell tent he shared with Birdie, he heard the distinct tone of Mac's voice followed by a burst of laughter from the others. The sound made him grin. Mac was in a good mood then. That boded well for the day.

Jacques got up and made quick work of wiping off with a couple of baby wipes before getting dressed and heading out to join the crew.

Somewhat surprisingly, Charlie sat in a camping chair beside Mac. An empty paper plate sat in her lap, and steam rose from a large mug. Wraparound sunglasses hiding her eyes was her only concession to the overindulgence in whiskey the previous night.

The usual greetings–variations on calling him sleeping beauty or announcing that the dead had risen–bounced from him as he got his own breakfast. He plopped down in a chair between Charlie and Birdie, with Rachelle sitting on the other side of the cameraman. Kiffer, as usual, sat in the RV doorway close to his equipment in case something went down.

They were all grouped close enough together that he didn't have to do more than slightly raise his voice to address the man. "Anything interesting to report?" It was a guarantee he had been up for at least a couple hours before anyone else on the crew even opened their eyes for the first time.

"Bit of this, bit of that," Kiffer said, then took a long drink from his bottle of iced tea. "Verified we have ourselves a Looper."

A looper was a ghost who performed the same sequence of events repeatedly. They did not interact with the world around them or show any awareness of the living. At first Jacques felt sorry for them, but he now thought of them more as impressions rather than actual ghosts. "Where?"

"First floor, path between the cafeteria and the emergency room."

Mac leaned forward. "The one you showed us yesterday?"

The technician nodded, getting to his feet to toss his plate into their trash. "Our ghost walks that path about every ninety minutes."

Bird slurped from a mug that revealed foul language as it changed colors. "Sweet. That'll be good footage."

"Oh, you haven't heard the best part yet," Kiffer said, grinning and looking at them with expectant eyes. "We'll want to reshoot this for the camera later, but get this. He's getting more visible."

Jacques raised his brows. "He?"

"Definitely," Kiffer plopped back down and drummed his

fingers on his thighs. "Wasn't obvious at first, but just wait until you see the side-by-side I put together earlier illustrating the differences between his first walk and his most recent one. Coolest shit I've seen."

Jacques resisted looking at Charlie. He couldn't remember much of his nightmares, but there was enough lingering sadness from them to make the idea of celebrating something resulting from her presence a little uncomfortable. "Anything else?"

Sounding a little disappointed, Kiffer said, "Some typical stuff. The mic near the bathroom caught the sound of running water a couple of times. One of the CCTV setups in the admin area caught a chair moving. In the pediatrics area, a toy was moving around at one point. The Looper's the best, though."

"I've tried to avoid that area," Charlie whispered.

"Why?" Mac shifted in her chair to face the brunette.

Charlie drank before answering. "Little kid ghosts are sad," she said. "I don't mind the adults so much, but I'd rather not encounter kids."

"Ah. Yeah, lives cut short sucks."

And it was getting too deep into emotional trauma for him so soon after waking. Jacques blew on his coffee. "So, what's our plan for the next few hours?" A lot of ghost-hunting was repetition. Sometimes they could go into a room once and catch an EVP or something. Other times it took repeated visits. If they got even a hint of something in one area, they'd return to it and put more effort into trying to get a more distinct reaction.

With the way Union Grace had acted yesterday, he had no clue what today was going to bring them.

"Looper later," Birdie said. "If it's getting more visible, let's just monitor for now and give it more time to develop. Then we can go in with the good stuff and see what happens.

Meantime, me and Chelle want to go visit the hallway from last night."

"Yeah, that was weird," Kiffer said. "That section of hallway is almost dead, pardon the pun. So, for it to suddenly go off the charts the way it did was insane."

"It was an all over event," Jacques said, considering. "You sure it started there?"

"Yeah," Kiffer said. "Spent some time last night between naps checking out timestamps and playing things back. It started in that hallway. Then the mic picks up the sound of Charlie screaming and then the lights go nuts." He paused and looked at Charlie, "Great scream, though. They could hire you for horror movies. You damn near blew out my eardrums."

"Thanks," Charlie said and took a long drink from her mug.

Kiffer blushed. "I, uh, didn't mean that quite the way it came out. Obviously, it sucks that you got scared like that."

The brunette waved a hand at him. "No worries."

"We sure Grace has no electricity going into her? No faulty wires in an old building?" Jacques asked.

Kiffer replied he was positive, and the group went back and forth on their game plan for a while before finishing their breakfast and getting suited up to head inside.

CHAPTER TWENTY-NINE

Two hours later, Jacques wondered if they'd entered an alternate dimension. Union Grace felt as abandoned as she looked. The lull when they first arrived had been understandable, but this was not. Especially the way things popped off last night.

There were some locations where ghostly activity seemed tied to a certain time, and he couldn't discount the possibility this was the case. But it just didn't feel like it. It felt like every trace of paranormal energy permeating the building had taken a vacation. And he wasn't the only one who noticed it, either. Birdie and Rachelle were trying with the Looper, but even he had gone still. They were determined to keep trying, though. See if they could do anything to get him riled.

Riling up the spirits was a bad idea. But sometimes it had to be done. They couldn't stay here forever.

"Going to look up in the administrative area," he radioed to the group. "Maybe if I move their papers, they'll move them back." And maybe find something to give me a hint about whatever Erschon is trying to hide. Jacques was not a gambler, and he didn't appreciate whatever Erschon was playing at. That brief comment about a demon being responsible still bothered him.

He'd gotten an email last night from the ex he'd reached out to shortly after being contacted by his old school colleague. Xavier was a slightly unhinged but delightful specimen who adored puzzles and gossip. It made him almost a perfect detective, except for the part where he forgot about things like the law. Both man-made and laws of the observable universe.

For someone like Jacques, who needed to keep the people he loved safe, it had been impossible to relax around Xavier after realizing this. The man would get himself killed one day, whether on a case or not. Likely from the inability to pay attention to his surroundings when fixated on something.

It hadn't taken long for the two of them to go their separate ways, but it had been an amicable parting. Jacques didn't hesitate to reach out to him to help fill in the blanks on a case if his team's WebFu couldn't handle the task. What Xavier found piqued Jacques' interest in the hospital further, pushing aside the dread that he'd been mostly ignoring.

After he hit the top floor and took a moment to get his breath back under control, he went into the Head Administrator's office. He figured he'd rehearse a brief voice-over summarizing what he'd learned before doing anything else.

The Head Admin's office was large and left untouched during the late sixties' renovations. The desk was made of thick, dark wood and looked heavy enough to require several people to transport it up to the room. Green-striped silk wallpaper, still gorgeous decades later, lined the walls. Large bookshelves matching the desk lined one wall, filled with titles Jacques had never heard of. Given the pristine condition of the titles, he'd doubted anyone had ever bothered to read them.

The leather chair behind the desk had not fared as well as the wood or wallpaper. Same the uncomfortable-looking duo of chairs in front of the desk. Years of neglect dulled the leather and bled the suppleness from it.

Overall, this was an office that screamed "I Am Important and You Shall Know This." He half expected to see or hear an ethereal remnant, but so far, no dice. He didn't know whether he was relieved or disappointed.

Jacques removed his mask long enough to take a sip from his water bottle and eyed the executive's chair. If they brought in some lights, maybe a couple of those battery-operated candles, this would be one hell of a place to do a proper voice-over. He wished he'd brought a suit and tie. It would have added to the atmosphere.

Smirking, he went behind the desk and sat down. He'd practice what he wanted to say now, then have Birdie film it later for maximum impact.

"June 6th, 1944 is a day that went down in history for millions of people around the world, though younger generations may not be as familiar with the date." He spoke slow and smooth, imagining he was broadcasting to a rapt audience, an expert in his field. "It was D-Day. Better known as the day Allied Forces stormed Normandy."

Dramatic pause here. He steepled his fingers. "But on that fateful day, something else happened that people should have taken note of. Something the papers almost entirely overlooked because of the drama on the shores of France. Something right here in Union Grace."

"Over 100 patients and hospital staff lost their lives here that day. To an invisible enemy that left no footprints, no blood. Just death. Death that touched all levels of the hospital in the early hours of the morning, sparing only a few lucky individuals."

Another pause, giving the audience time to wonder what the cause would have been. The explanation–gas leak–was a simple one, but there were enough questions surrounding it he could add a little flair. Besides, if Erschon was right, maybe there had been more than bad pipes at work. "They reported it as a gas leak. A tragedy because of poorly maintained piping and negligence from overworked staff. But there are questions that were never answered. Everyone seemed to want to put the tragedy of Union Grace behind them. We can understand and respect their thoughts and feelings there. But it's been long enough now that I think we can ask ..."

He leaned forward, lowering his voice to a stage whisper. "They built Union Grace in 1933. How did the pipes go bad in only 11 years? How did gas bad enough to claim the lives of over one hundred people permeate the entire building without anyone noticing and getting an evacuation started? Why does it appear that everyone simply stayed in the hospital even though the smell of gas had to be apparent to everyone?"

"Maybe," he raised his brows, giving his invisible audience a professorial look, "there were other forces at work. The question is what were they? Or, more accurately, who?"

He shivered and then grinned. He'd nailed it. Could feel the rightness clear down to his bones. It was the type of showmanship that made his toes curl. He loved this part of his job and knew that he did a damned good job of it.

Jacques sat for several minutes, basking in a job well done and imagining what their numbers were going to be like for this show before he remembered he'd come up here for a different reason. Then he got to work. Since he was already sitting in the boss's chair, he started there. He slid out the slim top desk drawer and started hunting, praying he'd find a false bottom and something juicy to share with everyone. This could make them. Make Banshee Investigations a Name. He just had to stop letting his nerves get the best of him and stick with it. He'd dig around up here, then head back to the basement and practice a little breaking and entering.

While he hunted, Grace started to stir.

CHAPTER THIRTY

An hour later...

Kiffer didn't like the trend he saw. He hadn't noticed it at first because the changes had been small, but in the last few minutes, they had been more dramatic. A few keystrokes pulled up a log of readings from the various instruments stationed throughout the building. The file was updated every fifteen minutes with time stamped blocks. He selected the last three blocks and asked the computer to display the results as a graph just to make sure he wasn't misreading the data.

He wasn't. The motion activated cams were registering far more frequently. The temperature readings were trending down. Voice-activated mics were being triggered, but not long enough to capture anything.

His gut told him something big was getting ready to happen. And this time he'd be prepared for it, unlike Grace's initial paranormal rumble from when they'd first arrived.

Get them out. The thought pushed itself to the forefront of his brain. He frowned, hand drifting to the radio. If they were all outside when Grace showed out, no one could say anyone was manipulating the cameras or whatever from inside the building. He could set a camera up in the RV or right outside to capture everyone. Prove they hadn't fiddled with anything. Release the unedited file afterward. No post-processing.

But he couldn't. He brought his hand back to the keyboard, verified all the feeds were online. Technically, he shouldn't warn them something was happening. Even the suggestion could influence their reactions. It'd be easy to claim they'd hammed it up afterward.

Get them out. They're in danger. He looked over his shoulder, feeling like someone was watching him. No one was there. Foot bouncing under the desk, he looked up at the monitor displaying their video feeds. Mac and Charlie had theirs off, but he knew they were on the second floor.

Turning camera feeds off wasn't something they were supposed to do, but they all did it. Nobody needed to see one of them taking a leak or something. Though in Mac and Charlie's case, the 'or something' would probably get them banned on YouTube. Jacques' feed showed a row of filing cabinets. From Birdie's, he could see Rachelle bending down to place a small vibration sensor on the floor.

They were adults and they could handle themselves. If he went full pussy and demanded they get out, Mac would never let him hear the end of it. Likely neither would Jacques. And Charlie had shot him down for reasons he couldn't dispute, but damned if he wanted to look like a weakling in front of her, either.

He eyed the digital readouts from the equipment again. The third floor was showing higher readings than anywhere else, although they were all starting to show out. He grabbed the radio, pulse starting to race. "Private time is over, ladies. Something weird as fuck is going on up there on the second floor. Talk to me."

Mac came back a second later telling him everything was fine. He stood as he answered her, letting her know the sensors were going wild but trying not to give her too much information. His eyes went to the screens mounted on the RV wall. There was movement on the CCTV camera overlooking the lobby. Not Rachelle or Birdie. He leaned in, studying the screen which was starting to go fuzzy with interference. It looked like someone about Charlie's size, but without her body type. They were yelling something at the camera, waving long arms overtop their head, but no sound was being picked up.

What the hell? Who was this kid and what was he saying?

Get them out. A flash flood of fear sent ice racing down his spine. Fuck what he *should* do. They needed to get out of Union Grace. Right now.

Kiffer pressed the talk button on his radio to tell them to come back to the van, and all hell broke loose.

CHAPTER THIRTY-ONE

E*arlier ...*

The thought of putting on her mask again was enough to make her shudder, so Charlie didn't bother. Between the hangover and the figurative flesh-eating ants eating her nerve endings, the Midol Kiffer had given her hadn't been enough. She'd popped a powerful painkiller a little bit ago. Adding any discomfort to her day wasn't an option. But at Kiffer's insistence, she let him hook up a small mic to the radio attached to her belt. Then he hooked up Mac similarly too, to Jacques' consternation.

"You both need to wear your masks," he told them, scowling from beside the van. "Remember the part where you could die from horrible cancer?" It amused Charlie to watch Jacques mother-henning the blonde. She remembered him trying to do the same to all of them when he was little.

"Thankfully, you give us good health insurance," Mac said. When Jacques opened his mouth to protest, she went on. "Jay, I am a grown-ass adult and this is a risk I am taking fully aware of the consequences. It's okay."

"It's stupid," he said, propping his hands on his hips. "It's not safe. And don't call me Jay!"

"I don't know if you've noticed, but most of Union Grace is incredibly well-preserved," Mac said, handling it more seriously than Charlie expected. "And most asbestos-related illnesses come from prolonged exposure and breathing in large amounts of the dust. I did my research before we came here. As long as we're not river dancing down the halls or burrowing through the inside of the walls, we should be okay."

"I-"

"It's okay," she said, stepping up to him and placing her hands on either side of his cheeks. "Thank you for caring. Thank you for being my friend. But so help me God, if I have to spend another hour in this heat trying to suck air through that mask, there won't be any point in worrying about my health twenty years from now. You get me?"

The two stared at each other for a long moment, and then Jacques nodded. Mac stepped back. "I promise no river dancing in the hallways."

He gave her a small smile of acceptance before turning his attention to Charlie. "I don't suppose I can talk you into wearing yours?"

"Sorry, Jacques," she shook her head, a throb of pain reminding her how the rest of her day was going to go. "Maybe if it was winter, but between the heat and the," she couldn't think of exactly how to put the oppressive feeling in the air into words, so she just waved her hand in a vague gesture, "everything, it's too much."

He sighed and pinched the bridge of his nose. "Well, might as well make the most of it with on-camera stuff," he said. "I'm going to swing by the administration area, then down to the basement. There's a storage room I'm determined to get into. See if I can find any evidence of shit going wrong that we can use for the show. Why don't you and Mac take one of the better handhelds and head up to the second floor? If Kiffer's right about the readings from yesterday and last night—"

"And he is," Kiffer said.

Jacques ignored him, continuing, "then it looks like there's pretty consistent low-level activity up there. While Birdie and Rachelle are trying to get a better look at our

Hallway Looper on the ground floor, you can have that floor to yourselves. Try some knocking and the usual."

"Got it," Mac said. It took her less than a minute to grab a camera and then she was linking her arm through Charlie's. "Come on, chica."

And Charlie went because the idea of being alone in the hospital after what had happened in the PT room unnerved her more than she cared to admit.

"He was bossy when he was little, too," Charlie said, tongue loosened by the meds, as they walked into the Overnight/Observation unit. She was holding the handheld while Mac had an infrared in one hand and laser thermometer in the other.

Mac made a noncommittal noise. Once they stepped inside the Observation Ward, she stuck the equipment back in her belt and headed straight to the back. Charlie followed her, wondering what was up. She was walking like a woman on a mission.

At the back of the area, a few cubicle-style three-walled rooms with a rod where a dingy, tattered pull curtain could be pulled across the front for a pretense of privacy. Charlie followed her back to the furthest one on the left. Once they were inside, Mac pulled the meshed-top, flower-printed material across to shield them from the camera Kiffer used to monitor the space.

The blonde radioed Kiffer she needed a moment, then turned off their GoPros. She patted the cracked padding of the room's bed. "Up."

Charlie raised her eyebrows. Mac was forward, which was fine. But she didn't read her as the type to shuck her job for a little fun while inside the haunted building.

Mac patted the bed again. "Come on, princess."

"You know the people in horror movies who have sex in scary places are always the ones that die first, right?" As soon as the words left her mouth, heat swept across Charlie's cheeks. She really needed to get laid if she kept bringing sex up like this.

Mac grinned at her. "You have a dirty mind. I like it. Up."

Unable to resist Mac's charisma, Charlie braced her hands on the mattress and, ignoring the sizzle of pain racing up from her toes, wiggled up onto it. There was the impossible smell of antiseptic in the air. Charlie had caught wisps of it in certain rooms early on, but it seemed to grow stronger, more prevalent. Or, she thought to herself, you've just had that damned mask on for too long, and your nose is readjusting to the smells of the hospital.

But still ... a smell lasting for fifty years?

Mac interrupted her thoughts by boldly pushing her knees a little further apart and stepping into the newly created space. The intimacy of the pose appealed to Charlie, and she brushed a strand of blonde hair back from Mac's face.

The quiet of the ward wrapped around them like a cocoon, and for a moment the two of them simply existed. Some of the stress winding the muscles in Charlie's neck and back slipped away. "This place terrifies me," she said.

"What you went through last night had to be scary as hell," Mac said. "But so far things haven't been so bad other than that, have they?"

She studied Mac's face, wishing they had decent lighting in the room instead of depending on flashlights and glow sticks. "Don't you feel it?"

Mac put her hands on Charlie's thighs, skimming upward until they were resting near her hips. "Union Grace is an old building. Some terrible shit happened here. It's dark, rotting where it stands, and haunted all to hell. But so are a hundred other places."

She didn't feel it, Charlie realized. It explained Mac's unflagging enthusiasm and willingness to go all over the building, and it horrified Charlie. She knew Mac was the "skeptic" of the group, but outright not picking up on how wrong things felt boggled her. Something must have shown in her face, because Mac tilted her head and said, "What do you feel?"

Something about the way she asked it was off. Like there were deeper layers to her question. Charlie shrugged the feeling off, concentrating on finding the words to describe what was so obvious to her. "Hunger," was the word that she landed on. "Most of the ghosts in Union Grace aren't really ghosts anymore. Can't you tell? I know you guys are getting activity, but apart from that ghost in the hallway, they aren't... individuals."

She'd witnessed it in other places, though she didn't know why. Sometimes ghosts just seemed to lose whatever had made them a distinct individual in life. The energy remained but the stuff that made them a person in some ways did not. In Union Grace, though, she couldn't help but think it was some way tied to the other presence.

"I think the other one is eating them up." Charlie knew how stupid it sounded the moment she said it, but it was the truth. Because it was doing it to her, too. She'd never felt exhaustion tugging at her quite the way it had until she'd spent a few days in Union Grace. And it wasn't the "I spent all day walking" sort of tiredness, but something deeper.

Mac frowned, and said, "I don't know what to think of you."

Charlie blinked, wondering what the hell she had to do with anything. "Okay?"

The blonde bit her lip as she stared at her, conflicting emotions appeared in the micro-expressions that flitted across her face. Charlie held her gaze, resisting the urge to push Mac out of her space. The space between them was filling with a tension not conducive to being close.

"You aren't a medium," Mac said finally, stepping back and pushing her fingers through her hair. "If you are, you're the strangest one I've ever met. But you're... something? Sensitive?"

Oh. That's what she was getting at. She couldn't even be offended, considering the entire pretense had been Jacques' idea. And Lord knows acting had never been her strong suit. But what could she tell Mac? Hell, she hadn't even had a proper discussion with Jacques yet. "Yeah. Sensitive is a good word for it."

The free admission she wasn't a medium seemed to ease some of the hard lines from Mac's face. But she looked confused. "So ... why are you here?"

Charlie's meds were fully kicking in at this point and she had that familiar lightheaded sensation that came with it. But this was a simple question. She liked simple questions. "Money."

The blonde's brows squished together. "Why did Erschon stipulate you had to be here?"

"Fuck-nuggets." She swore under her breath. Jacques was going to yell at her.

Mac's lips twitched but then her eyes narrowed. She put a finger under Charlie's chin, lifting it up. Charlie got happily lost in the dark green of Mac's irises until the blonde asked, "Are you high?"

Somebody's in trouuuuuuuuuble. Quick, kiss her and grab her boobs. That'll distract her! Suppressing the urge to giggle, Charlie commanded Emerson to shut up. As his voice retreated to the corner where it always lurked, she said, "Little bit." That much was true. It wasn't like she was incapable of thinking or going to do something dangerous. She was just a little... floaty at the moment.

"And is this a regular thing that you do?" Mac's tone was almost clinical, but there was no judgment in her eyes.

"Nope," she said, popping the p a bit. "Got a thing. Hurts a lot sometimes. Gotta take a strong pain pill." She hesitated, and then admitted, "That's why I need the money. There's this surgery that could fix things and my insurance sucks."

Mac considered it, then slid between her thighs and put her hands back into position. She rubbed her thumbs back and forth. "Damn," she said. "Healthcare in America, right?"

"Yeah." Charlie wondered what Mac would do if she leaned forward and kissed her.

Mac slid her hands up, creeping her fingers beneath the hem of Charlie's shirt. "Why was Erschon willing to pay you to be here?"

"Because I'm like a ghost battery," Charlie said reluctantly, understanding Mac would not let it go. Jacques was going to yell at her, but Mac made her feel safe and cared for right now. She needed that. "I spend a few days somewhere and whatever paranormal activity is present ramps up."

"Is that why you were at Union Grace before we showed up?" She was frowning, but it didn't look like an angry frown.

Charlie nodded. "Grant said if I stirred things up before you guys got here, we'd only have to be here a few days. Then he'd pay me and hook me up with someone who might help me stop doing this. And I want to stop doing this. I'm tired. Like from my toe bones all the way up and out, you know?"

The words were pouring out of her. She couldn't help it. Mac was listening and people didn't do that for her anymore. "I can't settle down anywhere because if I stay too long it's not just fun-for-ghost-hunting-TV that starts happening. It gets dangerous. People get hurt."

Quietly, her green eyes fastened on Charlie's, Mac asked, "People like Jacques' brother and sister?"

"Yeah."

"That fucking sucks."

The understanding with no cliché sympathy words made Charlie snort. "Yeah," she said again.

Mac tilted her head. "Need a hug?"

Kiffer's voice booming into the small space via the radio cut Charlie's answer off. They both jumped. "Private time is over, ladies. Something weird as fuck is going on up there. Talk to me."

"All good here," Mac said to Kiffer. She grabbed one of Charlie's hands and squeezed it. Then with quick, efficient movements, she turned on Charlie's camera before stepping back to fiddle with her own.

All hell broke loose as every door in the hospital slammed open and shut within milliseconds of each other. Charlie's heart rocketed into her throat. She covered her ears with her hands and stared at Mac with wide eyes.

Mac turned and ran toward the door to the observation unit, holding an EMF in front of her. Before she reached it, Charlie heard a high-pitched squeal, followed by a pop. Mac cursed and tossed the box away.

When it landed, a thin wisp of smoke curled up from the box before dissipating. Mac, seemingly unbothered that the EMF had blown up in her hands, was talking excitedly on the radio.

"The EMF popped a light on me," she said. "When was the last time we had that happen? Especially after an event had already happened." She paused, and in profile Charlie could see her frowning. "Kiffer? You reading me?" She unclipped the radio from her belt and fiddled with it before repeating herself.

When there was still no answer, she turned a knob on the top of the handheld and said, "Kiffer's not responding. Copy if you hear this?"

"Copy for me and 'Chelle," Birdie came back immediately.

They waited a few seconds. Not knowing what to do with herself, but wanting to be helpful, Charlie picked up the camera and aimed it at the blonde.

When Jacques sounded off, he sounded distracted and a little annoyed. "Probably just the equipment glitching. Check again in a few minutes."

"Alright. Bird, did things go sideways down there? Sounded like every damned door in this hospital slammed shut."

Static and then, "Yep. Sec."

"You guys okay?"

This time it took a few for anyone to answer, and this time it was Rachelle. Charlie slid off the bed and crossed the room to hear the girl's quiet voice better. "Um, we're fine. Birdie's trying to get the front door open so he can see why Kiffer's not responding. But it's stuck."

Mac turned, meeting Charlie's eyes. She inclined her head toward the door. Charlie nodded and went forward to try the handle. This time, no matter how hard she pulled—and she pulled until she thought she heard the wood creak in protest —the door refused to open.

Union Grace had followed through on her threat and trapped them.

Mac communicated the news that they were stuck to Birdie and Rachelle.

"Birdie says hold on. We're gonna come get you guys out and then we'll go from there."

Jacques told them he was almost through the door in the basement and as soon as he finished what he was doing, he'd join them on the third floor.

Charlie didn't understand how he could be so blasé about what just happened. That wasn't Jacques style.

CHAPTER THIRTY-TWO

Kiffer's head exploded with pain as the mics scattered through Union Grace screamed with the slamming of the doors. He cursed and tore the headphones off, throwing them onto the desk. The loud noise disoriented him, but he didn't hesitate. Instead, he leapt out of the RV and ran for the hospital doors.

"Talk to me, guys! What's going on?" He held the radio in one hand and tested the doors with the other. Behind the glass-encased wire mesh, figures of dust and spiderwebs circled the front of the lobby. All except for one, more solid in appearance than the others.

The person he'd seen waving at the camera stood still, eyes locked on Kiffer, accusing him silently. They had enough mass; he could tell his first impression was correct. A young male. All knees and elbows, feet too big and long-fingered hands, yet skinny as a rail.

He stared back, trying to ignore the expression on the boy's face while he wondered who he was. The clothing he was wearing was too recent for it to be a ghost associated with the hospital. After a moment, the boy broke eye contact, and tilted his head back, looking up at the floors above him.

And then he was gone, the particles forming him breaking apart and scattering into nothingness. It took Kiffer a second to realize the other figures disappeared as well. They didn't matter as much, though. They had been suggestions of shapes, echoes of lost memories. This kid looked like Kiffer could have touched him and felt something.

"Guys? What happened up there? The front doors are shut solid."

There was no answer. No feedback. Nothing. He frowned and hooked the radio to his belt, then grabbed hold of the door handles and pulled as hard as he could. Still nothing. But the doors had resisted them before only to be fine later, so he concentrated on the radio issue, hoping the other ghost fuckery would resolve itself while he did. It was possible whatever happened a moment ago drained the batteries. It was a frequent enough occurrence. That's why one entire cabinet in the van was stocked with nothing but spares.

He headed to the van, intent on changing out the batteries. Even as he took off the back cover of his radio and removed the rechargeable battery with pure muscle memory, the beeps and trills of his equipment in the RV yelled activity warnings. Like he didn't already know that. Like he needed equipment to tell him that something fucking bad just happened.

He changed the battery and verified the radio was operational. He tried again, first calling out to the team and then to the individual members. Still nothing.

Grace had his team, and she wasn't going to give them up.

The thought sent a shiver down his back and he set his jaw. He'd given up too soon before. He would never do that again, not when someone needed him. Kiffer got another radio off the charging deck and tried that one.

And then another. And another after that.

Five radios later, he sat down hard on the bumper of the van and admitted that the problem wasn't with the radios. Whatever happened in Union Grace had also cut him off from communicating with his team.

How could he help them out here when he had no way to

communicate with them? And why hadn't he been inside with them? He could have been in there, actively helping. Instead, he'd chosen to stay out here, where it was safe, and passively monitor the situation. And this is where it got him.

The memory of the whispers he'd heard over the mic last night crept into his mind, and doubt crept in. How could he help them even if he was inside? He was good with equipment. With coding. With things that didn't involve important shit like being the person someone else depended on when the cards were against them. He could fix a poor line of code. A mic with a loose wire.

He couldn't fix people. He just left them to die. Fooled himself into thinking that there were reasons for it. That it wasn't his fault. They were going to die, anyway. Not helping to save them wasn't killing them. He wasn't a murderer.

His heart pounding, hands shaking, Kiffer leaned over, resting his elbows on his knees, and pushing his fingers through his hair.

This wasn't the type of job that was supposed to put anybody at risk. It was the type of job that provided jump scares and laughter. Occasionally they got to experience some cool shit. But people didn't get more than the usual bumps and bruises. Except now they had, and for all he knew, they could be seriously hurt. Because he hadn't listened to his instincts. Hadn't made them leave.

His eyes caught on the words tattooed on the inner side of his forearm.

Be someone your loved ones can be proud of.

He froze, staring at the words. Letting them sink into his brain. He'd gotten them tattooed there for a reason. A promise to not repeat past mistakes.

Kiffer's pulse steadied. He could do that. It started with finding out if his friends were okay, and then he'd... he'd what?

CHAPTER THIRTY-THREE

Birdie and Rachelle got to Observation within minutes. Birdie immediately began putting his weight into the door from his side, trying to force it open. After a minute of repeated failure, he said, "You try pullin' while I push."

"Will do," Mac said. "Charlie can supervise." She nodded toward the big window behind the nurses' station.

Charlie looked over and jumped at the sight of Rachelle on the other side of the window, holding Birdie's weird multi-cam tripod thing. The other woman gave Charlie an enthusiastic wave. She forced a small smile and a brief wave in return. They'd just seen each other fifteen minutes ago. Waving was unnecessary. So was sticking a damned camera in her face.

She half expected a smart-ass remark from Em, or the remnant of him she'd cobbled together inside her head, but he'd gone quiet as soon as the shit hit the fan. So quiet she couldn't even feel him lurking in the corner of her mind, ready to snark like he normally was. That scared her almost as much as the external situation she was in.

But there wasn't time for her to contemplate this new level of craziness. She pushed the worry about Emerson out of her head and refocused on Rachelle holding the camera. It made her realize she was still holding the handheld.

Using it as an excuse to act distracted, Charlie fiddled with the rotating LCD screen. As she did, she walked around the nurses' station to stand behind one of the grossly yellowed Plexiglas dividers.

A wave of exhaustion hit her as she lifted the camera to aim at Mac again. The room swam in and out of focus. Something was building, pushing up to the surface like one of those bubbles in mushroom soup right before it splattered everywhere.

Charlie grabbed the edge of the nurse's desk. With her other hand, she sat the camera down on the edge of it. "Hey, guys?"

Mac turned to look at her, and the world shifted into slow motion even as Charlie's pulse raced like she was about to crest the hill on a roller coaster. Charlie said, "I really don't think it's done." It took forever to force the words from her lips, and she swayed on her feet.

Almost instantly, Mac left the door and came to her side, wrapping an arm around her waist. She said something, but Charlie couldn't concentrate as the energy drain on her system increased.

Everyone's lights started flickering.

Charlie swept her gaze around the room behind them but could see nothing happening. If not here, then? The food she'd eaten just an hour ago curdled in her stomach. She turned toward the window Rachelle stood behind in time to see the glass fracture.

Time snapped back to normal speed. A series of small pops went off, creating more jagged lines in the glass.

Understanding what was happening, but suddenly so exhausted she couldn't support her own weight, Charlie dropped to her knees. Mac let out a grunt as she dropped with her, unprepared for Charlie's sudden limp noodle act. As she did so, Rachelle said, "Holy shit, look at the glass."

She tried to yell at them, but the words were a near-breathless wheeze leaving her throat. As the intensity of the crackles and pops rapidly built, she fumbled for Mac's hand, squeezed it. 'S'not safe! Mac, tell them!"

Mac's brows drew together for a brief second, but then her eyes widened in realization. Vision wavering, ears ringing, Charlie watched Mac yell for the two to get down. Then the blonde covered Charlie's torso with her own, protecting their head with her arm.

CHAPTER THIRTY-FOUR

As soon as Rachelle pointed out the glass was fracturing in the frame, Birdie stepped away from the door. He plucked the camera rig from her unresisting hands and stepped back to get the full shot in the frame. Rachelle vibrated with excitement as they watched a web of fractures slither across the pane.

On the other side, Mac and Charlie were now out of sight. Birdie hadn't seen what had happened, but Charlie looked like she'd been about to pass out, so that was likely it. He didn't have the time to be concerned about it. He trusted his teammate to handle what was going on in there while he dealt with what was happening out here.

Birdie's skin crawled, but it wasn't the first time he'd been spooked, and it wouldn't be the last. He registered the feeling and ignored it, like always. Looking at the screens on his rig, he noticed a difference on the thermal camera. The area they were in was much colder than it should have been. A dark blue that made Rachelle's body seem impossibly bright.

"Temperature dropping. What should we do next, Chelle?" They could use this as a learning experience for her.

Rachelle tapped her EMF. He nodded, and she took it off her belt and turned it on. It peaked at four and held there.

"Feel anything? 'Sides the cold." His next breath formed a white mist that dissipated quickly. In his peripheral vision, frost formed in the middle of the pane, surging outward to meet the incoming fracture. On the thermal cam's screen, the cold spot was growing more concentrated.

'Chelle," he interrupted her jabber about her arm hair standing up, "can you do me a favor and take three steps to your right, please?" She was blocking some of the windows and he wanted to get the full effect.

Green eyes wide, Rachelle sidestepped as requested. The large pane Birdie aimed at was now so fractured it was a miracle it hadn't fallen out of the frame yet. The view into the Observation Ward was a distorted mess, but it wasn't what was on the other side of the glass that had his attention. It was what was forming on it.

The frost in the middle of the pane had somehow halted the window's fracturing. Weird enough on its own–as he was pretty sure the cold should have made the area more vulnerable–but then there was the shape the white had taken on. One that might not have been visible without the thin white film to highlight it.

Once he knew what he was looking at, it was impossible not to see. A humanoid figure, arms raised and hands pressed flat at shoulder height. Like they were looking into the Observation ward. He wondered what they were expecting to see. It was more a pose he thought people would take looking in through the glass to see babies or something.

"Oh my god," Rachelle said, voice cracking with excitement, "that's so cool!"

"Yeah. Think it's the first time I've ever seen an entity in the frost like this. Especially one that looks like it's gonna stick around. Boss, pretty cool shit. You comin' up?"

The line was silent.

"Can I use the spirit box now?" Rachelle shifted her balance from one foot to the other. "Bet we get something."

"Go for it but come away from the glass a bit." A shiver raced down his spine. He thumbed the radio as Rachelle got the spirit box turned on. "Charlie okay?"

Mac's voice was almost inaudible through the cracking and squealing of the radio though a few feet only separated them. "She's disoriented, but okay, I think. Give me a sec and I'll try the door again."

"Take your time," he said. The shot was damned near perfect, and he didn't want anyone else intruding.

The familiar crackle of static filled the air. "I'm talking to the spirit that's with us now," Rachelle said, her eyes darting between Birdie and the frosted glass. "My name is Rachelle. It is the afternoon of the twenty-fifth of June. What is your name?"

She paused, but there was no response.

"Were you a worker or a patient here at Union Grace?"

Birdie nodded in approval. That was a good, specific question.

Rachelle paused again for a response, but there was still none. She looked at him, and he made a rolling motion with one finger. She kept going, stepping closer to the frosted outline. He shook his head, beckoning her back. She ignored him, asking, "What do you want?"

"Die," the spirit box whispered, "here."

"You died here?" Rachelle asked, a sympathetic expression on her face. She took another step closer to the window, turning, fingers reaching out to touch the frosted outline. "I'm so sorry."

"Chelle-" He reached out to grab her arm, intending to move her away from the window.

"No," the Box replied. "You."

With the sound of a thousand matchsticks breaking, the window blew. Hours of training in his old life had him turning and ducking, covering the back of his neck with one hand even while he kept hold of the camera rig with the other.

It was over in an instant; the pieces hit the opposite

corridor wall before dropping to the floor. He stayed crouched as silence fell, half-expecting something else to happen. Gave it two breaths, then three, but everything stayed quiet. As the sting of hundreds of slight cuts told him he had not escaped unscathed, he turned, still in a crouch, just to be safe, and swept his camera over the aftermath.

The camera saw her before he did. Arm outstretched on pumpkin-colored floor tiles, hand resting palm up with fingers curled, dark splotches blossoming against the gray of her shirtsleeve. Her sleeve provided a directional line his eye followed; the camera moved slowly to take in more. The frame caught and hung on a pool of dark red liquid. He focused there for a heartbeat before panning the scene. Objectively, he knew what he was seeing was horrible, but his brain told him it wasn't real.

A large shard of glass glittered in the brightening camera light, buried deep into her chest under her collar bone. The fountain source of the red liquid revealed itself between the collar of her shirt and the black plastic of her respirator. Even as the camera–as he–watched, the force of the pulsing red lessened rapidly.

Recoiling from the grisliness before him, he panned upward, revealed a sharp chin and a small mouth with full lips seeping more red liquid. He wondered what they used to make the blood. Because, he realized, the momentary disassociation clearing from his brain, that's what he was witnessing.

While his brain struggled to process the realization, to tie it with what had just happened, his body continued to function. Years of filming had him continuing the shot until her entire face was in the frame.

Rachelle's lashes fluttered, and he saw her pupils change in size. Her eyes shift. Suddenly she was looking straight into the lens, into him, and all he could see was how scared she was. Her mouth worked, lips drawing back enough that he could see the blood coating her teeth.

And then reality hooked him. He wasn't watching a movie. Wasn't filming one. He was in Union Grace hospital and their newest team member were dying on the floor in front of him.

For the first time in his life, Birdie dropped the camera.

CHAPTER THIRTY-FIVE

10 minutes ago

Two floors below, in the basement, Jacques finished fiddling with the rusted door lock. He stood with a grunt. The sound made him flush in embarrassment. He'd have to make sure Kiffer edited that out. Old man grunts weren't good for his image. Neither was picking a lock and still being unable to get the door open. Stupid hospital really had it out for them.

Abandoning the pretense of civility, Jacques slammed his shoulder into the door. It gave a minuscule amount—just enough to encourage him. He kept at it even though his shoulder screamed it was a bad idea. The door opened a few inches on the fourth tackle with a screech straight out of a horror movie soundboard.

"Well, that took longer than expected," he said. "Our old girl here isn't eager to give up her secrets, but I used my manly charms and persuaded her. Now, what juicy details do we think she was hiding?"

The light from his flashlight speared the darkness with a stark glare as he pushed the door open. What greeted him was a sight to terrify even the strongest soul. An office worker's hell with metal filing cabinets haphazardly grouped together in the middle of the room. Some listed to the side, others had papers peeking out from the edges. Thick dust coated everything in his narrow field of view, but strangely, no cobwebs were in sight.

He never thought the lack of cobwebs (or mouse shit)

would be something that would make him uneasy, but it did. Abandoned buildings were never truly abandoned. Creepy crawlies and plague-carrying furballs always took them over. Except for Union Grace.

"Mes amis," he said, "welcome to the filing system of the seventies."

Happy for the protective respirator he wore, Jacques opened the door further. He nudged a nearby piece of debris he assumed had fallen from the ceiling under the edge to prop it open. "Given that Union Grace likes to keep its doors closed, we'll be keeping this one propped open."

He took a few steps in and panned the camera from left to right. "We'll be going through some of these later," he said, "though not to get at anyone's medical records. What we're looking for is much more interesting and," his eyes came upon a row of filing cabinets against the right wall, "and probably in these beauties."

These cabinets predated the metal clunkers in the middle of the room. Made in a time where beauty meant something. Even covered in dust, the appeal was undeniable. He crept over, doing his best not to stir up the thick layer of dust on the linoleum floor, and ran his fingers across the top of one in the middle. With the dust brushed away, the beautiful stained oak was clear to the camera's eye. "They just don't make them like they used to," he said, and sighed in appreciation.

Birdie's voice came over the radio, asking if he wanted to look at something, but he barely registered the man's voice. Right now, his palms itched to caress the wood of the cabinets. Union Grace needed him. Not only to review the files, but to help make her beautiful again. He'd review the footage of whatever was going on later.

Jacques pulled out a pair of purple nitrile gloves. He started to slip them on but paused. The oils from his skin would make the wood shine even more. He smiled and tugged on the drawer of the cabinet in front of him. He expected resistance, but the drawer opened with oiled ease to reveal thick files with some sort of compact script written on each tab. He frowned, squinting at it. "Doctor's cursive or alien language?" he asked the air. "I guess we'll find out soon."

He needed Mac down here. She was the only one who had a chance of reading the god-forsaken writing, and being able to read the labels would make this go a lot easier. Still, he started paging through the files and soon realized that the filing seemed to be grouped by year.

"Too easy," he said, going to the first cabinet. He already knew he could spend years down here, learning Grace's secrets. Before he could do more than lay his fingers on the first file in the drawer, a wave of misapprehension washed over him. It sent goosebumps racing up his arms and straight down his back.

It was weird and unexpected enough to make him take a step back from the drawer in surprise. He was about to make a crack about administrative ghosts, but then Mac's voice, strained to the point it cracked while she was talking, burst from his radio. "Rachelle's down, Jacques."

Dread pooled in his stomach and he thumbed the control. "Say again?"

"Rachelle's hurt. Bad. There was an event. Just get up here, Jacques!"

The file cabinets released their hold on his attention like a rubber band snapping. He turned, shot through the door, and ran toward the stairs. He hit the hallway door hard enough that it slammed through the disintegrating rubber doorstop and lodged into the wall and took the stairs two at a time.

By the time he hit the second floor, his heartbeat like a machine gun on full auto. At the intersection, he turned left and smacked straight into a wall of disbelief that held him back as effectively as brick. Blood, glass, and the too-still form of their newest ghost hunter, surrounded by the rest of the team, stamped itself into his brain. He couldn't move. Couldn't speak. Could only stare in horror.

Mac looked up, her hands pressing against Rachelle's neck. "Call 911 and get the first aid kit," she said sharply. "Hurry."

Jacques' gut told him there was no point in hurrying, but her words gave him the ability to move again. Breath caught in his chest, he spun on the ball of his foot and headed back down the stairs.

CHAPTER THIRTY-SIX

Jacques hit the front entrance doors of Union Grace at a speed that should have sent them careening off their tracks. Instead, the doors stayed closed while the force of the impact sent him stumbling backward and falling on his ass.

Scowling, bony ass aching, he hopped to his feet and went for the door again. This time, he used the push bar. The bar worked, giving in to the force he exerted with minimal resistance. The door, however, did not. "What is it with this goddamned building and its doors? No wonder it closed down, fucking death trap."

He keyed his radio and cringed at the heavy static. "Kiffer, come help me with this damned door."

Once they got them open, he'd wedge them open. Something he should have done the minute they recognized the doors were a potential problem.

Kiffer didn't answer. Jacques tried again, doing his best to keep his breathing under control. This time when there was no result, he pressed his face to the reinforced glass, cupping his hands around his eyes to block out the extraneous light. On the other side, about twenty feet away, Kiffer sat on the bumper of the van, shoving his hands through his hair.

"Kiff," Jacques yelled, relief flooding him. He smacked the glass with his open palm. "Let us out! We can't get the door open."

Kiffer made no move to show he'd heard him. Didn't even flinch. Jacques started beating on the door. He kept at it until his palms were bright red and stinging from the force of the impact as his heart did a drunken two-step inside his chest.

Kiffer had to hear him. There was no way he didn't, right? He wasn't thirty feet away. How could he not? Sucking in air through a throat wanting to close from sheer panic, Jacques called up his theater training for making his voice carry. He took a few deep breaths and hollered Kiffer's name as loud as he could. At the same time, he started beating his fists in unison against the glass.

When he ran out of air, he paused with his forehead against the door. On the other side, Kiffer abruptly stood and disappeared into the van. Jacques held his breath, hope making him giddy. Hope or perhaps just a lack of oxygen. If Kiffer couldn't hear him, did that mean Union Grace had sealed itself off airtight? Would they run out of oxygen?

A second later, Kiffer returned with a large crowbar and strode back toward the doors. Determination etched itself on the man's beautiful face.

Jacques whooped and stepped back. With the reinforced wire, it'd take a couple of hits, but the door would break. "Come on, baby," he said.

Kiffer wasted no time smashing the crowbar against the door, and he went at it with a rabid energy. But, apart from a few nicks, the door appeared unharmed.

Jacques couldn't believe it. Kiffer wasn't a big guy, but he put in time at the gym to make sure he could haul around the heavy equipment bags with ease. Unless the glass was like three inches thick, it should have fractured.

Panic returning, Jacques stepped close to the glass again. He waved his hands in front of Kiffer's face, trying to get his attention. But even though only inches separated them, it could have been a thousand miles. Even vigorously waving his hand in front of Kiffer's face brought no recognition from his equipment tech.

"Shit," Jacques cursed, turning to look around the room. His eyes lit on one of the ugly yellow waiting room chairs. It had to be heavier than a crowbar, right? Or maybe if they were both hitting the glass from different sides, it would make a difference. He grabbed it by the back legs and carried it over to the door. Swinging from the waist, he launched it into the glass.

The chair thunked against the glass and fell to its side on the linoleum.

The door remained intact, but Kiffer reacted. His sound tech halted in mid-swing, his brows drawing together.

"Yes!" Jacques screamed. "Yes, Kiff! I'm here!" He picked up the chair again, swung it at the door.

Kiffer frowned, the crowbar dropping to his side. He stepped forward and tried to peer through the glass. Jacques got right in front of his face. "Thank god. Listen, I think you–"

Lips pressed into a grimace, Kiffer stepped back. Jacques watched him lean his head back to take in Union Grace. His lips moved as he muttered something before disappearing back into the RV.

Disappointment and disbelief threatened to crush Jacques. But the sound of Mac blasting over the radio interrupted him. "Need that kit, Jay!"

"Working on it," he said, resisting the urge to scream at her. Did she think he was down here just playing fucking tiddlywinks while Rachelle was up there dying? He picked up the chair again. He'd beat the fucking door down if he had to. And as he tried to do just that, he remembered.

And while he did, black particles seeped from the door and wall of Union Grace, settling in around his body.

CHAPTER THIRTY-SEVEN

Watching Rachelle pass on terrified Charlie. For all that her ability was so closely associated with the afterlife, Charlie had only seen someone die on two occasions. Emerson and Ana's joint death had been the first. Then her father.

In the former case, things had been too chaotic to pay attention to what happened directly afterward. The latter had been a peaceful transition while she was sleeping.

She and her dad had been spending the night in an old BnB. With plans to head off to Yellowstone for a homeschool science study the next morning, they'd both gone to bed early. He had complained earlier that his arm hurt a bit, but neither had thought much of it.

Around midnight, Charlie awakened to a presence standing over her bed and a warmth wrapping itself around her. As she registered the intense feeling of love, she opened her eyes to see her father there. He watched her with a rueful yet loving smile on his face. There was a fragility to his appearance, and she remembered thinking sleepily that she shouldn't be able to make out the chair behind him. Like he said, people made doors better than windows.

He'd reached out, brushing his fingers along her cheek before lightly tapping her nose with his finger. It was a move he'd made since she was little, and it never failed to make her smile. Then, in the time it took her to exhale, he faded into non-existence.

He was dead. She was sure of it, but it didn't stop her

from rushing into his room to save him. From screaming for help. Hadn't stopped her from breaking his ribs during CPR to get his heart beating again. He had left her. The only one she could count on in the world was gone. Charlie was officially alone.

But even though she had grieved, and hard, she clung to the memory of him saying goodbye and of his transition. She knew with absolute certainty that her dad had passed on, and he'd been okay with it.

What happened with Rachelle had been nothing like that.

Soon after the pool of blood surrounding the slim young woman stopped growing, a wisp of white rose from the body. Her father's shape had been exquisitely detailed, but Rachelle's spirit was a barely defined slip. She could still remember how even the individual hairs in his mustache and beard had been visible.

The apparition wandered back and forth in the immediate area a few times, giving Charlie the feeling of uncertainty. That had been fine. Expected. Traumatic deaths such as hers could leave a spirit confused afterward. After the initial appearance, Charlie watched her wanderings from the corner of her eye. She'd made the mistake of interacting with a relatively new ghost (although she hadn't known it at the time) a few years ago. Once the young man figured out that Charlie could see him, her entire trip had gone off the rails. She'd ended up leaving the area early when the spirit had turned violent in denial of his death.

When Rachelle set off down the hallway toward the stairs, slowly forming into a reasonable likeness of the body she'd left behind, passing Charlie without acknowledging her existence, Charlie followed. A mix of curiosity and a sense of not-belonging to the few gathered around their teammate's body propelling her on. If nothing else, she figured, she would at least be able to view Rachelle's transition and reassure them that their friend had not stuck around. Or that she hadn't. She suspected those who died in Union Grace were at the mercy of the hospital or the thing that controlled it.

Rachelle's figure radiated unease. She floated down the stairs to the first level with the creeping speed of a terrified child. Charlie wondered if it was because she didn't realize she was dead yet or because she feared something worse than death was coming for her.

They came to the first floor and Rachelle slipped through the closed stairwell door. Charlie was right on her heels but slowed enough to make sure the door opened and closed as quietly as possible. So far Rachelle hadn't noticed her, but that could change, especially since Charlie was sticking so close to her.

Past Rachelle, she could see a bright spot of light engaged in a rhythmic movement which had to be Jacques' flashlight. The light kept disappearing into the haze that grew denser around him as she watched. The muffled sound of metal on metal followed his movements.

Rachelle headed straight for him.

As they got closer, Charlie willed him to turn around. To see them. But Jacques seemed as lost in his own world as Rachelle's spirit. It was only the reassuring solidity of his form amidst the haze of black wrapped that kept her from freaking out.

Rachelle didn't seem to notice him, but her form became more defined. She went straight to the doors, arms extended to push them open. As soon as her non-corporeal hands contacted the metal, thick claws of black smoke sprang from the door and shot through her body. Rachelle threw her head back, mouth open in a scream of agony as she thrashed desperately in Grace's hold.

Charlie clapped her hands to her mouth to hold back her own scream as Rachelle's body arched, her head bending back until Charlie could see the curve of the young woman's throat. It was the perfect view to observe her spinal column cave to the pressure with such a visible shift Charlie imagined she could 'hear' the pop that left Rachelle's head hanging by ephemeral flesh alone.

Rachelle's eyes locked onto hers, wide and desperate. Seeing Charlie for the first time and pleading to be saved as the jagged tip of her broken spinal column pierced through the flesh of her throat. This injury that would have caused instant death in life did nothing to ease Rachelle's pain in the hell she was now trapped in. And Charlie could only bear witness to the convulsive movements and the asphyxiation of the ghost hunter who still did not realize she was already dead.

Charlie screamed. Jacques' EMF reader shrieked. The two combined seemed to snap the man out of the trance-like state he'd been in. Shouting in surprise, he dropped the chair he'd been striking the door with and threw himself backward. He landed hard on his ass and did an awkward scramble on hands and feet to get away from the door.

The tendrils, at least six, forced their way through so much of Rachelle's form that Charlie could barely make out the white.

Charlie, already so tired she barely registered the drain on her energy as sick anticipation spread throughout her body, could only whisper, "Please don't."

With a sudden burst of movement, the tendrils forcefully yanked in different directions, obliterating the slender white form.

"Holy fuck, holy fuck, holy fuck," Jacques said from somewhere to her left. Charlie couldn't answer him. All she could do was stare as the smoky appendages curled up on themselves and retreated into the structure of Union Grace.

It was a long moment after the last trace of tendril disappeared before Charlie could drag her eyes away from the door. When she did, she saw Jacques staring down at the LCD screen of his camera, muttering to himself.

As if he felt her gaze on him, he looked up. "Did you see that? It came out of nowhere and ... and ripped that spirit to pieces. Holy shit. It just decimated it! And I caught it on camera. I didn't turn my camera off while I was trying to get through the door, so I caught it on camera."

"The spirit that got ripped apart was Rachelle's," Charlie told him, the words rotten and unwanted in her mouth.

She knew the instant her words registered. Jacques' hands slowly stopped their fidgeting with the camera, and his eyes closed for several seconds. Finally, he whispered, "Are you sure?"

Charlie nodded once.

"Shit," Jacques said. "Shit, shit, shit!" He took his glasses off and wiped his eyes. "I tried," his voice cracked. "I tried to get through the door. But I couldn't. No matter how hard I tried, I couldn't."

"I know," Charlie moved to his side, placing a hand on his shoulder. "I saw you, and I know you were trying. And I think it's clear why. Union Grace doesn't want us to leave."

"Well, we'll just get Birdie and the rest of the crew down here," Jacques said, grabbing her hand in both of his and squeezing it. "All of us working together can get through it."

"I don't think that's a good idea," Charlie said reluctantly, not wanting to put her thoughts into actual words. Afraid that it would make them real if they weren't already.

"Why?"

"It was surrounding you." At his look of incomprehension, she elaborated. "I was more interested in what was going on with Rachelle, but before she touched the door, the smoke was getting pretty thick around you. I think it was building up to an attack before she gave them an easier target."

"Then we get out of here before it attacks us again."

"And how many of us will die trying to get the doors open? Who are you willing to let die in the hopes that we might be able to defeat Grace with sheer physical power?"

Jacques said something in French, harsh and filled with frustration. He muttered to himself for a moment, then scrubbed his face hard with his hands. "We need to go talk to the others," he said. "Figure out what to do."

"Yeah."

"Shit," he said again, and thumbed his radio to no avail. Frowning, he tried a few more times before beckoning for hers.

She shook her head. "Dead, too."

"Okay. Let's go." He didn't head straight for the stairs, though. Instead, he stopped at the receptionist's desk and grabbed a neon bag. "Protection," he said at her inquisitive look.

"What's cold iron going to do against ... whatever that is?"

"I don't know," he whispered, "but I have a feeling we're going to find out."

CHAPTER THIRTY-EIGHT

When Jacques and Charlie arrived back in the hallway, Birdie was finishing wrapping Rachelle's body in one of the grimy room-dividing sheets taken from the Observation Ward. They watched in silence, so close together their forearms touched. After enshrouding her, Birdie placed one hand on the round lump of Rachelle's covered head and crossed himself. Jacques had never seen the camera man be overtly religious, but the prayer didn't surprise him. He bowed his head deferentially but kept his eyes on the scene. Someone needed to keep an eye out.

After a moment, Mac joined him, wrapping an arm around his shoulders. Jacques's heart hurt, and guilt ate at him, searching for a hole in his defenses. Telling him that if he'd been there, if they hadn't split up, he would have seen what was coming. Would have been able to save Rachelle. But right now, all he could think was Rachelle had died knowing he didn't want her on the team.

The two distinct lines of thought combined into the realization that if he'd released her prior to the investigation, as he'd been tempted to do, she'd still be alive. He made a fist and rubbed it hard against his sternum as the ache spread.

Charlie's hand warmed his arm as she gave it a gentle squeeze before she walked away. He knew he should call her back. That they shouldn't split up again. But he couldn't. All he could do was stare at his team, knowing he could never make this right. That they were all trapped here, even though the rest of them didn't know it yet.

The idea of having to talk to Mac's mom or Kiffer's parents—of having to look them in the face and tell them their child had died, and it was his fault—hammered into him. The hallway intersection swam in and out of focus.

Cold metal touched his arm, and he ignored it. It bumped into him harder. Did it again. He looked over in consternation to see Charlie pushing the end of a stretcher against him. Brows drawing together, he tilted his head in question.

She left the stretcher in place and came to his side to whisper. "We need to take her to the morgue." When he didn't respond, she snapped her fingers in front of his face. "Jacques, even without electricity, the morgue is the coldest place in the building. If we put her in a drawer, it'll preserve the body more than just letting it stay up here where it's warm."

He pressed his lips together. She was right, but he wasn't ready to deal with it. He needed a moment. They all did. Didn't she understand that?

"Jacques, we have a lull right now," she said, voice urgent. "Feel it! We need to take care of Rachelle's body and then figure out what the hell we're going to do." Her eyes softened; voice gentled. "I know you're hurting right now, but your team needs you. I need you. You got us out of this once, right?"

Her last words cut through the shock like fog of grief and fear he'd wrapped himself in. She was right. His team needed him. If he couldn't get his act together, there was no telling how many of them would make it out of Union Grace alive. If any would. Jacques inhaled, the breath expanding his chest to the point of pain. Purpose cleared his head.

Charlie relaxed a bit when she realized she'd gotten through to him.

"You're right," he said. "Let's move."

Together, they wheeled the stretcher to the base of Rachelle's feet. Jacques moved to crouch down in front of his team. "We need to get Rachelle moved down to the morgue," he told them. Mac's eyes narrowed as she searched his face.

Birdie wiped his eyes with a thumb and forefinger. "This investigation is over, boss." His normally placid face grew darker. "What are you thinking? Team first. We need to get out of here."

"I tried," Jacques said, gut twisting. "But Grace wouldn't let us out. I couldn't even break down the door."

"Because you weigh about sixty pounds soaking wet." Birdie squared his shoulders. "I'll go handle it. I can get us out."

"It was going to kill Jacques," Charlie said, voice sharp. "But it got distracted by ripping Rachelle's soul to shreds. But by all means, if you think you are somehow magically stronger than whatever asshole entity is keeping us in here, go for it. Risk your life and your chance at the afterlife."

"Charlie," Jacques snapped as Birdie and Mac went pale.

"It got Rachelle's soul?" Fresh tears welled in Birdie's eyes. "Are you sure?"

Eyes downcast, Charlie nodded. "I saw it happen. I'm sorry."

"I saw it too," Jacques said. "But before that... it wasn't just me trying to open the door, Bird. Kiff was on the other side, and he was trying to break it with a crowbar."

Mac ran her fingers through her blond pixie cut, making sections of it stand straight up. "You saw Kiffer?"

Jacques inclined his head, but said, "But he didn't see me."

"So, what's the plan? We just stay here and wait to be picked off one by one?"

"No," he told Birdie. "But we have to find a different way. One that might actually work."

"I don't like this," Birdie said, "but I'm not stupid. You've never led us wrong before, especially when it comes to safety stuff. Let's get 'Chelle somewhere safe." He crouched down and slid his arms under Rachelle, picking her up with a small grunt. Jacques stepped back as he laid her on the stretcher.

Charlie helped the cameraman fasten the belts around the body. She chewed her lower lip for a second, and then whispered, "I'm not very strong." Her cheeks flushed as she spoke.

Jacques joined her at the foot of the stretcher, placing a hand on her shoulder. "It's okay," he told her. "I've got this." Rachelle was his responsibility. No way he would let Charlie be the one to help Birdie take her downstairs, anyway. Still, as she stepped away and wrung her hands, he understood the need to do something.

Conscious of the weight of the neon bag on his shoulder, he undid the zipper and pulled out a two-foot-long iron rod. He hefted it, pointing one end at her, and Charlie's eyes widened in realization. "Got my back?"

She nodded and grabbed the other end of the rod, holding it to her chest as he released it. Her flushed cheeks were wet with tears, and her upper lip glistened with snot. She wiped her face with the sleeve of her free arm, then got a two-handed grip on the rod. "Let's do this."

"Here's the plan," he said, handing her the rest of the bag as past and present merged once more. "Birdie and I will carry Rachelle." As Mac stepped up to Birdie's side, he continued, "Mac, I'll need you to open doors for us. Charlie, there's salt and holy water in there. Glowsticks if our lights crap out. Crack one and shake to activate. I want you on Mac's heels, okay?"

She slid the bag onto her shoulders, then choked up her grip on the rod. "And after?"

He didn't have a plan that stretched that far ahead. "Let's concentrate on the right now. Okay?"

He looked at them each until they all answered affirmatively. "Grace caught us off guard," he said, forcing confidence into his voice. "It won't happen again."

Mac squared her shoulders and started past him to the stairwell, Charlie hot on her heels. Birdie nodded and put his hands on the push rails. "Let's do this."

Because there wasn't an immediate need for him to be at the other end of the stretcher, he turned toward the rest of the crew, keeping a hand on the rail to keep it straight as Birdie began walking it forward. "Mac, there's a bag in the basement on the other side of the stairwell. Grab that as soon as you're through."

"Got it," she said.

"Kiffer, if you can hear this, we're taking Rachelle down to the morgue now. Please get help getting us out of here."

There was no response.

Jacques prayed that in destroying Rachelle, both in body and spirit, Union Grace had exhausted (or satiated) itself, at least for a little while. He hoped it was the case, and the thought weirded him out. His life had turned upside down. Only one other time in his life could he have imagined rooting for a lack of paranormal activity. But this wasn't a normal investigation anymore, and his life had come full circle.

Union Grace had thrown out the rulebook and written her own. Unfortunately, she'd chosen to clue none of them into what those rules were.

CHAPTER THIRTY-NINE

Charlie had demanded Jacques snap out of it, focus on saving them, but the truth was cotton wool had enveloped her own brain. She knew it was her body's way of dealing with what had happened, and she welcomed it. Operating on autopilot was the best way to get through the upcoming hours. She feared what would happen when she had no choice but to resume manual control. Paranormal activity around her was always high, but when she was emotional? It So much worse. And she'd not only watched someone bleed out, but she'd witnessed the decimation of their spirit.

The door to the basement opened like the hinges were freshly oiled. The faint scent of sanitation chemicals lingered in the air. For a moment, Charlie swore she heard muffled conversation happening behind closed doors. Union Grace felt livelier here and now than anywhere else.

Mac pushed the door all the way open, then flattened herself to the wall beside it. Charlie readied herself to swing the first time a ghost so much as looked at her cross-eyed.

There was nothing to swing at. The sounds of conversation faded so quickly she put the sounds down to her imagination. Shaking her head, she turned to see if Jacques and Birdie needed any help maneuvering through the door.

They came through okay, both with shoulders squared and eyes staring off into the distance. The two never looked down as they sat the stretcher down on its wheels and pushed it toward the morgue doors. She didn't blame them. She didn't want to look either.

Mac brushed past her, her hand skimming the small of her back. The blonde paused with a hand on the metal doors of the morgue and wet her lips. She glanced back, and Charlie knew Mac felt it too. Union Grace wanted them down here, in the basement. The only question was why.

Charlie took a deep breath and held a finger up, signaling she needed a minute. It didn't take her long to fetch the large Maglite from her backpack. She turned it on and adjusted the beam to its widest possible setting. The flashlights attached to their harnesses were not bad, but this one was better. The familiar heft of the light comforted her, but she wouldn't be carrying it while in the morgue. Not for long, at least. Tucking it between her shoulder and ear, she got her bags back into position, grabbed her rod, and stepped up to Mac.

The blonde raised her eyebrows.

Charlie said, "Just in case." She cut her eyes toward the door. Mac's mouth opened, then closed again. She took in an audible breath, then pushed one door open as wide as she could.

Charlie darted in, and when nothing came at her from the dark, she stepped off to the side and kneeled. Putting the Maglite on the floor, she balanced it on one end so it spread light upward. It wasn't enough to fully illuminate the room, but it gave them an element of visibility that didn't depend solely on the positions of their harness beams.

Then she was back on her feet, batter's grip on the rod again as she visually swept the space. Everything was the same as the last time, but goosebumps crawled up her spine.

As the guys rolled the stretcher into the morgue, Mac stood beside her. She was fingering a loop on her tool belt, her dark brows drawn into a low frown. She watched the room as the men settled the stretcher near the closet row of morgue drawers, but she didn't move until Jacques called her name. At his murmured request, she approached the middle drawer in the row.

As she grabbed the handle, Charlie sucked in a breath, not knowing what was going to come from the darkness, but positive it would be nothing good. To her surprise–and Mac's too, given the sigh of relief that she heard–nothing leaped out at them.

After a long moment of staring into the darkness as if waiting for some sort of delayed reaction, Mac grabbed hold of the inset metal slab and pulled it out to the end of its track. Then she stepped back, saying, "Okay."

In sync, Birdie and Jacques undid the belt buckles securing Rachelle's body to the stretcher. Then Birdie slid his hands under her shoulders and Jacques took hold of her legs.

Jacques started counting, but before he could get to three, the cloth-encased body writhed on the stretcher.

He yelped, pulling his hands away and leaping backward. "Nope. No. No. Fuck this shit. She moved. Oh my god, she moved." His voice was high and tight, the strain threatening to make him a falsetto.

Dread filled Charlie as she understood which way this was going to go. She knew she needed to pay attention to the rest of the room, just in case, but she couldn't tear her eyes away from the scene at hand.

Birdie had the opposite reaction to Jacques. Instead of pulling away, he found the seam where the ends of the sheet overlapped with each other and pulled them apart.

'Chelle? Shit, we–" he stopped, going rigid with a mix of fear and anger. "You're not Rachelle."

"Nope." Rachelle's voice was unfamiliar. Deeper, darker.

Birdie took a slow step back.

Mac got a two-handed grip on her own poker.

With no effort, the corpse raised its torso until it was sitting up. Sitting and staring straight at Jacques. A sliver of Charlie's mind noticed it had not used its arms to accomplish the task. "Hello, Squirt. If that is my brother underneath that... thing on your face."

Jacques went white, a feat considering his natural deep brown color. So did Charlie. It had been a long time since she'd heard that nickname for Jacques. And only one person had ever got away with using it.

Jacques hesitated for a moment, then loosened the straps on the respirator and removed it. Charlie saw the imprint of the mask on his face as he licked his lips and said, "Ana?"

Rachelle's chin tilted down with slug-like slowness before she went still again. Not still with the slack immobility of death, but the anticipatory stance of a predator awaiting the perfect time to strike.

Charlie's stomach dropped like an elevator with the cable cut, ending up at her feet in about three milliseconds. There was no way that was Ana. No fucking way.

"Not happy to see me?" Ana's accent was a weird mix of the French nasal and Rachelle's Southern accent. It grated against Charlie's ears, emphasizing how wrong the situation was.

"It's, uh, not exactly how I imagined our reunion would look," Jacques responded after a moment. The corners of his mouth tugged up in a small smile about a million miles away from reaching his eyes.

Charlie sidled over until she could get a better look at Rachelle's face, holding the poker so tight her hands were hurting. What she saw made her want to recoil. To puke. To cry.

It wasn't just Jacques' dead sister's voice coming from

Rachelle's body. The features of the corpse had undergone subtle alterations. Her eyes, normally a light green, were now brown. Her cheeks and the line of her jaw looked stronger and more pronounced. Like her flesh stretched over the bone structure of someone with much more defined features.

There had been no life in Rachelle's body when she'd lain askew on the floor. Her body had been unprotesting weight in Birdie's arms when he placed her on the stretcher. If, by some chance, she had been unconscious, the trip down two flights of stairs would have roused her. All these pieces of knowledge came together in an instant, and Charlie understood what she was looking at. Someone using her body like a rentable meat sack. Someone who wanted them to believe she was Jacques' sister, Ana. But who? And why?

"Oui, et moi je ne pensais pas d'être morte, mais c'est comme ça."

Charlie didn't know a lot of French anymore. Hanging around with Em it had been inevitable she'd pick some of it up, but after thirteen years of non-use there wasn't a lot of vocabulary in the memory banks. Despite that, she got the gist of what the Rachelle-puppet was saying. Something about not expecting death.

Out of the corner of her eye, she saw Mac's head turn as she looked around the room.

Jacques said, "I'm sorry. I missed you. Every day."

Ana rolled her neck like she was trying to ease tension from the muscles. The movement was quick enough that an audible pop made Charlie cringe. Growing up before The Event, Charlie loved horror movies much to her father's delight. So, she'd seen many instances of dead bodies moving in unnatural ways. And how Ana moved? It didn't fit in with any of Charlie's horror movie logic. Admittedly, not a great thing to base one's expectations off, but still.

Ana should be slow, jerky. Should move like she needed to

think about how to operate the body she occupied. Not springing into action like she'd taken some super serum.

"Mm," Ana said, falling back into a statue stillness as unnatural as her rapid movement had been, "You left me alone, Squirt. Left me to die in the fire." The pitch of her voice rose, imitating stressful tones. "Why didn't you save me?"

"I tried," Jacques said, voice fraught with emotion. Charlie saw his throat work as he swallowed before continuing. "I tried to keep you safe. You left the circle! You shouldn't have left the circle!"

"You should have tried harder. I died all alone because of you," Ana accused him.

The sheer anguish on Jacques' face twisted Charlie's heart. It also solidified her belief this thing was pretending to be Ana. There was no way in hell Ana would be cruel to her little brother. Why couldn't Jacques see this wasn't her?

"No, she didn't," she said, unable to keep quiet. "Ana and Emerson died together. And if you were really Ana, you would know that."

Jacques looked at her with guilt and grief etched into his face. She focused on him, finding it easier to look at him and watch the possessed body indirectly out of the corner of her eye. His breath crystallized in the air as the remaining warmth leached from the room.

"Hiya Charlie," the Rachelle-Ana thing snapped its head toward her. Charlie reacted to the quick motion in her peripheral vision, whirling in that direction. She blanched at the sight of the rictus grin and doll-like blank eyes with dilated pupils fixated on her. "I missed you."

The sheer glee in its voice snared the breath in Charlie's chest, sending waves of panic racing through her. Hating herself, Charlie dropped her eyes and tried to calm down as the atmosphere grew thick, and the morgue drawer doors began to rattle. If she didn't keep herself under control, things were going to get much worse.

"You know this is all your fault, don't you?"

Their flashlight beams flickered again, casting everyone's faces in deep shadow. The chains on the hanging scale squeaked as it rocked back and forth. The putrid smell of rot hit their senses a second later, causing a couple of them to gag.

"Emerson and Ana would still be alive if it wasn't for you, wouldn't they?"

"Yeah, I'm gonna need you to shut the fuck up." Mac's voice overrode the Ana-thing, voice loud and filled with anger. As she spoke, she stepped toward Rachelle's body and swung the rod.

It was the wrong thing to do. To give warning before action. In a heartbeat, Rachelle's corpse pushed off the stretcher, lunging toward Mac with a furious scream.

Jacques yelled something in French. Adrenaline surged through Charlie, making everything in the room suddenly visible with hyper-realistic clarity as the lights above the morgue table surged to life, only to shatter and go black.

She was already moving, ignoring the changes to the environment as she tried to stop the attack. She was close enough to Rachelle's corpse that she didn't have to move, just swing for the fences with her rod aimed straight for the head. But she was too late.

Instead, she could only watch in horror as the corpse barreled into Mac, fist flashing out and impacting the blonde's chest. It hit her hard enough to send her crashing into the stretcher. The ancient metal contraption tipped over even as she somersaulted over it.

Mac grunted as she hit the floor, but then went completely, deathly silent. Charlie brought a shaking hand to her mouth. Not again. They'd already lost Rachelle. They couldn't have lost Mac too. Her fault. Her fault. The phrase was burning itself into her brain. She was here, and now more people were dead. The last breath she'd taken was locked inside lungs that refused to expand.

And then the abomination inhabiting Rachelle's corpse attacked Jacques.

CHAPTER FORTY

The thing masquerading as Ana came for him, defiling the cooling body of his newest team member by wearing her skin like a meat suit. She was fast, so damned fast. There was no time to move. He threw his hands up in front of his face as Mac thumped to the floor, certain he was going to get his ass kicked.

But the expected impact never came. The looming threat chilled him through, but the killing blows he expected failed to materialize. He lowered his hands enough to see over them, and his vision tunneled in until all he could see was the being in front of him. Ana stood staring back at him. The real Ana, with brown eyes now filled with affection. Rachelle's body shuddered, individual muscle groups flexing beneath the skin. Her long, skinny fingers curled into claws, then fists, and relaxed, only to repeat the process over again.

"Ana?"

She jerkily nodded before her head twitched hard, forcing her to look up and away from him. Her mouth opened, and an irritated hissing sound came from it. She clamped her jaw shut, turned her attention back to him. He could see the fight for control in the shifting micro-expressions on her face. She put her hands behind her. "I told you to be careful, Squirt."

It was her voice, clear and beautiful. Tears blurred his vision.

"Ana, I'm sorry. I'm so sorry."

"You were a kid, Jacques. We all were." She twitched again and her head tilted too far back. He heard the bones crack in her neck. Her abdomen bulged out, a softball sized lump appearing under the blood-caked shirt, worming up toward her throat.

He heard words from Charlie and Birdie, but he couldn't make out what they were saying. Couldn't find it in him to care. All he could do was watch his sister as she battled the evil inside Rachelle's body for control.

Ana grunted, and the lump stopped at the hollow of her throat, descending a few inches before disappearing. She straightened her head back up. "I can't hold it for long," she said, voice strained. "I love you. Em loves you. You did nothing wrong. We did. We didn't listen."

He brought a hand to his chest, felt the rapid thump of his heart, and the easing of a band that locked in place around it that night. "I love you," he whispered, tears tracking down his cheeks.

"I know," Ana told him. She brought a hand up, tried to touch his face, but her fingers splayed wide. Too wide. The webbing between digits and palm tearing open. Her fingers curled into talons. She huffed out a breath and pulled her hand back, putting it behind her back again.

Ana gave him a sad smile and then turned around to face Charlie and Birdie. The two were standing a few feet apart. Charlie had her weapon at waist height, end pointing toward Ana. Confusion and hope warred on her face. Birdie held a container of salt in one hand, a pile of the white granules in the other. His eyes flicked between Rachelle and Jacques and back again.

"You need to save him," Ana said, addressing Charlie directly. "He can't do it without you."

"I... I can't," Charlie whispered. "I don't know how."

"By being the person Em knew you could be, not the scared little mouse you've become," Ana said, her voice dropping into a growl at the end. Charlie's eyes widened more than the growl called for. She must have seen something on Ana's face.

A heartbeat later, Ana spoke again. Her voice was tight, but normal. "Control the Force. Jedi that shit. But right now, you need to kill this body."

"How?"

"You're holding a weapon, dumb ass. Figure it out." That was teenage Ana, exasperated, amused, and sarcastic.

Charlie's eyes dropped to her weapon, and her cheeks flushed.

"Now do it," Ana hissed.

Indecision warred on Charlie's face.

"Now!" His sister screamed the word and sprang at Charlie.

Charlie reacted, thrusting the iron rod into the corpse's torso, right below the ribcage. It penetrated the body completely, end poking out from beneath Rachelle's shirt in the back.

A shriek of enraged fury buffeted the room as the entity stumbled back, ripping the rod from Charlie's hands. It whirled away, trying to run. Jacques stepped into its path, grabbing for the rod.

The entity swung, and though a physical blow did not connect, Jacques slammed into the wall. As soon as he made contact, an invisible force gripped him by the throat, shoving him upward until his feet left the ground.

He grabbed at the air, but there was nothing to latch onto. No way to ease the pressure. He was losing the ability to think, blackness creeping in on the edges of his vision.

"Yo, bitch," Mac's voice cleaved the air. Ana's head whipped in the blonde's direction. Mac rammed the rod into the left side of her chest. The blonde didn't stop there. Instead, she leaned into it, determined to pin the possessed corpse to the wall.

Suddenly, Jacques was down, sliding to the floor as his knees gave out, while Mac forced the dead woman's body sideways.

Before the two had gone far, Birdie grabbed the possessed corpse, wrapping one large arm around it. He clapped his free hand over its mouth, grains of white slipping between the contact points and falling to the floor.

A muffled scream rose from the possessed body. It convulsed and bucked furiously. Jacques tried to get up, to run and help hold her, but his knees were jelly, and he couldn't rise.

Mac dropped her hold on the poker, twisting her slim body between the two rods, and wrapped the dead woman's front in a bear hug.

There was no fucking way he was letting his team deal with it alone, Jacques crawled the few feet on hands and knees and timed a grab for the corpse's feet, wrapping his arms around them and then putting all his weight into keeping them down.

The entity fought for what felt like an hour before the body went slack.

Jacques let loose of her feet and forced himself to his. Mac and Birdie shifted their hold. Mac slid the iron rods out of the body, the wet sucking sound turning everyone's stomach. Birdie picked up the body and laid it upon the waiting metal slab. Charlie came over to Jacques, and he opened his arms to her. She went into his embrace without hesitation, and they clung to each other.

They all looked at each other in silence, and then Birdie pulled the respirator down his face, tucking it under his beard. "Don't think cancer is worth the hassle of worrying about right now," he said.

Jacques touched his throat, "Yeah. Be happy to just be

alive in fifteen to have the damned cancer." He added, "Good thinking, mes amis."

"Job's not done," Birdie replied. "Still useful."

He knew what he meant. The salt had only temporarily cast Ana–and whomever else that had been–out of Rachelle's body. To make sure that they couldn't come back into it, they were going to have to make the body uninhabitable.

His stomach churned with sudden nausea. He took an unsteady breath, trying to muster the will to do what needed to be done. "Okay," he said, and swallowed back gorge, "okay. I, uh... "

"Take Mac and Charlie into the hall," Birdie said quietly. "Mac got hit pretty hard. Check on her."

"I'm fine," Mac protested, pressing a hand to her chest. "You're right. We need to-"

Birdie gave her a look and held out a hand. Mac's voice trailed off. She handed the poker to him before turning to Jacques and saying, "Maybe help me see if she actually broke all my ribs or just feels like it?"

Jacques realized what Birdie was doing, and even though he knew he should protest, should stay and help, all he could do was give the bearded man a small smile of grateful relief. He kept his arm around Charlie as he led Mac from the room.

They both tried very hard to ignore the sounds of poker meeting flesh coming from within the morgue.

CHAPTER FORTY-ONE

Outside Union Grace, Kiffer hopped out of the van and kicked the front tire. Something was going on inside the building, but all he could get was staticky glimpses of familiar forms from the RV screens. Split second flashes before the screens would go black. Union Grace taunting him with the knowledge that his friends were in danger, and he couldn't do anything about it. "You son of a bitch," he yelled as he made contact. "You evil, fucking son of a bitch!"

The van hadn't started when he'd given up and exited the RV to try his luck with it again. The engine hadn't even deigned to sputter. He'd done all of Birdie's tricks to get it going, but it just sat there as placid as the man himself. Even when he'd begged and promised to buy it a new transmission.

"I'm trying," Kiffer yelled, slamming his fist on the front side panel. "I'm trying. I just don't know... " Why hadn't it worked? He'd received a sign. While he'd sat there, trying to plan, someone (or something) had rained yellowed paper confetti down the side of Union Grace. When he gone to investigate, he discovered that the confetti consisted of the numbers 9 and 1 that looked like they had been ripped from newspaper headlines. There had been double the amount of 1s. Even if he'd been an idiot, that message had been clear. Call for help. It was a sign letting him know that God was present, but he was expecting Kiffer to do the work.

Had God been there this whole time, guiding him, even

though he hadn't recognized his voice at first? Get them out. But then He hadn't taken a heavenly form, had he? He'd taken the form of a young boy, one with desperation and disappointment in his movements. A ghost, albeit not one that looked like it belonged to Union Grace. Too modern.

Too modern. He frowned at the thought. While he had no doubt that God could make miracles happen, hastily ripped confetti telling him to call 911 did seem a little too on the nose. But if it was someone who had recently died that was trying to communicate with them, it would make perfect sense. Especially a kid. They were always trained to call 911.

Kiffer went to the back of the van and opened it. He dug around until he pulled out a Ouija Board from the back of one shelf. Jacques hated the things and refused to use them, but sometimes they were a useful tool. Viewers loved to see a good old-fashioned shot of the planchette darting across the board.

He briefly considered setting up the camera but discarded the idea and set the board up on the table. Sitting, he placed his fingertips on the planchette. "I seek to contact the spirit that has been trying to communicate with me. Are you here with me?"

The planchette zipped to YES.

He exhaled through pursed lips. God did not communicate through Ouija boards. His methods weren't that direct. So, there was a little disappointment, but it was far better to have this outcome than to assume the omnipotent being he tried so fiercely to believe in had been either fucking with him or was so helpless he couldn't win against one hospital and whatever was controlling it.

"Do you have anything you'd like to tell me?"

Some people preferred to say the individual letters out loud. It was great for dramatic effect. Not him.

"DUMBASS."

The bottle of water sitting untouched on the table since breakfast wobbled hard and then tipped over, sending a stream of liquid sloshing toward him.

He grabbed it and swiped most of the water off the table. He put his hands back on the planchette. "I deserved that. And I'm sorry. But I need help. I don't know what else to do."

"CAMERAS."

"Check the cameras? Again?"

The planchette didn't move, but the water bottle started to wobble again.

"Alright," he said quickly, getting to his feet. "Checking the cameras." He didn't know why. He'd seen nothing useful the last hundred times he'd looked. But that didn't stop him from hopping up into the back of the RC. Most cameras were off, feeds indicating they were receiving nothing. However, one screen was on. Charlie's GoPro, he thought. While the quality of the footage wasn't great, it was better than anything he had been receiving. What he saw on the grainy footage horrified him.

Unable to hear anything from the radios, Kiffer could only watch as the situation played out in complete silence, like a twisted silent film horror movie. He couldn't tear his eyes away from it. Not until Birdie placed a gentle kiss on Rachelle's forehead before lifting the iron rod up. Part of him wanted to bear witness, to tell his friend later that he hadn't been alone. But he couldn't. Both because of his own helplessness and the fact that Charlie chose that moment to leave the room.

When he looked back at the screen, it surprised him that the connection was still solid. Grainy, dark, and sometimes only a few frames at a time, but there. He saw the back of heads and stairs. When he eventually lost them for a brief second, he held his hand over his mouth, praying until the connection came back.

When it came back on, he was looking at Jacques, seated at the end of a conference table. Acting on hours of instinct and muscle memory, Kiffer double-checked to make sure the feed was being recorded, then maximized that camera's view so that his boss's face took up the whole screen.

CHAPTER FORTY-TWO

When the camera was on him, Jacques felt like the best version of himself. He wasn't Jacques, the poor little rich boy who'd lost his sister and brother in one fell swoop and then watched his family fall apart after. He was Jacques De Molyneux, the somewhat dramatic but always charming host of Banshee Investigations. But even though part of him wanted to wax eloquent, to protect himself with the persona he'd begun to craft, he couldn't do it. There was too much on the line right now. If by some chance they got out of Union Grace alive, he'd redo the footage. Right now, he just needed to make sure someone heard the damned story. There had to be a recording in case none of them made it out of here.

He started with the story he'd been told of Union Grace and the subsequent questions raised. It was almost painful to keep it as brief as he did, but he was cognizant of the fact that they were in danger. It made sense to kill two birds with one stone and explain the truth of Union Grace as he knew it to both his crew and the viewers at home. And recounting this let him push the thoughts of the morgue—of Ana—away.

Most of what he said was available in their dossiers, but he didn't know what Charlie knew. When he hit the end of the known information, he steepled his fingers and fell silent. From behind the rig, Birdie flashed a thumbs-up.

Jacques leaned toward the camera. In his mind's eye, he saw the thing masquerading as Ana wrapped inside Rachelle's body, launching herself at him. His heart leaped, but he forced the image aside. "Now," he said, "we need to digress a little bit. I've told you the history of the deaths at the hospital, but I haven't told you the history of the Erschon family and how Union Grace came to be. And that information that may be vital to figuring out the puzzle we find ourselves trapped in."

He paused, swallowed, and added quietly, "Or you, if you're watching this from within the hospital and we're dead."

Charlie's chair creaked as she leaned forward, eyes wide with curiosity.

"We accept that gifts can be passed down through generations. Usually, it's children inheriting their parent's physical abilities, but it's no different with other types of gifts. Psychic gifts. And one family with this lineage is the Erschons."

Ana, wrapped in a shroud of fire, screaming as she fell to the floor. His fear as he'd screamed for her, for Emerson. Too scared to leave the circle to try and help and hating himself for it.

He bit the inside of his cheek hard. The copper tang of blood edged his tongue. It helped him focus again on what he was doing. Grant was going to hate him for this, but the man wouldn't be able to do anything about it. Jacques never agreed to anything without having some sort of contract on hand, and that included when he checked out haunted buildings on behalf of old school chums.

"You see, in the Erschon family, there is a gift tied to the women in the family. One that gives them the ability to interact with the dead. One that—" He paused again.. He could feel himself sliding into the eloquent, loquacious role. He needed to resist the urge and keep things moving. "The men of the family weren't shy about taking advantage of." He wanted to make eye contact with Charlie desperately, but he didn't know if he'd be able to stay on track, so he kept looking at the camera.

"Then in 1930, Charlotte Erschon decided she didn't care for the way her family used their gifts and decided to do something about it."

Rachelle's body sitting up.

The rictus grin and dead eyes.

Anxiety seeped past the wall he was trying to keep in place. He swallowed hard, unable to suppress the shudder that rippled through him.

"Using the inheritance set aside for her when she turned twenty-five, Charlotte broke ranks with the family in a dramatic, public manner which made the gossip columns. Willing and able to live within or even below her means, Charlotte established her own residence and made friends with those her family considered undesirable. And then she did something unthinkable then. She used a large portion of her inheritance to a dear friend to fund a charity hospital in the area since they were sorely in need."

"Now, after a few years of finding other benefactors, Union Grace was built on March 3rd, 1933. A date specifically chosen by Charlotte's dear friend—Emerick Marple—who had an interest in Numerology."

Behind the rig, Birdie sat up straight. Jacques allowed himself a small smile. Birdie dabbled in Numerology, and this would have rung a bell. Three has long been thought to be the perfect number, even before Numerology became a thing. It is, after all, the accepted number of divinity. However, in Numerology, it is an Angel number."

Birdie frowned and stroked a hand down his beard. He lifted a finger, the signal to Jacques to pause, and cleared his throat. It surprised Jacques. Birdie had only interrupted Jacques a handful of times during these dialogue-heavy sessions and it was generally because of technical issues. That wasn't what this turned out to be.

Instead, Birdie said, "Three has negative connotations as well. It's thought to be an angel number, but in truth it can go either way. Three is in six, and we all know how people love that number. Three in thirteen, which is unlucky. People latch on to one aspect of a number and run with it, but you must consider all aspects. Three is also a number that magnifies whatever power you use it for."

That was interesting. He frowned, considering it. Very interesting. He couldn't help but wonder if it had anything to do with what he was coming to believe. That a demonic entity possessed Union Grace. People didn't get possessed just walking down the street, minding their own business. There were always contributing factors. Maybe the same was true with the hospital.

His body started to hum with anticipation, like there was a current running through it. He pushed it aside and nodded to Bird to let him know he had heard him before continuing. "When you play with power, sometimes the results aren't always what you'd expect. Grant Erschon admitted to me that his family had apparently made some sort of 'mistake' that was linked to the hospital. That Union Grace wouldn't see peace until that mistake was rectified."

"And now. . . " He couldn't ignore the feeling any more, and he could see that all of them were starting to shift restlessly. The idea made him want to giggle. They felt it too, whatever it was. He had to get it out. Had to finish this record. Even if they got to say no more, when people came to find them, they needed to know what happened. That Union Grace was a dangerous place. He fought back a chuckle. "We are missing the final member of our crew. Less than two hours ago, Rachelle Mason's life was lost as a direct result of paranormal activity. And then her body was used in an assault against me and other members of Banshee Investigations."

"Maybe we're wrong. But spirits don't possess the bodies of the dead, at least not for very long. That takes a lot more power than they have. The type of power you'd associate with a much higher power... or should we say a much lower one? And whatever we're facing here definitely has more power than it should."

Saying that out loud, he realized what an amazing thing Ana had done. She shouldn't have been able to enter Rachelle. Let alone take control from whatever it was that was already in Rachelle's body like she had. The sheer willpower and determination that had taken was amazing, but not surprising. His sister had always been willing to kick ass for him. Why would it be any different in the afterlife?

He paused for a beat, lifted a hand palm up to the camera, trying to ignore the strange swell of amusement and something else he could feel building. Something wrong. "One can only imagine what went down on June 6th, 1944. One can imagine–" The feeling of anticipation was growing stranger. So hard to ignore. He wanted to... to what? He had to keep going, to remember to keep his words vague enough to avoid accusations of slander. "One can imagine a deal or a promise made that would lead to the deaths of over one hundred people early that morning. And if the records are to be believed, they died within an hour of each other. One can only imagine what the Erschons had bargained for."

And then the laughter tore out of him, scraping his throat, forcing his mouth open until his jaws hurt. The sort of belly laugh that echoed off the walls, edged with frantic hysteria. Laughed until tears streamed down his cheeks and the laughter had segued into near screams.

It was terrifying, trapped in a body that was reacting against his will. Unable to stop it, to get control back. Feeling his heart hammering in his chest, his pulse pounding in his temples as his vision began to go gray.

Mac saved him with a slap that threatened to dislocate his jaw.

It sobered him at once and he put a trembling hand to his mouth. "I didn't... that wasn't me," he whispered. "That wasn't me."

CHAPTER FORTY-THREE

While Jacques laughed, Charlie tried her damnedest not to puke. The malicious energy she'd first encountered in the OR crept into the room while they'd focused on Jacques's words. Instead of brute force, it used a gentle touch, wrapping itself around them like a vine that slowly crept up a tree. She hadn't been expecting it, and its slow growth had gone unnoticed with her distraction.

When it struck, viper quick, her stomach rebelled so violently it was only a lack of food that prevented projectile vomiting. Carefully, she bent over and took a deep breath, trying to calm her racing heart.

Slender fingers touched the back of her neck, and the warm strength of them kept her from a panicked flailing fit. A faint voice spoke, barely audible. She had trouble understanding his words, but she didn't care. The words didn't matter, but the way they said it - with a tone of comfort and reassurance. She clung to that comfort as the hand gently kneaded the muscles of her neck, helpless.

Charlie detested feeling helpless, a feeling which had dominated so much of her life. It controlled her by keeping her on the move. It was as responsible for her inability to achieve a sense of normalcy as much as her ability itself. The acknowledgment of that hatred, that self-disgust, brought so many memories to the forefront of her mind. Nobody understood what she went through. Living at the mercy of something she couldn't see, couldn't touch, that meds or doctors couldn't fix. Em, her dad, both acted like she was amazing. Special. And Em ended up dead because of it. Special, her ass.

Even before her power fully manifested, it scared her. People shouldn't be able to do what she did. Spirits shouldn't react to her like they did. And even before she'd lost anyone, she'd understood not all spirits were kind. Like the mean one at her house. The one she refused to name. She would wake up in the middle of the night feeling it watching her. Sense its anger. It would take things she loved, and only the other spirits could lead her to them again.

She had known, deep down inside, that if it could hurt her, it would. It just hadn't been able to. Its weakness had kept her safe. Then her ability fully manifested, and her entire life had changed.

The nausea eased finally, but she didn't move. She hadn't thought about that spirit in forever. Somewhere between then and now, she'd started to believe she was safe because... Why? Because she helped them? Because, surely they wouldn't hurt the person who gave them energy back. Hadn't she? Or perhaps, she had buried the knowledge of her own vulnerability deep within her psyche, along with the memories of Em and Ana's death.

She knew the answer. She was a coward. The knowledge struck like an electrical shock. She'd spent so much of her life telling herself that she ran to keep other people safe, but it was just as much to keep herself safe. The realization horrified her. Coward wasn't a word she'd ever thought applied to her, but it did. And this was the life she was doomed to lead.

What were the chances that Grant really knew people who could help her? If anyone had been able to help her, it would have been her dad. And he was gone. Gone like Em. The only person who could help her was her. And had she ever even tried? No.

An angry heat swept through her. She'd spent her life

running like a dog with its tail tucked between its legs, doing nothing but feeling sorry for herself along the way. Even remembering her willingness to give up her own life if that was what it took to get forgiveness from Emerson stunk of cowardice because death would be a release from the life she was living.

A life that might very well end here at Union Grace, the way things were going. The duality of the situation with the event that transformed her life didn't escape her. Trapped in the middle of nowhere, surrounded by things that scared the shit out of her, and stuck with people that would end up dying because she couldn't...fucking...do...anything...to...stop...it!

Her pulse pounding in her ears, vision tunneling in until the grain of the table was all she could see, Charlie surged to her feet. She wasn't doing it this time. Would not be the helpless fucking damsel in distress. Union Grace and the evil bastard riding it could just get fucked. She screamed at the room, at the entity, at Union Grace, "Get. The. Fuck. Gone." and slammed her palms down onto the table.

As her hands struck the wood, a heady sensation that felt like it sent her individual atoms vibrating shot exploded out from inside her, pushing against the festering evil infecting the room. Forcing it away from them.

She had a split second of relief before consciousness left and she crumpled.

CHAPTER FORTY-FOUR

Charlie came to with Birdie's big hands cradling her head, his chocolate brown eyes filled with concern. She inhaled, noticing right away that something was different. The heavy odor of neglect and rot inundating the room had fled. In its place, she could smell the faint traces of what she assumed to be Birdie's cologne.

She struggled to sit up, and he helped her. For a moment, what she'd done stayed lost in the fog that came with regaining consciousness. Then the memory snapped back in place like plucked elastic, and she looked around the room.

"It's okay," Mac said. "You... chased it off." She was smiling at her, eyes glazed with relief. Charlie couldn't help but smile.

From beside her, Birdie asked, "You ever done that before?"

Charlie shook her head. "I don't even know what I did." It wasn't like she'd thought about what she was doing. She'd just reacted.

"I think, cherie, you just bitch-slapped the devil," Jacques said from the end of the table, and laughed. It was a blessedly normal laugh.

Rising to his feet, Birdie offered her a hand. She took it, grateful for the help. Once she was on her feet, Charlie realized she felt better than she had in several hours. Tired, but better. Whatever she'd done had taken a lot out of her, but it was worth it.

She briefly opened her senses to the hospital, hoping she'd

find the rat bastard gone for good. Disappointment cut when she realized it was still present. What she'd done hadn't been enough to get the entity to relinquish its hold on Union Grace. Just to get it to retreat for a while.

It was enough. Now they could think instead of just reacting. React in a way that didn't involve running. Charlie was fucking tired of running. "Well, unfortunately I didn't slap him back to hell," she said, sighing. "So, you should finish your story if there's anything left to tell while you can. Then we need to figure out what happens next."

She sat back down, ready to hear the next part of Jacques' tale. Silence fell in the room. Charlie looked around in confusion. "What?"

"Just like that? You... yeet... an evil entity to the other side of the hospital, something you've never done before, and now you want me to just keep talking?" Jacques was still in his chair, but there was a protein bar wrapper in front of him, and he held a water bottle in his hand. She'd been out for a few minutes at least.

"Yeah?" Nothing was going to get accomplished if they sat on their ass doing nothing. And while she wasn't a big damned ghost hunter like Jacques, even she knew if they didn't find an explanation for what happened here, they weren't making it out alive.

Mac shook her head, half-smiling and giving Charlie a look she couldn't read. "The lady's right, boss. Time to finish your story or plan. Whatever we do, we need to do it now."

CHAPTER FORTY-FIVE

The absence of light made Jacques realize it must be nighttime, although he had lost track of time. They were heading into the morning of June 26th, if not already there. He'd resumed his position for the camera a few minutes ago, but his fragmented thoughts drifted just out of reach. Most of them attached to the feisty brunette watching him with all the expectant energy of a Grade A nerd on the morning of an intense lecture.

Even when they were younger, she'd been the definition of 'smol but fierce.' Barely taller than him, even with the age difference. And cute. He'd been able to see it. Damned sure knew Emerson had. Especially after the Lord blessed her with boobs. He grinned at the memory. Realistically, he knew childhood friendships rarely survived into adulthood. Relationships were almost certainly set to fail. But Em and Charlie? They'd had that magic. That spark that when you looked at them, you thought, "These two are gonna have each other's backs when they're old and gray."

And then Emerson and Ana died, and the world shifted into some sort of alternate reality. One that had taken him too long to accept. One that had broken Charlie. He understood that now. Pieces of the feisty teen were still there, but the sheer amount of glue holding her broken pieces together overpowered so much of who she had been. She once needed Emerson. Someone who unconditionally accepted her and grounded her. The world wasn't meant for someone with

Charlie's ability to drift through alone. She'd gotten lost to it and now they were paying the price.

It had blown up in their faces because he'd not listened to his gut. To Ana. Instead, he'd let himself be driven by the viewer count Union Grace could give them. By the popularity that would get them on the map. And now there was another death added to his ledger, and likely more to come. An hour ago, he would have said more deaths were a guarantee. But then Charlie... Charlie'd.

That was the only word he had for it.

The paranormal world ran on a set of rules that he—he'd thought—mostly understood. Knowing those rules was how he kept himself and his crew safe. Even Charlie had her own set of rules. They didn't really match up with the rest of the paranormal world as he understood it, but they were still there and, in their own way, they made sense.

Until she'd slammed her palms down on the table and told the entity to get the fuck out ... and it had. No rituals, no instruments. Just beast-be-gone and it had be-goned. That sort of thing worked with low-level entities if the person knew what they were doing. But dark entities like the one they were facing? Christ, it should have laughed—he shuddered, remembering the laughter he couldn't stop—and ripped her a new asshole.

The game changed. He remembered Ana's words. She'd been so confident Charlie could save them. Control the force. Jedi that shit. And Charlie had done such, possibly for the first time. But was it something she could repeat?

"Boss?" Birdie's calm voice pulled him back to the present. "You good?"

"Yeah." He took a fortifying breath and squared his shoulders. At least it felt easier to talk this time. "Yeah, Bird, I'm good. We rolling?"

"We rollin'."

"I'm sure you all have questions about what you just witnessed, and hopefully we'll have time to address that later. But for now, let me just take a moment to reassure you that everything is fine, and we shall continue with our tale."

"Please keep in mind that the rest of the information I have is barely more than an outline. After the events of June 6th, 1944—a date our viewers who know their history will recognize as D-Day—the hospital closed. The timing may be why there was so little initial coverage of the fact. Much more important things took the front page, even in a little town."

"Locals were paid a sizable amount of cash—something desperately needed—by unnamed persons to help ease the pain and suffering because of the sudden loss of life. And it is here I need to mention that in our research we could turn up no evidence that there was an investigation to substantiate this. Take that as you will for now."

He'd already spent a lot of time talking. Too much more and he'd lose his audience. Much more and they'd run out of time before they could make plans. But he still needed to lay the rest of it out. Fuck the Erschon family.

"And then, in the early 70s, Union Grace reopened to deal with the influx of troops returning from the Vietnam War. But the events of 1944 had left an indelible mark on the hospital, and Union Grace was no longer the place of peace and healing it had once been. It hobbled through the end of the war, tainted by the evil that touched it. The locals believed it was cursed. That if anyone stayed there long enough, they became different. Darker."

He dropped his voice, leaned in toward the camera. "Like their soul had spoiled."

Jacques straightened up, drummed his fingers on the tabletop, natural showmanship returning to him. "And then Union Grace closed its doors for the last time. The Erschon family assumed full ownership within days. They allowed no visitors, no investigations, but chose not to raze the hospital to the ground and either sell the land or build something new here instead. Curious."

"But when you add to this Grant Erschon's talk of a demon inhabiting the hospital and mistakes made ... Well, it doesn't look good, does it? But whether demon or something else..." He hadn't intended necessarily to be this direct, but he couldn't risk the loss of lives of those who might come after them. "Please understand this. There's something evil walking the halls of Union Grace, and if we don't make it out, do not investigate. Do not recover our bodies. Instead, burn this building to the ground and salt the ashes. I mean it."

He looked at Birdie instead of the camera. "We're done."

"Done," his cameraman agreed.

CHAPTER FORTY-SIX

The plan was made. Charlie and Mac were going to try to find an entrance to the roof. There had to be one for maintenance, if nothing else. While they did that, Birdie and Jacques were going to go back down to the basement and check out the file room while everything was still quiet. Birdie hoped they could find some sort of clue. It didn't seem likely, but Jacques had said firmly: "The more money you have, the more arrogant you are." Hence, they couldn't rule out the possibility of finding something buried in the paperwork stored in the old file cabinets.

Both groups had the neon safety bags with them. Mac carried the one for their team and Jacques the one for his. Everyone had an iron rod in their hand as well. Birdie carried his rig and kept his iron rod under his arm for quick access. He felt a little silly carrying the tripod contraption given everything going on but couldn't deny the feeling of security it gave him. And if everything went to hell, maybe the camera would survive. Shot of a lifetime and all that.

Promises to be careful all around, they set out. Since Jacques had the free hand, he led the way to the stairs. They went silently, which was a rarity for his boss. At the doorway to the second floor, Jacques paused, reaching out a hand to touch the metal.

Birdie waited.

"We should salt the blood," Jacques said after a long moment.

Birdie frowned. They didn't know how much time they

had before things started to act up again, and it didn't feel like the most judicious use of their time. "Never worried about that before."

Jacques curled his fingers into a loose fist and rapped his knuckles lightly once against the door. "Never went toe-to-toe with a demon before. Blood has power, Bird. I don't know if that applies to the blood of the dead or just the blood of the living, but blood has power. We can't take the risk."

"Let's get it done, then." Though his mouth dried out at the thought of going back to where Rachelle died, it needed to be done. Calling on training he hadn't had to use in years, Birdie—whose real name was Richard Fowler—forced himself to breathe calmly as his boss pushed open the door.

When Jacques went through, Birdie was right on his heels. And as a result, almost rammed his rig into the other man's back when he stopped a few feet inside the hallway.

"Holy shit." Jacques exhaled with a disbelieving sound.

He frowned and stepped around him to see what had made Jacques react. And then he said much the same thing.

The blood was gone. Completely. Rachelle had bled out, and even though she was tiny, the blood had made a large pool around her. Yet there was no trace of it. He was fully aware that no one had bothered to clean it up, and even if it had seeped through a crack, residue should have been evident. But there wasn't and there was no way it had just evaporated.

The second thing he noticed was that the floor was clean. Not just the floor, but the hallway itself. And not just clean, but brand new in appearance. The change started about six feet in front of them and extended to where the wing joined the main building. Gleaming pumpkin-colored tiles replaced the cracked and dusty dull orange one that were previously there. He fancied he could see an obvious line where the yellowed paint of the Union Grace they knew was being pushed back by a vibrant white.

"It's spreading," Jacques said. "What in the hell?"

He was right. He could see the advance most clearly on the floor, the way marked against the dark lines of the square floor tiles. Lines that were lightening in a steady roll in front of their eyes.

"Time slip?" It didn't feel like it, but it was the closest thing he could deduce. They'd experienced it once before. In a house that the owners had all but abandoned, too afraid to do anything with it. Banshee had gotten permission to go in there and see what they could find. Their plans were simple. Find evidence of who (if anyone) was haunting the building and help the owners find someone who could cleanse the area. They'd done it several times before. But that time was different. When they'd opened the kitchen door on their preliminary walk through, they'd found a grimy-faced man collapsed on his side, clutching a hand to his chest and writhing in pain.

Jacques ran to assist, but the camera glitched out and showed a different version of events before he even got to the man's side. Got to his side and realized it wasn't a man, but a corpse. One who had been there long enough that scavengers had stripped the meat from his body and left his clothes nothing but threadbare rags.

That bit of footage never made it to the website. Or to the police. They couldn't be sure they wouldn't somehow be held responsible for what had happened to the man. So instead, they'd called the cops, and Birdie had erased the footage from his camera.

"Don't think so," Jacques said.

The line of advance was now a couple of feet away. "What you want to do? Could be dangerous."

Jacques pulled a glow stick from his pocket and snapped

it, then lobbed it into the clean area. They both watched, tense and ready to run, but nothing happened. The glow stick remained untouched.

They watched for a little longer and then by unspoken agreement entered the area. Birdie shifted his grip and rig around a bit so that he could grab Jacques and pull him with him if the need arose.

It wasn't necessary. The changed area remained benign even as they tromped through it. And while there was some low-level chirping by the EMF, for the most part the area seemed normal. Disturbingly so. Birdie was almost relieved when they continued down to the basement.

CHAPTER FORTY-SEVEN

Just entering the basement made Birdie's heart beat harder in his chest. None of the nightmares he'd struggled for years with after getting back to civilian life came close to the reality of this. Hunting ghosts had been a distraction. A way to ignore the ghosts of his past. But the lines were blurring now, and this was a horror of its own sort. It was an entirely different experience, but just as unsettling as the haunting memories he had been working to move past.

When Jacques started to head to the storage room, he put a hand on his shoulder, holding him back. "Hold on a sec," he said. Like the second floor, too much shit had gone down here for him to be comfortable. He looked through the cameras, paying careful attention to the thermal cam. Nothing. The hallway was cold overall, but there were no spots of concern. He continued to observe, holding his breath, until he was sure he wasn't missing anything. Only then did he let loose of the other man's shoulder.

Jacques looked over his shoulder and gave a small, close-mouthed smile. Then he headed to the storage room. He wrenched the door open, hopping back a bit like he expected a mummy to fly out at him. When it didn't, he asked Birdie to hand him a chair, which he wedged under the knob before stepping inside. Given everything, the cameraman thought it was an intelligent decision.

Once they were inside the cramped space, Birdie realized beyond being Jacques' emotional support human, he was useless for the task at hand. Reading had never been his strong point. He could do it, it just took forever. He couldn't stand here twiddling his thumbs, getting in the other man's way, and slowing him down. "Gonna set up a salt line in the doorway," he told him. "Hopefully, buy us more time."

Jacques didn't even look up from the first batch of files he'd pulled from one drawer. He just said, "Bet," and shrugged off the neon bag. He handed it over to Birdie and resumed thumbing through the files.

Birdie got into the bag and pulled out the table salt. Kneeling, he put the tripod down on the floor beside him and laid a thick double line on the threshold. The morgue doors caught his attention as he straightened up. He cast a glance over his shoulder at Jacques, stroking a hand over his beard.

Birdie knew Jacques would likely have a fit if he left the room, but there was a time and place to listen to a man just because he was your boss. This wasn't it. Birdie respected Jacques. He was a good man. Did his best to keep everyone safe, but he didn't have the instincts that had been drilled into Birdie. Sometimes a man had to take risks to keep his family safe. And as much as he trusted Jacques, he was a slim little shit more built for running than doing anything that required actual muscle.

Laying some extra protection in front of the morgue might keep anything lurking in there from coming out to them. Other doorways to protect, as well. Maybe use the chairs and anything else he could get his hands on to wedge the doors shut. Keep the ghosts—and the dead—where they belonged.

CHAPTER FORTY-EIGHT

[*CCTV camera #4 - Location: 1st Floor, Original Structure - View: Left side of main lobby, showing emergency room exterior through to cafeteria entrance]*

No one is paying attention now. The multiple eyes inside this beast wearing the corpse of what was once a place of healing broadcast their signals to a system that is incapable of retrieving them. A system hijacked by a brother and sister doing all they can to support a connection between the Observer and his family trapped within. However, the camera continues to watch, as it was designed to do so. And it alone bears witness to the moment that is the beginning of an end.

He is no longer graveyard fog woven into a threadbare towel. The figure is so clearly defined that as he walks toward the camera in that halting cadence, one can make out the dried spatter of dark fluid that covers his gray scrubs and the mask laying untied against his chest. The movement of thin lips as he speaks. Whether his words are to himself or to a memory of someone walking beside him is unknown. What is known is that this is a man lost in his own world, to his own thoughts.

Lost until he comes to the turning point in his loop, where he is close to the blinking red eye of the impartial observer that has been a consistent feature in his journey over these last few days. The pause he takes here has lasted a little longer each time, but inevitably he must give in to the source of his nature now. To the destiny that has doomed him to walk the halls of dead space.

He has completed this journey, fading to nothingness, over the years since the hospital closed in the early seventies. Since the one who whispered to him of the rewards he should reap if he was unafraid to embrace the power offered whirled into a fearsome rage on that final night. The night that would lead to the hospital's closure. The night he offered everything only to be denied anything, including a chance to shrug off the existence he'd maintained and move on to whatever awaited him when his flesh had been returned to the earth.

Now, for reasons he does not understand nor can ponder more than briefly because his thoughts are scattered, incoherent things, he is changing. Gaining strength and form. Now he is more than he was even in the first days following his demise, when he was still struggling to understand the changes to his world.

And then, for the first time since this change has occurred, the eye bears witness to the dawning realization on his face as he understands what the eye is. That he is, in fact, being watched. And in that moment, the voice returns. It weaves words like silken knots into the momentary quiet space inside him. Reminds him of the promises it had made, of the offer he had accepted but never fulfilled. He cannot remember then, for it will not let him, that it was the cause of this contract being left unsigned. That its rage cut things short when he was on the cusp of doing what it had requested.

Instead, all he remembers is promises. The bargain they had struck. The blood he had promised to spill as he turned his back to the Hippocratic Oath in search of the power he craved.

His smoke-formed hands clench into fists at his side as he remembers. As he yearns for what slipped away from him.

For what had bounded off his fingertips that night, slipping into the ether.

And in that moment, though imperceptible to the eye and ear of those who watch, the voice beckons and assures that there is still time. That he has another chance to fulfill his end of the bargain. An opportunity to affix his signature onto this contract with the blood of the living now walking these halls. But only if he acts now.

All of this takes place before a full minute has passed as the surgeon looks up at the red light anchoring him to the present. But he needs no time to think. Thinking, he remembers, is why he lost this opportunity before. He dwelled too long on consequences and lost everything that night.

He moves now, but he no longer goes toward the wall he has disappeared into so many times before. Instead, the surgeon turns and heads toward the stairs. Heading toward the one who has made himself vulnerable and alone.

CHAPTER FORTY-NINE

1 *hour ago*

She was there, and then she wasn't. Charlie stared, uncomprehending, at the wall that had swallowed Mac. A blank wall where a door existed not five seconds ago.

They'd been working through each room in the upper story, their second pass. Nausea had steadily grown in Charlie's stomach as they started on their second pass, but she'd been doing her best to ignore it.

Bad things were going to happen. Bad things already happened. But she couldn't give into the fear anymore. Cowering in a corner would not save them. Charlie'd been so lost in her own thoughts, poking the ceiling tiles with a broom they'd found in a janitor's closet, that Mac's bemused "Where'd you come from?" startled a shriek from her.

She'd lowered the broom and turned to see Mac looking at a wooden door. Charlie was positive had not been there when they'd come in. Charlie frowned. "That wasn't there. Right?"

Mac looked over her shoulder, smiling briefly. "Or we Captain Oblivious'd it because we're exhausted."

Charlie couldn't dispute the possibility. The earlier refreshment had long since faded, but none of them had been able to stomach the idea of napping. But still. She was pretty sure she'd remember a door in a wide expanse of blank wall like that. Especially one all gleaming and new, with its warm cherry tones. Too new. Charlie turned to look at the door of the office. It was propped open–they wedged all the doors open now because they weren't stupid–but she could still see the dark, heavy stain and the brass knob that had grown tarnished and dull.

Why would the doors look so different? Even if it had been a door replaced during the renovations, it had been years since anyone had been inside Union Grace to take care of it. The door should have been showing its age.

"Mac," Charlie said, "Compare the doors."

The soft click of a door opening answered her. Charlie whirled to see Mac standing with her head tilted to the side, looking into the black opening beyond the threshold. "Huh," Mac said, voice distant. "Guess I've found our exit. I see sunlight."

"No!" Whatever Mac was seeing wasn't real. The darkness she was staring into concealed something dark and dangerous. Like it had in the PT room downstairs. "Mac, don't!"

"It's fine. Don't be a worrywart." Mac stepped through the doorway.

Instantly, the door slammed shut behind her. A foreign sense of satisfaction flooded Charlie's senses.

Charlie ran to the door, grabbing for the knob and screaming Mac's name. But her grasping hands met nothing but plastered wall as the door disappeared before her eyes.

She screamed Mac's name again, pounding on the wall, then put her ear up against it to listen. For a second, she thought she heard the blonde's voice, like she was walking away into the distance. But it faded into nothingness quickly.

"You son of a bitch!" Charlie yelled, smacking the wall with open palms. She wasn't doing this again. She wasn't losing another friend. Not again. Not like this. "Give her back! You give her back!"

But Union Grace or the entity possessing it didn't listen.

Rage swelled in her, pushing fears and insecurities aside. "Fine," she spat. "I'll fucking take her back then."

CHAPTER FIFTY

Birdie finds himself interested in the sterilization room against his will. He doesn't want to be interested in anything he sees. He wants to do his job, to block the doors and lay down salt. To do what he can to keep his team safe. But how can he turn down the chance to see an area of the hospital responsible for keeping everyone safe? Maybe he was a nerd, but seeing how they managed large-scale sterilization back then is tempting as hell. He envisions a wall of ovens where workers manually sterilize equipment like overheated automatons.

The mental imagery is so rich, saturated with colors and noises he can imagine it happening in front of him as he peers in through the small inset window of the door. Can see the sparks of flame inside the ovens, metal contraptions made with one purpose only. He puts a hand on the doorknob and turns it, promising himself he'll just take a peek.

When he opens the door, a sweat-damped woman dressed in white, with black bangs clinging to her forehead, gives him a distracted smile. Her eyes are a vibrant green, reminding him of someone whose identity flits just out of reach. Over the clamor of oven doors opening and closing, he can barely hear her speak. He steps further into the room to hear her better. To talk to her. He needs to know what they're doing down here? Don't they know the hospital is closed? There's no point to sterilizing anything.

"Sorry, say again?"

She tsks. "I said close the door. If we don't keep it closed, the morgue complains about the heat."

Freckles are sprinkled like fairy dust across her nose. He'd always been a sucker for those little melanin spots because they spoke of someone who was unafraid of the sun's kiss.

He released the door. It closes quietly behind him. "Sorry about that. Just wanted to get a better look at what's going on."

"What's going on?" She laughs and turns toward the open oven she'd been standing in front of, reaching inside and carefully removing a tray of instruments. "When you could watch the doctors and nurses saving lives, you're interested in us doing a bit of tidying up?"

"I am," he says. "Without clean instruments, the people the doctors work on would succumb to disease and infection. What you do here is important, even if it isn't the work that everyone else sees. Every person on the team is important. They all have their role to play." He means it with his whole heart. It was a lesson he'd learned well in his life before Banshee.

Banshee... He has something important to do. With them. For them. He shouldn't let her distract him. The thought tugs at the edges of his awareness. But she's got a demeanor that draws him in. An attractive confidence as she sets about sorting the instruments on the tray into individual containers and smiles at his words. It would be rude to just walk away from her now.

"Well, that's lovely," she says. "To think of it like that. That we all have a role to play." The way she speaks is a little unusual, but he likes it. Could listen to her for hours. She reminds him of someone.

Cool air brushes against his back, and he welcomes the relief from the heat that bakes this room. He cannot imagine being down here for hours on end, facing the heat from the ovens.

Birdie does not think of the reason for the cool air. He is not aware of the door which is closing again behind him, as she asks, her eyes still on her job at hand, "And what role is it you play, Richard?"

He does not remember giving her his name, but he must have. And it sounds so elegant coming from her lips that he cannot muster up the disdain for the ill-suited moniker his parents foisted upon him. "I..."

He pauses, frowning. His left hand curls around the handle of a device that isn't there as his mind pushes through a sudden fog brought on, he thinks, by the heat. The answer is right there, on the tip of his tongue. What he did was important. Is important. There are people depending on him. But he can't keep hold of his thoughts long enough to answer her question.

Her hands still when he does not immediately answer, and she lifts her head to look at him. She glances at something behind him, and her facial expression shifts briefly before returning to puzzlement. "Cat got your tongue?"

He chuckles, aware of someone moving past him in the edges of his vision. Slipping a gloved hand into the bin where she's sorted things. A glove with red smears on it. Dirty. The contrast draws his eye, but when he glances over, there's no one there.

"Uh–" Brows drawn together, he looks back at her. She's acting like nothing weird just happened. Looking at him with those brilliant green irises framing oddly dilated pupils and smiles. It is a wide smile that blossoms into brilliance for a fraction of a second. But then it pushes past the point of beauty, exposing all her teeth, drawing her lips back until they are fixed in a familiar, horrific grin he'd seen just hours ago.

The clanking of the oven doors faded away. Suddenly,

Birdie's conscious of the heat blasting through the room like the gates of hell had opened around him. And still, she holds his gaze. Holds his gaze and smiles that horrible smile as the overhead lighting fades to nothingness, and her face is caught in sharp shadows cast by his harness light.

His mouth dries, but he keeps his breathing steady and slowly lifts the container of salt he still held in one hand up.

"That won't work this time." The words are a whisper brushing against his ear even though she faces him dead on, a mockery of intimacy that disgusts him to his core.

Keeping his eyes on her, he takes a slow step back, dragging the heel of his foot along the floor to make sure there's nothing behind him to trip him up. It hits something thick, almost viscous, and shortly thereafter his back and a part of his leg make contact with the same odd, out-of-place pressure.

Dread rolls through him.

For a large man, Birdie can move quickly. His speed has always surprised people who consistently underestimate him. He spins to the side, throwing himself backward as the gleam of something small and silver slices through the air. It comes from a figure dressed in gray scrubs; a bloody mask now tied over the lower half of his face. The movement saves the major vessels in his neck, but the scalpel still digs into his throat. The iron rod he has tucked under his arm falls to the ground.

Pain sears through him as he stumbles backward, falling hard on his ass to the concrete floor. Birdie presses a palm to his throat as he scrambles backward, trying to get away from the figure already stepping toward him, coming in for another flick with the tool he dimly recognizes as a scalpel.

Birdie's foot hooks on the corner of the cart the entity stood behind, and he pulls it toward him as hard as he can. The cart topples onto its side in a resounding crash that bounces off the unforgiving surfaces of the room, the metal instruments pinging off the floor as they drop.

He screams for help as he backs away. Or, at least, he tries to. All that comes out is a high-pitched wheeze of air and a strangled gurgle as his vocal cords try to come together but fail. His heart skips a bit in his chest. He understands what has happened. The scalpel might have missed his blood vessels, but it has severed his vocal cords. It didn't matter how much he tried to scream; he cannot make any sort of significant sound now.

The surgeon pauses in his advance and pinches the front of his mask, pulling it down underneath his chin. His lips move in a speech that the cameraman cannot hear, but the smug smile following the words tells him everything. Birdie's back comes up against the wall of ovens, and he grabs blindly for one of the handles. He needs to get to his feet. He can't scream, but if he can get out of the door, he can still get help.

His hand touches one of the short handles, and he grabs onto it, pulling his feet underneath him so that he can stand.

Quick as a striking snake, the leering figure lunges forward, scalpel darting out.

Through the adrenaline, Birdie can't feel the pain, but his hand stops responding to his commands and when he pulls his arm toward him, his fingers slide limply from thc handle. He knows he is going to die. But he will not go down without a fight.

As he looks around the room, he sees the container of salt just out of arm's reach. There is a thin dribble of salt beneath the opening, but since he has already used so much blocking the other doorways, hardly any has spilled out.

Before the coherent thought can fully form, he throws himself toward the salt, grabbing for it with the hand that had been pressed to his throat. His hand lands hard on it, but the contact sends the cylindrical container skidding out from beneath his palm, rolling further away. Cursing, he tries to push himself after it in an awkward belly crawl since his one arm cannot support his weight.

He has to get it. Has to escape. Warn Jacques and the others. He can feel the specter coming up behind him, knowing without looking that he is straddling his legs now. Screaming breathless screams, he scrambles faster, not caring now that one hand is folding under his wrist the wrong way. Ignoring the pain as multiple bones break from the weight. Pain doesn't matter. Warning Jacques does.

And then, a sharp sting at the back of his neck. Like a murder hornet had made him its bitch. But the pain lasts only a second and then disappears, taking his ability to move his arms and legs with it. He collapses to the floor, chin hitting the concrete hard. For a moment, all is quiet and still. Then he is rolling over, turned by invisible hands, and staring up at the monster looming over him as it kneels and brings the scalpel in a straight line down his body.

Delicate, long-fingered hands move the remnants of his shirt to the side with a lover's gentleness. A gentleness at odds with the evil burning in the pitch-black space beneath the surgeon's thick brows, and the downturn of his mouth as he takes in the sight of Birdie's bared torso.

The scalpel lifts again, comes down in an agonizingly slow movement. Birdie tries to react. To move away. To wiggle. To lift a hand and shove him away. But he can do nothing. His body refuses to respond to him. Even breathing fast becomes an impossible thing, and his vision is graying around the edges.

Unfortunately, he is still alive when the blade slices into his stomach, though he is lucky enough to be unable to feel it. The blade slices through the thick padding of fat, then the abdominal muscles still strong through regular workouts, and then deeper. As black dots swirl in his vision and his consciousness fades, he is aware of pressure pushing down into the slit the surgeon has created, and then a tugging sensation as the surgeon pulls something dark and ropy into the dim lighting.

In the last blessing he would ever receive, Birdie Fowler dies before the surgeon goes back for another handful.

CHAPTER FIFTY-ONE

Tears making dark streaks in the dust coating her cheeks, Charlie leaned her forehead against a now heavily pockmarked wall. She'd lost herself for a while to a dangerous combination of rage and panic that had seen her running to each of the rooms adjoining the one they were in previously, pounding on the wall and calling Mac's name. Trying to track her progress into Grace's bones. But Mac hadn't answered. No other doors had appeared, not even when Charlie had dared Grace to do the same to her. To take her the same way it took Mac. Grace hadn't answered either.

Realizing her efforts were futile, Charlie had gone back to the room where Mac had disappeared, determination filling her. She'd tear through the wall if she had to, beat it to nothing but chunks of plaster with the iron rod she carried for protection. Whatever it took. But Grace never reacted to a single blow, and no matter how hard she tried, all she'd managed to do was send asbestos-laden dust into the air while small chips of wall covered her shoes.

"I'm sorry," she whispered to the air, muscles quivering with exhaustion. She'd tried to call the others, but her radio had gone dead. "I can't do it alone. I'm sorry. I'll be back, Mac. I'm not giving up. Not on you."

With that, she'd made her way back to the room where all of them had agreed to meet up after their tasks were complete. She figured it was safer than wandering the halls, potentially missing each other. But Charlie was also determined not to sit there, twiddling her thumbs like a helpless maiden while she waited for the menfolk to show up. Last time she was in here, she'd done two things. While she still wasn't sure how she'd done the first, the second one had been a deliberate action.

She closed her eyes and opened her senses.

Unlike the other time she'd done it, this time she sensed more than the big bad sulking in its corner. This time she sensed energy signatures throughout the building. Many of them.

She knew Union Grace had ghosts, obviously. She'd been scared to come here for precisely that reason. But the time she'd spent here before Grace showed her ass had lowered her expectations. She'd assumed most of the spirits had faded to the sort of nothingness which left only indistinct impressions and low-level activity. She'd laid most of the vigorous activity at the feet of the malignant presence possessing the building.

That was not the case.

She pressed her lips together, brow furrowing as she did mental math. Jacques and crew came on the fourth day. They had the one-night camping outside the hospital, but had been inside for the second night. It had to be early in the morning now. That meant she'd been on site for six days.

She tilted her head back and huffed out a breath. "Fuck."

She concentrated again. She could feel the entity's presence, but something about it had changed. It wasn't as much of an obvious hot spot on her mental map. It felt like it was everywhere now, tendrils of power working its way through the entire building. What the hell was it doing?

Her eyes snapped open, and she sat upright in her chair. She looked at the surrounding room. The walls were a delicate cream color, unmarred by the passing of time or the accumulation of dust. Pushing to her feet, she ran out into the hallway. The orange tile gleamed like new. Before her eyes, a doorknob closer to her lost the patina of age and began to shine.

It didn't take a genius to figure out what was happening. The entity was feeding off them and merging with Union Grace. Bringing it back to life.

"Jesus Christ," she breathed, heading back into the room and sitting down at the table once more. She leaned forward, propping her elbows on the table and shoving her fingers through her hair. What was the point in possessing a hospital? It wasn't like it could shape shift and walk off. Why make it shiny? What purpose did it serve? Had Hell's renovator set up shop in Union Grace to ... advertise its services?

Charlie groaned. Not to advertise. That was stupid, but this would get attention. Would draw crowds when Jacques' footage aired. The pieces began to fall into place. With more people, the evil lurking in Union Grace could hurt more people. Gain power from them. She remembered what Jacques had said. Evil had been lurking in Union Grace, especially the second time the hospital had opened. Desperate to gain more than a toehold in this world. But it was greedy. Too greedy. Ultimately, it had failed to control itself, and that led to the shutdown of the hospital. But now it had the opportunity for a second chance, and it wanted it.

It wouldn't have to possess people, to cause harm individually. A hospital was a place of healing, but it was also a place of suffering. If it made the hospital part of itself, it could feed endlessly from it. From the minor aches and pains to the agonizing deaths and everything in between. Who wouldn't come to a miracle hospital?

And if she stayed—if they couldn't get out of here in time—it was possible it would have all the staff it needed when the dead gained corporeal form.

"Son of a bitch," she said with a strong exhale, exhaustion hitting her. "Son. of. a. bitch."

She closed her eyes, lids heavy as the exhaustion returned, throwing itself over her like a weighted warm blanket on a wintry day. She needed Jacques. They needed to make a plan. To get Mac back. To put an end to Union Grace. But right now, she needed to rest. Nothing would harm her if she just closed her eyes for a few minutes. As a false sense of security wrapped around her, Charlie folded her arms on the table and rested her head on them, childlike. She'd just rest for a moment.

CHAPTER FIFTY-TWO

Jacques had a one-track mind for reading, especially if the subject was interesting. He'd get wrapped up and the world would fade away. His mom always laughed about it. Before the events in the cabin, she'd said the house could burn down around him. After the cabin, fire was a dirty word.

What he found was interesting, even if it wasn't the smoking gun they were looking for. He found documentation supporting the Erschon family's donation to the hospital after the death of Charlotte Erschon in 1940. Documentation which included stipulations for additions to the building. Stipulations including bringing the Erschon family's presence on the board of directors up from one—Charlotte Erschon until her death–to three.

This change alone effectively gave control of Union Grace to the Erschon family. Under any other circumstances, he would have shrugged it off. Power plays like this were what his peers did. But this just added to the mystery. Why had the Erschons wanted it so badly? Had the entity already been present? He jotted down his thoughts, then moved on to the files spanning time after the renovation through the final closure.

He knew there had been reports of problems within the hospital, but what he'd been told didn't come close to explaining how extensive the problems had been. Reading between the lines, he suspected more incidents had occurred but not been recorded. Perhaps brushed off as hysterical over imaginings of easily excited females and distracted orderlies slacking on their duties and trying to excuse the behavior via wild stories.

Something had gone rotten with Union Grace, and at a certain point the desperate denial shone through even the carefully formulated words. And then he found the meeting minutes detailing the motion to close Union Grace hospital once more. He scanned the paper, his eyes widening. "Bird, check this out. Get a clear shot of this with the good camera."

When the cameraman wasn't instantly at his side, Jacques frowned and tore his eyes from the paper. "Hey, man, wake up."

Bird had an uncanny ability to catch a catnap anywhere, but this was taking it to a new level. He looked around the room, seeking his friend out. It wasn't until his second sweep that he saw the tripod sitting on the floor, camera angled out to the hallway.

Trepidation cloaked him. He picked the tripod up and rewound the footage until he saw Birdie exit the room. Watched him lay salt down in front of the morgue doors and then head off down the hallway.

"Shit," Jacques murmured. And though he damned well knew it probably wouldn't do any good, he still keyed the radio that he'd detached from the mask wiring and lifted it to his lips. "Birdie copy?"

No answer.

"Anyone copy?"

Still nothing.

"Bird's wandered off. Going to look for him." Even if they couldn't hear, the act of keeping in touch was reassuring. He folded the minutes from the meeting and stuffed them between the pages of his leather journal, then stuck it down in the large pocket on the side of his cargo pants. Scooping up his iron rod from beside one of the filing cabinets, he went looking for his friend. He wasn't too worried. Not yet. If anyone could take care of themselves in this place, it was Bird. Didn't mean he wasn't going to tear him a new one for wandering off, though.

A few minutes and door openings later, Jacques pushed open the door to the sterilization room and stopped. A cart lay overturned, scalpels and other instruments he could not name splayed across the floor. Thin lines of white etched bright swirls across the floor. It was not the tidy room they performed sweeps through earlier. A moment later, the smell hit him. Sewage and rot, with an underlying hint of metal that left a nasty film on his tongue.

Jacques gagged, then tried to call his friend's name. It came out a broken rasp. He swallowed once and then again, trying to bring moisture into a throat suddenly coated with sawdust and cotton. "Bird? Brother, this isn't the time for fooling around. You know that."

There was no answer. No sound. This room was as much of a tomb as the morgue had been, before... that. Not letting himself think about what he might find, Jacques grabbed the first thing off the floor that looked like it would hold the door open and wedged it into place. Then, death grip on his iron rod, Jacques pushed further into the room. He chose his steps with care, avoiding the white scrawl and scattered instruments. Faintly, he let himself by reassured that there was no blood. If there was no blood, then it could still be okay.

It only took a few steps before he saw the boots that his friend had loved so much, he'd pay to have them resoled rather than buy another pair. The pale, hairy legs disappearing into cargo shorts. And then he saw the mass resting on his friend's abdomen. For a long moment, what he was seeing made no sense. Long loops of pink material wrapped around each other, tightly wound across each other in the center. The ends of some of the loops had been neatly sliced and had been arranged to lay flat over Bird's shirt, which was stained red but tucked neatly underneath the mass on his chest.

Jacques remembered then. There had been no blood in the hallway where Rachelle had died when they had gone back to investigate. Jacques forced himself to step to his friend's side, collapsing onto his knees beside him. "Mon cher ami," he whispered. From up close, he finally noticed the other details. Birdie's eyelids had been sewn shut with small, neat crisscrosses of black thread. Similar thread could be seen along the seam where his lips should have parted, holding the bluing flesh closed. And now he could see that though Birdie's shirt had been sliced open, someone had taken the time to tack it back together. To make him look whole. Left him like a present for Jacques to find.

And that was when Jacques understood that the weird mass atop his friend's abdomen was a bow. One meticulously crafted from Birdie's intestines.

In frozen horror, Jacques stared at his friend, unable to think, unable to act. Ana and Emerson had burned to death, bodies ravaged by the flames. Yet somehow it seemed less evil than this macabre presentation done with such care. Evil had shown itself to them multiple times now, but it had been nothing like this. Union Grace had woken another of its residents.

He didn't know how long had passed before he snapped back to the present, but he was shocked when he laid a hand gently on his friend's forehead. His body had passed the cooling down stage and was now outright cold. Jacques knew he'd been buried in paperwork for a while, but it took roughly twelve hours for the human body to be cool to the touch after death. There was no way he'd been at it for that long.

He stared disbelievingly at his watch, even bringing it to

his ear to verify he could still hear the ticking. According to it, it was 1 o'clock. He wasn't sure what time they'd come down to the basement, but it had been nighttime and close to, if not beyond, midnight already. As cold as Birdie was, blood congealed around him, that meant that it was likely one p.m. in the afternoon. Unbelievable. Unless, a quiet voice made itself known inside his head, it's even later than that. What if it's 1 a.m. and you've lost a whole day?

Nothing was outside the realm of possibility when the paranormal was involved, and that scared the shit out of Jacques. He looked down at his friend. "I'm so sorry," he whispered.

He remembered what had happened to Rachelle's spirit. The thought of that happening to Birdie horrified him. That it could keep happening to anyone foolish enough to enter Union Grace made him want to throw up. He had to figure out a way to prevent it from happening.

Tears welled in his eyes. He pressed his fingers to his lips and touched them to Birdie's forehead. "I'll come back for you, my friend."

He rose to his feet. He couldn't do what Birdie had done to Rachelle. The idea of destroying his friend's body threatened to cut the thin thread holding his sanity intact. So instead, he did what he could to secure the room that Birdie's body was in. If Grace got her feelers into Birdie like she had into Rachelle, he didn't think he could handle it.

Then Jacques headed up the stairs. He needed to see if it was light outside. To see if Kiffer had brought help. Then find Charlie and Mac.

CHAPTER FIFTY-THREE

Jacques was so goddamned tired. He leaned back against the wall of the tiny chapel room, legs feeling like wet noodles. When they buckled underneath him, he didn't halt the downward slide to the floor as his emotions finally overtook him. First Rachelle, then Birdie. Who else would he lose?

He hadn't been able to raise anyone on the radio, and he'd screamed his throat raw, but hadn't heard even the faintest return shout. They were supposed to meet back up on the third floor, but what if he went up there and they weren't there? What if he was the only one left in this godforsaken bitch of a building? Why hadn't Birdie listened to him? Why didn't any of them ever listen to him?

Tears stung his eyes. He leaned his head back and closed his eyes, letting the tears trace their way from the corner of his eyes into the stubble coating his cheeks. So goddamned tired.

"That's mom's ringtone," Ana exclaimed, eyes fixed on her bright pink phone where it lay on the coffee table. "I need to answer it."

Jacques grabbed his sister's arm. "You can't step out of the salt. It's the only thing keeping us safe!" Already he was wishing he'd chosen some place more secure. Maybe tucked into a corner where things couldn't fly at them from all sides. But the way the girls had been circling them, and with things coming off the walls at him, the only thing he could think was to get them inside a salt circle. So, they'd ended up in the kitchen with him and Charlie spreading salt they'd grabbed right in the middle of the kitchen while Emerson and Ana clutched cast-iron pans and batted at the spirits who came too close.

"Mom can bring help," Ana hissed, shrugging her arm from his grasp. "It's just a few feet away. I can get it and come back here."

A knife flew past them and buried itself in the wood wall of the cabin. Ana and Jacques both stared at it and then looked at each other. For a second there was fear in Ana's eyes, and he thought she understood. That she'd stay there safe with them.

But then his sister swallowed hard and straightened up. "I'm in charge," she told them all. "It's my responsibility to protect you, not vice versa."

"The salt is doing its job," Emerson said. "Jacques knows what he's talking about. They can't touch us here!"

"Maybe not," Charlie said, "but they can affect our environment." There was something in the way she said it that had them all turning to look at her.

She was staring at the stove. One burner had already been lit, and as they watched, the knob for the second one finished turning. Seconds later, the third knob turned with agonizing slowness. Like the spirits were taunting them. Reminding them they weren't as smart as they thought they were.

"At least they're not lighting them," Jacques said.

"It's gas, Jacques," his sister said. "Just because there's no flame doesn't mean it's not dangerous." She inhaled. "We need to turn the stove off and take the knobs. I saw mom pop one off by accident yesterday so I know we can do it. That'll keep them from turning them again. And I need to grab my phone. We need to let mom know to bring help."

"Ana–"

"We can't risk her getting hurt too, Jacques," she said. She put her hand on his shoulder. "I'll be fine, baby brother. I'll grab the knobs, get my phone, and come right back before they even realize I'm out. Track team, remember?"

"That was two years ago," he said, wanting to cry. "And you sucked at it!"

"Asshole." Ana stuck her tongue out at him.

"You can't," Emerson said, and when Ana made a sound of frustration, he continued, "It needs to be two people. One to do the stove, the other grabs the phone."

"I'll do it," Charlie said, her brown eyes open so wide Jacques could see the white all the way around the iris. "They haven't really tried to hurt me."

It was true. The ghosts had gone after their dad, and when he had left, they'd turned their attention to Emerson and Ana. But Charlie and Jacques seemed to be in the way more than anything else. He didn't know why.

"No way," Emerson said. "I'll do it. I'm the next oldest."

"By a week," Charlie hissed at him. "I'm safer, and you know it. Don't be stupid just because you're a boy!"

"She's right," Jacques said. He believed it, but also, he didn't want both his brother and sister out of the safety of the circle. If something happened to them both, he didn't know what he'd do.

Charlie and Emerson stared at each other for a second, and then Emerson pulled Charlie in for a fierce hug. "Don't just drop them on the floor," he said. "We don't know if they'll be able to put them back on. Bring them back with you. Understand?"

"Got it," Charlie whispered, hugging Emerson back. She looked at Ana. There had been tension between the two since Emerson spilled the beans about how ghosts were always more active around Charlie, but there was no trace of it now. Instead, the two had some sort of conversation with their eyes and reached an agreement.

"Charlie should go first," Jacques said, thinking quickly. "She's got less of a distance to go, and they don't seem fixated on hurting her as much. She can distract them. Then when she's grabbing the knobs, Ana can run for the phone." He really didn't want her to run for the phone, but she had a point. They had to think about their mom and

what might happen to her if she came back to the house unaware of what was happening.

Charlie gulped, then nodded. She turned around to face the stove. "Ready," she said.

"Set," Emerson continued.

"Go!" Ana yelled, and sprang out of the circle, running for her phone.

Charlie didn't see it because she was already darting to the stove and yanking the knobs off, but Emerson and Jacques did.

Cursing, Emerson darted out of the circle after Ana, head twisting from side to side as he tried to keep watch all around them.

Ana picked up the phone, thumb swiping over the surface, and held it to her ear. "Mom? Mom, is that you?"

No. No no no. That wasn't what was supposed to happen. Ana was supposed to grab the phone and come back to the circle. She could make a phone call from within the circle. "Come here! Come HERE!"

Charlie's voice joined his. She'd made it back to the circle, four stove knobs clutched in her arms.

Then, like a cord had been cut, the activity in the cabin stopped. Items swirling through the air clattered to the floor. The air calmed, and the shrieks battering their ears quieted.

In the silence, the four looked at each other in disbelief. Ana licked her lips and said into the phone, "Mom, are you there?"

Jacques felt Charlie press closer until they were touching along their upper arms.

"Baby? What's wrong?"

In the dead silence, he could hear his mother's voice, though it sounded tiny and distant.

"Mom, you need to bring help," his sister said, her eyes locked on Jacques. There was some sort of knowledge in them. An awareness that Jacques wouldn't recognize until several years later. At that point, somehow, his sister knew something terrible was about to happen. She put a hand behind Emerson's back and shoved him toward the circle.

Emerson wasn't expecting it and did an awkward two-step shuffle, one of his shoes coming down on the untied lace of his other shoe and sending him sprawling forward. He hit the ground hard, smacking his chin against the floor and crying out. His skillet flew out of his hand with the impact and slid toward Charlie and Jacques, coming to rest just inches outside of the circle.

Emerson moaned, cupping a hand to his mouth and standing.

And then fireplace exploded, flames shooting forward to engulf–

Jacques jolted awake with the memory of his sister wrapped in a halo of flames. Sweat slicked his skin like he was back in the cabin all over again. His pulse hammering in his throat, he scrubbed his face hard with his palms.

Ana hadn't listened. She hadn't listened, and he hadn't tried hard enough to make her. He failed her. Failed her, failed Emerson. Failed Birdie. Everyone important to him died because he couldn't do enough to keep them safe. He wasn't smart enough or strong enough or quick enough.

"You were nine, Squirt." Ana's voice came from right beside him.

He turned his head to see the shimmering, moonbeam-etched form of his sister sliding down to sit beside him. She was translucent, but he could feel the weight of her presence. "You were nine, and I was seventeen. There was no way you could stop me. You need to understand that. Our deaths were never your fault. We all did the best we could."

"I ... If I hadn't–. There was a Ouija board." He'd never said the words out loud before, but the memory of that damned board haunted him.

"You were nine, Jacques," his sister repeated, reaching out to cover one of his hands with her own. Her touch was butterfly soft, a whisper of weight, but he felt it. "Whether or not you'd used that board, we would have been attacked. Those girls were so full of rage and desperation that they would have come after us, regardless."

"If I hadn't... if Charlie hadn't been there..."

"We could play this game all night. There are a thousand things you could assign blame to. A thousand things you could say. "If this hadn't happened, then..." It wasn't your fault. It wasn't Charlie's fault. You can't blame someone for doing something when they either didn't know what they were doing or they couldn't control it. You know that." She tapped the top of his hand with an index finger. "I know you know that because I've sat in on those therapy sessions, willing you to forgive yourself."

Suddenly there was an impossible lump in his throat. "You were there?"

"Of course I was," Ana said. "You're my baby brother. I needed to make sure you were okay." She paused, looked around the room. "Which is why I tried to warn you away from this place."

"I didn't know," Jacques said, throat hurting.

"I know," his sister told him. "It was so damned hard to communicate with you before this. Like I was screaming at you from miles away and could barely get three words out to you. But with Charlie here, it's easier."

"Yeah?" He wanted her to keep talking. He didn't care what she said, as long as she kept talking. As long as she was here.

"God, Jacques, you should feel her. It's like– I don't know. It's indescribable. She puts off energy like water down Niagara Falls or something."

Her tone changed, losing the wonder. "She's restoring the spirits here. The bad guy . . . he's feeding off her as much as she can, but the others are getting some of it too. They're starting to break free because of that. She needs to use that."

"How?"

"She's the key to them escaping this place. Without her, they'll be stuck here forever. Losing more of themselves to the darkness. Becoming empty wisps again. Make her use that. Make her understand that she can use that."

Ana dimmed suddenly, voice growing faint.

"He's feeding again," she said. "He's getting desperate. Find her, Jacques. Find Charlie before it's too late."

"Where is she?"

Ana's next words were so quiet he could barely hear her. "Conference room."

Jacques pushed to his feet and ran.

CHAPTER FIFTY-FOUR

Jacques halted in the conference room doorway. He'd pulled open the door half-expecting to see Mac and Charlie sitting there, asking what had taken him so long. What he hadn't expected was Charlie sleeping like a little kid at the table. No sign of Mac.

Stomach sinking, he called Charlie's name. When she didn't respond, he feared the worst. Anxiety banded around his chest. He forced himself to approach her, lay a shaking hand on her back. His breath imprisoned inside him as he waited to feel evidence of hers.

A gentle exhale that brushed his hand damned near brought tears to his eyes. He stole a moment to just stand there, feeling her breath, and trying to ground himself. Reminded himself the two of them had done the impossible before. They could do it again. He had a hell of a lot more knowledge and experience now. And he trusted Ana. If she said Charlie could pull this off, he believed her. His sister might not have always listened to him, but when it came down to it, she always had his back.

He exhaled deeply and then gently shook the brunette's shoulder. "Wake up, Charlie."

It took a few more nudges, but eventually, she lifted her head from the table and stared at him with bleary eyes. "Jacques?"

"Hey," he said, sitting down in the chair next to hers. "You okay?"

She sat up, rubbing her face with her palms, and yawning. "Yeah," she said, and yawned again. "I was just waiting for you." She went still, then looked around the room. When her eyes came back to his, he could see the sadness manifesting in her eyes. "Birdie? Did the hospital take him too?"

Her choice of words was peculiar. "Take him?"

"Yeah. Mac... there was this door." She lifted a thumb to her lips and nibbled at her nail, her brow furrowing as she stared off into the distance. "It wasn't there, and then it was. She went in and then it disappeared again. I heard her after the door closed though, so I don't think she's... gone." She shifted her eyes to him. "It didn't take Birdie like that?"

He pressed his lips together and shook his head.

"Dammit," she whispered. She took his hand and gave it a gentle squeeze. "He seemed like good peoples."

"The best peoples," Jacques agreed, his throat tightening. He coughed to ease it.

"So, Mac is still alive. Grace is just holding her hostage," he stated. He didn't let it be a question. He couldn't believe it was a question. It was a statement. Mac was still alive, and that meant she could be rescued.

Charlie nodded.

"And Kiffer is trying to find a way to help us," he said. He believed that, one hundred percent. "But for now, we're on our own." His talk with Ana in the chapel came to the forefront, and he managed a small smile. "Well, not entirely alone."

At Charlie's inquisitive look, he relayed what happened in the chapel.

When he was done, she was smiling. Though sad, comfort also existed there. "Then it was Emerson," she said, and a tear tracked down her cheek. "He was the one who wrapped his arms around me in the PT room."

It was Jacques' turn to nod. There was comfort in the

thought, knowing that his big brother and sister were there with them, watching out for them. But —

"But if they're here, then they're in danger," Charlie said, eyes large with fear. "They're in danger like Rachelle was."

He chewed on his lower lip. "Yeah."

Charlie looked down at the table, nodded to herself, and then inhaled deeply. When she looked back up, her eyes were fierce with determination. "I was mad when Grace took Mac," she told him. "Determined to get her back. I still am. But there is no way in hell that I'm letting this hospital or its demon hurt Emerson and Ana. Nobody is hurting them. Not ever again."

"Then we need a plan," he said, squeezing her hand.

Charlie grinned. "That's your job, boss. Always has been."

"You know, no plan ever survives first contact with the enemy." He had to say it. Had to warn her. Even if he made the best plan, there was a chance neither of them would make it. He finally understood that. He couldn't control everything.

"Yeah," Charlie acknowledged, then pursed her lips for a second. When she spoke again, her voice rang with confidence. "Then let's see them survive the next contact with me."

He was gay, Jacques reminded himself. He was absolutely one hundred percent gay. No question about it. But the sheer confidence that Charlie exuded at that moment was sexy as hell.

CHAPTER FIFTY-FIVE

Offering of blood and flesh received, knowledge denied upon his awakening unfolded within him. Knowledge of the hospital's heart entwined itself so fiercely with desire that the two could not be separated. The heart, pulsing with dark and foreign energies, needed the figure. Needed a service only he could perform. And the voice, an incubus without form, whispered to him he could do what he pleased with the vessel awaiting him.

Leaving the cooling form of his offering, the figure went to the spandrel beneath the basement stairs. Had he been human, he would have opened the slim door, pushed aside janitorial debris, and entered through the second door with a key that few, trusted staff had been entrusted with. But now, with scarcely more than a thought, he was ensconced within a space that had once thrummed with power.

It would again soon.

So narrow three humans could not stand abreast in the space, the heart had length enough to contain a decades-old chair, coated with dust and dark spatters of dried fluids, and a slim metal table with implements of pain and promise neatly arranged. Above the chair, a single surgical light on an arm shone directly into the face of the female vessel curled up like a small child on the deteriorating seat cushion.

There would be pleasure in adorning her pale skin with the words the voice whispered, satisfaction in the precision cuts which would prolong her suffering even as it provided the scarlet ink that would adorn her brow, breasts, and abdomen. Exquisite satisfaction in turning her from a vessel filled with sanguine fluid to a prayer book and exhibition of death's beauty.

The figure picked up the glinting silver blade, a twin to those he had saved and sacrificed so many lives with. A flick of his wrist and a red tear welled to the surface just below the vessel's left eye. The light illuminating her flickered and dimmed considerably. Eyes widened as they saw what had caused the wound. For the first time since he entered the heart, he had her attention. Now he would have her fear.

First, the vessel's pupils dilated, then her body stiffened. Had he still human form, her fear would have teased his nose and tongue with promises of what was to come. He took a gliding step forward, turning the scalpel so that it would catch the remnants of the light.

Focus shifting to the blade as if it alone were the danger, her hands searched for the armrests. Fingers dug into the cracked and dull padding. The vessel spoke, but the words meant nothing to him. They all spoke. Begged, pleaded. Offered him anything to make this moment end. Even the fire lacing her voice was unusual only because it was typically male subjects who dared to think they could overcome the situation with anger.

It was less the impertinence and more a need for perfection that scored a matching line beneath the right eye.

He had time enough for a brief flicker of satisfaction before the vessel's eyes narrowed, and she lunged at him with fist raised. Pain unlike any his human form had experienced ripped his ability to think, to cohere, temporarily away.

CHAPTER FIFTY-SIX

The more she and Jacques talked, the more Charlie craved Emerson's presence. The more that happened, the angrier she got about the fact that she could rouse some evil fuck, but she couldn't bring her best friend back. No matter how hard she tried. And she had. She'd tried and failed too many times in the past. And when they'd buried him, she'd also buried the part of herself that could reach out and make friends. Make meaningful connections.

Her transient lifestyle and inability to work much with electronics had worsened that. But still... even if she'd been able to make friends again, they wouldn't have been Emerson. Em had been her ride or die. She'd been his. Regardless of her emotional state, she understood that wasn't something people found every day.

Emerson could push her to do things that scared her. To do things she didn't think she could do. Jacques was good. He was smart, and he obviously cared about his people. He unfailingly treated her kindly even though he had reasons to hate her. But he wasn't her best friend. They weren't even friends at all. Not anymore.

She sighed. Union Grace had to be destroyed. That much was obvious. But there were two issues. One, the protective asbestos in the building. Two, the demon. It would do everything it could to protect the building once it figured out what they were doing. Considering how it could do things like make the building inescapable, Charlie doubted it would have any problems dealing with the fire.

So, they either had to vanquish the demon and then set the building on fire or set the fire and distract the demon until the blaze got too big to control. Coming out alive would be a big bonus if they could pull it off. But if not... it would be worth it. And she'd finally be with her Emerson again.

Charlie was lost in thought, trying to figure out the plan, when something caramel colored was suddenly thrust in front of her eyes, causing her to jump. She swatted instinctively.

Jacques jerked away. "Relax, woman, I was just offering you a protein bar!"

She blinked rapidly. "Sorry. I was thinking. You surprised me."

"I know," Jacques said, extending the bar again. "But right now, you need to eat. We both do. Our next moves are going to take energy. So, stop for a moment and eat."

It made sense. She took the bar and, suddenly ravenous, chipmunked it.

"The 'a moment' didn't mean less than five seconds," Jacques said, mild disgust on his face as she struggled to chew the bar with her mouth closed and cheeks puffed out. "You could have even taken an entire minute if you were feeling daring. Two, even."

A little ashamed but too hungry to really care, Charlie flipped him off and dug in her backpack for a bottle of water while she continued to chew. When her questing hand located one, she downed half of it to help get the remnants of the bar down. She eyed the one Jacques was unwrapping. One hadn't been nearly enough. And that wrapper looked familiar.

She realized he'd gotten into her backpack when she wasn't paying attention. He'd taken her food! The outrage must have shown on her face because he said, "Don't worry, this one's for you."

She made a grab for it, but he quickly moved it out of her reach. "I will eat it in at least three bites, Jacques," he said in a high-pitched tone.

"Give. me."

He repeated himself, eyebrows raised.

"We don't have time for this," she grumbled.

"We have time for you not to accidentally off yourself by choking on a granola bar," he said. "You die and for all we know whatever sort of paranormal nuclear reactor you have in you might go into meltdown."

"I will eat it in at least three bites. Give me." When he handed the bar over, she broke a piece off, unable to trust herself not to chipmunk it again, and then cocked her head. "Paranormal nuclear reactor?"

"Do you have a better word for it?"

She remembered the way he'd told her Ana had described her, thought about the way she got no peace. How she was always putting off energy. Paranormal nuclear reactor sounded stupid, but it fit. Something else about what he said niggled at her, but whenever she tried to latch on to the thought, it darted away. Knowing herself well enough to understand that she just needed to let her subconscious chew on it for a while, Charlie let the thought go and said, "Sounds pretty accurate, I guess."

They ate two more bars a piece in complete silence, emptying the box without worrying about future meals. She knew and thought he did too, that this was their last meal in Union Grace.

But they still had no plan. There was no guarantee that Charlie could call the ghosts to her. She'd cleared them out through brute force, and she could power them up unwillingly, but she couldn't command them to help her. And without the ghosts' help, the chances of succeeding were slim to none. Especially when the demon fed off the energy she emanated.

Jacques interrupted her thoughts, saying, "Just try."

Brows furrowed, she eyed him.

"We're overthinking this," he said. "We've spent so much time thinking about how to do it when too much is unknown. Call them to you."

"I don't know how." But she took a deep breath and closed her eyes, dug her fingernails into the arms of the chair and did that thing where she opened her senses to Union Grace. They were even brighter beacons in her mind. Separate, for the most part. Lost in their own pieces of the hospital, their world. "Come here, please," she projected to them. "We need your help."

None of the spirits paused in their movements, let alone started coming toward her.

She relayed the information to Jacques. He frowned. "Tell them to come to you. Don't ask them."

She didn't think it'd work, but she tried again. This time she articulated the words out loud, wondering if saying them aloud would help anything. "Come to me. We need your help." She felt like an idiot saying the words. Like some sort of psychic fraud.

"You are a fraud," Jacques agreed, startling her. She wasn't aware she'd said that out loud. And the words hurt once they registered.

"What the hell?" she said, disbelief filling her. He was pulling this shit now?

"You pretend to have everyone's best interest at heart, but you don't. You're a coward and a fraud of a friend." Jacques' eyes were hard and his jaw set. "If you were really Emerson's friend, you wouldn't be sitting here doing this pansy-assed attempt to save him. To save Ana. To save Mac and Birdie.

You don't care if any of them die the way Rachelle did, as long as you don't get hurt in the process, do you?"

What the fuck did he think she was doing? Heat swept Charlie's cheeks. She was the one who vowed she'd get Mac back from Union Grace. The one who promised to save Emerson and Ana from the same end that Rachelle's soul had met. She was the only one who could do it. He was just along for the ride. Wind stirred in the room.

"Instead," Jacques kept talking, tone ice cold, "you depend on everyone around you to solve the problem for you. Just like I solved it when we were kids. You could have stopped things then, but you were too fucking scared and weak to do anything about it. So, it fell upon me. A nine-year-old kid, youngest of all of us, to do what you failed to do."

"Don't you fucking talk to me like that," she spat at him. "I would have given my life for Emerson, and you know it. It's not my fault he didn't listen!" Her backpack skidded across the table, and she grabbed it by the strap, yanking it back to her. She was trying. If she died saving them, it would be worth it. She just didn't know how to do what she needed to do.

"He wouldn't have had to listen if you were anything other than poor little Charlie!" Jacques slapped the table. "Poor little Charlie, cursed and alone. Cowardly little Charlie, so afraid of her own goddamned shadow that innocent people are going to die. Delicate little Charlie. You'll ride that train for the rest of your life, won't you? Nothing's your fault because you can't control it. But what they don't know is you can't control it because you never fucking try. Too afraid to risk it."

A vein throbbed in her temple. Charlie got to her feet. "I'm not the one who saw my brother and sister murdered and then decided, "Oh yeah, I should totally go investigate the type of things that killed them. That makes perfect fucking sense."

"At least I'm living," he snapped. "I have a life. Friends. A job."

"I can't do that," she was having trouble seeing now, tears clouding her eyes. She didn't know whether they were from the hurt, the anger, or both. "It puts people at risk. They could get hurt."

"It puts people at risk," he mocked, sneering at her. "Did you even try to get help?"

"Who was going to help me, Jacques?" It wasn't like there were specialists in what she did. She'd never even found proof anyone could do what she did. Part of the reason she was even here was because Grant had dangled the possibility in front of her.

"I would have tried." He stood, stepping into her space. His face was inches from hers. Anger was there, but something else, too. Something she couldn't name. "I've spent my life trying to understand the spirit world, Charlie. If you'd have come to me at any point, at any fucking point, and said, "Hey, can you help me figure out how to do control this?" I would have done it. I would have found a way to help you. But you're so convinced that you're meant to spend your life alone that you can't even fucking ask for help, can you?"

"Then fucking help me!" She screamed the words at him, pain pushing the anger to grow bigger and stronger. She felt a familiar sensation, as when Jacques lost his shit in this same room. A tingling, a vibration that started in her core, radiating outward. She needed the help. He couldn't help her. Nobody alive could help her.

But the dead could. And if they didn't, they were no better than she was. Too afraid to risk anything for the chance of losing the slightest bit of what they did have.

"Fucking help me," she screamed again, this time

directing the words to the spirits within Union Grace. She grabbed on to the power building up behind the dam of her anger, and flung it outward, sending it towards the spirits themselves, visualizing it hooking into them and them alone. The fucking demon wasn't feeding on this.

The cheap 70s paintings on the walls trembled, shifting back and forth in the corners of her vision. The table wobbled like it was trying to jump out of the way. "You know he's going to destroy you. Like he did her. That's why you hide and get weaker every day. I'm the one helping you now. Giving you strength. So fucking help me," she flopped down in her chair, the burst of energy leaving her feeling empty and trembling. "Help me," she said hoarsely, "or lose yourself all over again."

Their next breaths crystallized in the suddenly freezing air.

CHAPTER FIFTY-SEVEN

Jacques' next breath fogged the air, and a winter's chill nipped at his nose and fingertips as the dead began to flood into the room. He shivered and took out the handheld thermometer on his belt, aiming it at the far wall, showing a thirty degree drop in temperature in less than two minutes with the number still dropping. "Shit," he whispered, sticking the thermometer back in his belt with hands already hurting from the sudden cold. This was the most insane temperature drop he'd ever experienced. And then the dead got his full, horrified attention.

They came from everywhere, through walls and doors and floors. Most were only wisps when they first entered the room, though they took on a humanoid shape shortly thereafter, while others ranged from well-defined but translucent to damned near corporeal. A doctor wearing scrubs with a mask flat against his chest, covered with splatters of blood, looked so real Jacques thought if he pushed him, he'd meet physical resistance. He looked like an evil sonuvabitch and Jacques felt the hair on his nape prickle as the ghost stared at Charlie.

Jacques knew the danger the dead posed, born the trauma of what just a few angry spirits could wreak. That he was able to keep his calm and maintain rationality did not mean that the dead lacked the ability to scare the hell out of him. But apparently the events of the hospital had pushed him past the point of rationality, because why the hell had he suggested Charlie call the dead to them?

Determined not to show his trepidation, he tucked his hands between his upper arms and torso to ward off the cold and took in the rest of the room. Most of their forms were clear enough now that he could see a mix of doctors, nurses, and patients. Some stood close enough to each other that their figures blended together, whereas others hovered at the edges of the room, as separate as possible from their brethren. A determined old lady in the corner was wearing her gown backwards and open in the front, making everyone uncomfortable. She was baring her gums in a wicked grin. A man stood near her, wearing nothing but tattered pants. He was skeletally thin, and one side of his chest curved inward, echoes of jagged bone poking through ghostly skin. Just looking at him made Jacques' own chest ache.

All were united in two things. All were giving the one bloodied doctor wide berth, and all were staring at Charlie. The expressions on their faces ranged from hunger to confusion, as if they'd answered her call involuntarily and were trying to figure out what was going on.

Jacques had rarely seen spirits this close to corporeal. Most of the time they were suggestions of form, or flickers seen out of the corner of the eye. Sometimes they'd been lucky enough to see a face or a part of the body. For the most part, spirits made their presence known through the tools they used to interact with them, or how they manipulated things in their environment. He put a hand to his chest and inhaled. Between the cold and the atmosphere that had grown thick with ghostly presence, it was hard for him to breathe. Anxiety played a part in it as well.

He reminded himself that they had called them here. That he was sure they would listen to Charlie. He exhaled and shrugged his shoulders to relieve some of the tension. The movement reminded him of the GoPro on his shoulder, and he could only pray that the device was still working.

More came into the room as he watched, and he anticipated the arrival of Ana and Emerson. However, the influx stopped abruptly after a few more minutes, with no sign of his brother or sister. Or Birdie, for that matter. He could only hope that his friend had been able to pass on instead of being a victim of Grace's a second time.

He made eye contact with Charlie, who did not look nearly as cold as he felt, but looked like she could fall asleep on her feet. She raised her eyebrows at him, a quizzical expression on her face. She asked, "Now what?"

It was time for him to take over. To tell them all how he planned on getting the living out safely. Jacques swallowed hard, fighting back memories of the night he lost Ana and Emerson. He'd failed that night. What if he failed this time? They'd already lost Rachelle, Birdie, and potentially Mac.

Charlie put her hand on his forearm, and the skin there almost burned with her heat. He felt a charge of something akin to static electricity race up through the point of contact. There was sorrow and understanding in her eyes, like she was reading his thoughts. Something else, as well. Something he couldn't identify. "I listened to you that night, and I survived. *We* survived, Jacques. We will this time, too."

"You don't know that."

She shrugged. "Premonitions was my mom's power. Not mine. But I trust you. I trusted you then, and I trust you now."

He frowned. He hadn't been able to find out what Madeleine Erschon's gift was, but he'd assumed it was something like Charlie's. "Your mom had premonitions?"

"Not the time, boss." The familiar voice jolted him. He turned toward it, and Charlie's heat left him as her hand fell from his forearm. Birdie stroked a hand down a beard that glimmered with silver like it had been painted with moonlight. His other hand was against his abdomen, clutching the grotesque bow of intestines.

"Oh, Birdie," Charlie whispered, grief in her voice. "I'm so sorry."

"Not your fault." Birdie gave her a kind smile, and behind him the ghosts shifted and drew closer to them. He shifted his attention to Jacques. "Or yours either. But there's a time for grieving and pity, and this ain't it. Now, sorry I'm late, but this maneuvering without a body thing takes some getting used to. So, what's the plan, brother?"

"The plan?" Jacques asked stupidly as grief and happiness at seeing his friend again played emotional ping-pong with his heart.

"You didn't call us up for shits and giggles," Birdie replied. "You don't make a move like that unless you've got a plan."

Jacques licked his lips and struggled to get his thoughts together. There were several parts to what he wanted to do, but what it boiled down to was something he couldn't believe he was suggesting. "Kill it with fire."

A little warmth returned to the room then, or was he imagining things? Had he gotten used to the temperature? Or had some of the ghosts fled when they heard what he said? A glance around the room showed him that the room was basically as full as it had been, but he felt like something or someone was missing.

Brow furrowed, he turned his attention back to the living.

Charlie's eyes were wide and filled with fear. "Fire?"

He nodded. "We didn't start the fire then, but it ended things. It should work here."

"Or maybe it stopped because we got out of there and they were dead, Jacques!" Charlie's voice went up an octave or two and then cracked.

He didn't blame her. He didn't want to face fire again like that either. But he didn't see any other option. He did, however, need to get her on board. He knew Bird would back him. "You just said you trusted me. Were you lying?"

She put her hands to her mouth, hiding it from view, but then shook her head. "No. I meant it."

"Then act like it," he said simply. "Trust me to do what I do."

She took a deep, shuddering breath, and then gave him a resolute nod. "But how? There are no active gas lines and we'd have to start the fire in multiple places at once, or else it'll just get tamped out. Also, asbestos?"

Her brain was going in the right direction. She was with him now. Good. He inclined his head in the direction of the spirits who were now just a few feet or so away from them. "That's where they come in."

At first it didn't seem like the spirits were listening when he began to lay out the plan. Like Charlie was all that existed for them. Once she noticed, she commanded them to listen to him. After that, things went better. He knew what they were asking was a lot, and there was no guarantee that every one of the spirits would help them, but the more that did the better their chances.

As he talked, the spirits moved closer to Charlie. Unhampered by the need to respect the mass of physical objects, many of them walked or floated through the tables and chairs until they could touch her. None of them did it for long, but the ones who did suddenly seemed more present than they had. With the first few touches, Charlie visibly shuddered, but she stood calmly as he talked, eyes fastened on him.

When he was done, the spirits began departing. He could only pray that they'd disappeared to do what he'd asked. They'd find out soon, either way.

As Birdie turned to leave, Charlie called his name. He stopped, turning back to look at her. "Mac," she said quietly.

"Mac disappeared. Grace took her into the walls somehow. Can you... can you find her? Please?"

Birdie flicked a glance at Jacques. Even in death, he still respected his friend's leadership. When Jacques nodded, Birdie said, "One big Mac, coming up."

And then he was gone, and it was just the two living alone in the room again. He held out a hand. Charlie stared at it for a few seconds, and then placed her hand in his. They stood there for a moment, drawing strength from each other. Then, feeling the need to lighten the mood, Jacques grinned. "You know, I think the day Emerson noticed you developed boobs was one of the most disconcerting of his life. Suddenly, you were a *girl.* He didn't know what to think, but he sure as hell couldn't stop looking."

When she blushed, he laughed. Together, they got to work.

CHAPTER FIFTY-EIGHT

Birdie'd been aware of his new existence for just a few moments before Charlie called them all to the conference room. Long enough to have seen his mutilated body and worked out the basics on how to move just before the undeniable call pulled him away from the room and toward what had been a bittersweet reunion with Jacques and Charlie.

Now he was on a search and rescue mission on which Mac's life depended. And after that? Maybe then he'd give in to the rage and desire for revenge that had fueled him since he woke up in this form. He'd find the one who'd murdered him and put a permanent end to that psychotic motherfucker's existence. Bird was already sure he was going to hell for the kills he'd committed in service to his country, so what did one more matter? At least this one would feel good.

So, while the living and the dead put their plan into action, Birdie headed for the basement. There was a chance Mac was somewhere else, but Grace—or whatever entity inhabited it—clearly considered it their home base. As soon as he hit the bottom of the stairs, he knew he was right. There was a spring of energy somewhere here. One that hadn't been present when he'd first awoken, and one that beckoned to him like a supreme meat lover's pizza and a bottle of beer.

The only question was where? He didn't have time to search every room. Grace wasn't exactly the type to stash Mac somewhere safe and offer her tea. He decided he'd play a quick game of hot and cold. He hadn't sensed Mac's presence until he got down here, so it made sense there would be some area affect happening. Quickly, he set off down the hallway. Almost immediately, her energy began fading. He back-tracked, pushing into the morgue. Memories of the fight they'd had against the thing possessing Chelle, of what he'd done afterward, made the search difficult. Even more so when he stuck his head through the drawer where they'd put Rachelle, just in case the sick fuck had stashed her on top of him. Luckily, the search went quickly as the further he got from the hallway, the 'colder' his search got.

In the hallway again, the feeling of Mac's energy zipped through him. She was somewhere nearby, but if he yelled, would she hear him? If he yelled, would that spur whoever was holding her captive to hurry up? He couldn't risk it. He went into the file room, with the same results. Frustration had him slapping a hand against the wall, only to be denied the sensation of impact as his hand went through it.

As he started to step back into the hall, he became aware of another presence that had just entered the basement, resonating with an evil that he intimately recognized. Peeking around the door frame, Birdie watched the spirit disappear into a door underneath the basement stairs that he hadn't noticed. A second later, Mac's energy flared, bolstered by fear.

He wanted it. Wanted to bask in her energy, to feed on it. As disgusted as he was by the thoughts, he couldn't deny the truth behind them. And if he wanted it, then surely the asshole who had offed him did too. Mac was alone with him somewhere in there. It had taken him just minutes to kill Birdie. How long did Mac have?

Birdie ran into, and through, the janitor's closet. He entered the small room just in time to duck as something flew at his head, as Mac yelled at the figure to go fuck himself with a rusty scalpel. Pride bloomed fast and hard in him. That was his Mac.

He straightened up and caught a look at her as she dodged behind the back of a restraint chair. Blood coated her cheeks from just below her eyes down, and her blonde hair was sticking straight up, streaked with red like she'd run her hands through it. Blood traced figures on her arms as well, though with her movement he couldn't get a clear look at them.

The figure, which he could now place as a surgeon, stepped forward with clear intent to just go through the chair to get to Mac. In response, his friend stabbed out with something she clutched in her hand. The movement was enough to make the surgeon stop his forward movement.

Neither of them seemed to have noticed him, and since Mac was holding her own at the moment, he took a second to look around the room. He needed a way to help his friend, but t none of their traditional protective gear was in the room, and he hadn't had time to even see if he could bring anything solid with him.

"Birdie?" Mac's voice grabbed his attention. He looked over to see her staring at him, mouth slightly open. "What happened?"

The surgeon made his move while she was distracted, lunging toward her. Birdie knew what he was about to do was stupid. That he'd just fall right through the other spirit. However, if it even just distracted the man long enough for Mac to get safe again, it was worth it. He put everything he had into a tackle that hit the figure squarely in the chest.

The impact tore grunts from both of them, though at least in Birdie's case it was more from surprise that impact had happened than from the force of the collision. They hit the wall to the right, phasing through it as if it were nothing more than a curtain of air and landed in a small alcove already occupied by a mummified corpse.

The surgeon dissipated, slipping through Birdie's grasp while he knelt there, knees halfway into the floor, mind cataloging what he was seeing, gazed fixed on the long, blond braid draped over one shoulder and the iron chain wrapped around her head and torso. Mac's yelp jerked him back to the present. Acting quickly, apologizing as he did so, Birdie grabbed the chain—and oh shit, touching it was excruciating—unwound it. Fighting the desperate need to drop it and stop the pain, he threw himself back through the wall, hoping with everything he had that the chain would come with him.

The chain landed near the chair, and he landed on top of it. Searing heat bit into his torso, and he rolled to the side to get away from it. Pain ate at the very atoms of his existence, and his ability to think was being consumed along with it. It was all he could do to try to hold himself together and pray that Mac understood why he'd brought the chain to her.

Mac did. Fresh blood streaming down one arm, she dove for the chain even as the surgeon swiped at her with the scalpel again. Birdie saw red well on her back as she went down, but then she was coming back up, arms full of iron links that she tossed at the murderous spirit.

The surgeon screamed, form exploding into black mist at the touch of the chains. And his Mac, his beautiful, wonderful, foul-mouthed Mac, didn't just fall to the floor in relief, thinking it was all over now. Instead, forgoing the horror movie damsel bullshit, she picked the chain up from where it landed and quickly wrapped it around her neck and torso, the loose end going twice around her hand with several links hanging from her clenched fist.

"Try to get me now, motherfucker," she spat.

Birdie laughed, and the eerie connection he shared with his murderer lessened. "I think he ran for now."

"Good," Mac said, but kept the chain around her as she turned and knelt beside her friend. Her expression was sorrowful, but her tone was light as she said, "Not the best look for you, bud."

"Looks better on me than you," he told her, meaning it with all his heart. God, he needed to rest. To recharge. But he couldn't. Not before he got her to safety.

She put a hand to the outline of his shoulder, and he felt her life's energy—nothing like Charlie's but powerful in its own right—start to flow into him. He was dying of thirst and she was a gallon jug of ice-cold water. He needed everything she could give. That was enough to have him shaking his head. "Don't touch, Mac. I'm... feeding off you, I think."

"Then have a snack," Mac said, not moving her hand. "But if you go for the Thanksgiving feast, I'll smack your ass with the chain, we clear?"

"Crystal," he said, and let the energy flow between them until she started to sway. It wasn't enough to get him back to full strength, but he wasn't worried he was going to lose himself again just yet.

Once he'd figured out how to go from horizontal to vertical again, he told her what the game plan was as soon as they'd gotten her out of the room. He could see the doubt in her eyes, but she said nothing, instead choosing to start tossing the room looking for a key to the door.

CHAPTER FIFTY-NINE

Charlie and Jacques were piling papers from the filing cabinets under the table in the conference room when the sound of a door opening sent them jolting upward. Charlie smacked her head into the underneath of the table and fell back on her ass. A long-fingered, feminine hand entered her field of vision. "Full of grace, I see."

The voice was warm and smooth. The hand made of flesh and blood. Charlie grabbed hold of it, letting Mac pull her to her feet. She fell into the other woman, wrapping her arms around her neck and squeezing her. She'd never really expected to see her again, or at the very least see her alive again. Birdie had carried out a miracle. "You're stupid," she muttered, wanting to kiss her and smack her all at the same time. Take her out to her camper, clean her up, and check her all over for wounds she could kiss better. Instead, she said, "We split up. We weren't supposed to split up." She pulled back so that she could look at Mac, but kept her arms around her. "Have you never seen a horror movie? Seriously?"

Mac bit her lip. "I couldn't help it. I wasn't in control of myself until it was too late."

"Well, that makes me feel a little bit better. I hadn't had you pegged for a complete idiot." It matched, too, given Jacques' behavior earlier. She leaned back, studying the blond, taking in the blood coating her face and arm. "What happened? Where did you go? What happened to you?"

Mac shook her head, her eyes going dark. It was clear

she'd been through something bad, and equally clear she had no desire to talk about it.

Birdie said, "Think we should concentrate on the getting out, do the catching up later."

"Yeah, I suppose." Charlie gave Mac one last squeeze and t stepped back. She looked over at the cameraman, now standing next to Jacques. He didn't look quite as present as he had when he left to find Mac. Like he'd used himself up in some ways.

For the first time, Charlie found herself fleetingly thankful that she could do what she did. Because while she couldn't bring Birdie back from the dead, she could fix this. She stepped over to him. "Permission to kiss you, sir?"

"Don't think you can, Princess," he said, looking genuinely regretful.

"Wanna bet?" She concentrated, not on him, but on herself. Remembered the tingly feeling that came through her with exerting control over her power. Her emotions running high because of Mac, it was easy to wrangle a small piece of the energy. To wrap it around her hands. It took a heartbeat to do. Maybe less. Hands feeling like they were just waking up after the nerves had fallen asleep, she placed her palms on either side of Birdie's face.

The contact was barely detectable, but it was there. Real. Birdie's eyes widened in shock, and she heard Jacques say something in French right before she pressed her lips to Birdie's. She kissed him, hard but chaste, then stepped back, grinning at him.

"Huh," she said. "Ghosts can blush. Who knew."

"Hmph," Birdie grumbled, tugging at his beard. He was now almost solid in appearance.

"What in the hell did I miss?" Mac asked, going to Jacques. He wrapped her in a hug, lifting the blonde woman off her feet. Mac gave a childlike sigh.

"Figured out how to help Charlie channel her energy," Jacques replied.

Without missing a beat, Mac said, "Pissed her off, didn't you?"

Charlie snapped her head in Mac's direction. "How'd you know?"

"Tropes exist for a reason." She winked at her. "Pissing someone off is pretty much the go-to key for unlocking power."

At Charlie's narrowed eyes, she continued in a light voice, "You aren't the only one who watches horror movies, Sweet Cheeks."

Mac clearly wasn't okay, but neither were any of them. If this ridiculousness would get them through it, Charlie was willing to roll with it. "Sweet Cheeks?!"

Jacques clapped his hands together. "Alright, let's focus, people."

Charlie blushed as she shifted her focus to the lead ghost hunter, feeling like she'd been called out for not paying attention in class. "Sir, yes sir!"

Jacques' lips twitched. "Glad to see you know your place."

Birdie guffawed.

Jacques turned his attention to their body-challenged friend. "Can you leave the hospital? Rachelle tried, after, but ..."

"I think he can," Charlie answered for him, approaching the exterior wall and carefully touching her fingers to it. Time to test a theory. She closed her eyes for a second, letting herself feel the energy threading through the materials. "It feels different up here." She opened her eyes. "It's strongest on the lower levels. I don't know if it's because it is thinking like a human or because it just isn't strong enough to exert full control up here like down there, but it's weaker. We can't get through, but I bet he can."

Jacques nodded in her direction, then turned his attention back to Bird. "It's a big risk. There's a chance Charlie's wrong. It could ... You could ... I don't want to ask, but can you get to Kiffer? Try to communicate with him? Let him know what's going on? If you don't want to risk it, I understand. We'll figure something else out."

"Got it, boss," Birdie said. "Don't worry." He walked over to the wall. "Banshee Investigations saved me," he said to the room. "Didn't really ever talk about it because I didn't want to, but it did. Even with how this mission turned out, I don't regret a thing. I would have died sooner without you all."

He disappeared through the wall.

Charlie watched him go, then said, "No, uh, tentacle things. I think he made it through okay."

Jacques and Mac both made sounds of relief.

CHAPTER SIXTY

Going through a wall was a disconcerting experience, even though he'd had to do it a few times now. Hovering in thin air several feet in the air afterward? If Birdie'd had any bodily fluids left, there's a strong chance he might have pissed himself.

As it was, Birdie had to reassure himself for at least a minute that physical rules no longer applied to him while hovering in mid-air before he could focus on moving. It wasn't easy. Every action took a lot of concentration. Old habits still had him scanning the area for danger, though. His eyes brushed over Charlie's truck several times on the way down.

His progress slowed when the beginnings of an idea clicked in his brain. The truck was old. Old enough it predated any computer chips if memory served him right.

Finally reaching the doors to the RV, he got his own surprise when he looked inside. Kiffer was not alone. Another ghost was already there, standing beside him while he sat on one stool, eyes fastened on a monitor. Kiffer's screen showed a low-quality image of Jacques, Mac, and Charlie piling papers under the conference room table.

The other ghost, who appeared to be a teenage boy, holding onto a wire and muttering encouragement. Bird stepped into the RV. The screen fuzzed completely and went out. The boy looked around him and scowled as Kiffer made a sound of despair.

Spotting Birdie, the boy said, "Stay outside the RV, bro. It can't handle both of us."

Heeding the wisdom of his words, Birdie resumed his position just outside the RV doors. The kid was familiar. Looked like the one in the family picture that Jacques pulled out to look at sometimes when he thought no one else was looking. "Emerson?"

Looking surprised, the kid gave him a chin lift, then looked at the screen again just as another ghost, one Birdie didn't recognize, entered the room. Wishing they had sound, Birdie watched as Charlie talked to it, then dug something out of her pocket and laid it on the table. It was too small to tell what it was.

Shortly thereafter, the three living left the room.

Emerson frowned and jiggled the wire. "Come on," he hissed. "Where are you?"

"Have you tried talking to Kiffer?"

"Yeah," Emerson said, not taking his eyes off the screen. "He's kind of oblivious, though. It's taking all my concentration just to keep him plugged in to this." He cut his eyes at him briefly. "How'd you get out?"

"Top floor. Weaker up there. You? Or have you been out here the whole time?"

"Time it right, you can get in and out on the bottom while the bad guy's distracted. Wouldn't try it now, though. He's got a good hold on things. Where are they?"

"Your sister here too?"

"Yeah. She's got her own job. Where the hell are you, Chuck?"

"I need to try to talk to him," Bird said, pointing at Kiffer.

Emerson glared at him.

"I'll be quick," he said, "but I know my way around this equipment. Think I can make things easier on you, too."

Emerson's lips disappeared into a thin line, and his brow furrowed. He huffed out a breath and dropped the line, heading toward the door. "Be quick," he said. "I don't like not having eyes on them."

"I will," Birdie reassured him, and stepped up into the RV. He came to stand beside Kiffer and stared at the keyboard and mouse. It was going to take a lot of work, but he felt like he could do it. Charlie's quick kiss had given him an energy jolt akin to drinking a triple espresso. Huffing, he maneuvered the mouse and opened the system's basic notepad system.

Kiffer didn't even look at the screen.

Rolling his eyes, Birdie typed, two fingering the keyboard. In life, his fingers would have been flying. In this existence, though? Pressing keys was damned hard work. Two was all he could do. But he did it as fast as he could.

He was halfway through the note by the time Kiffer looked at the screen and, as anyone who knew him could have predicted, startled violently. His friend read the words on the jumping screen and said, "Birdie?"

Birdie chose not to answer him. It was hard, but things were moving too fast right now for him to deal with his friend's grief. He ignored the question and kept typing. Finally, he was done. He stepped back away from the screen, which settled down.

Kiffer finished reading, foot bouncing. "That'll work," he said. "Has more chances than anything else I can think of, anyway." He grabbed a flashlight and headed out of the RV, stepping right through Emerson. Birdie followed him and waited while his friend searched for Charlie's keys.

Kiffer declared them nowhere to be found after a minute of frantic searching.

Birdie sighed. Things had just gotten a little more complicated. He considered things, and as Kiffer stepped aside to lean against the truck, peeked his head in. The hood latch was nowhere to be seen, but there was a picture on the back of the visor that had to be Charlie and her family. She was a cute kid, but what really caught his attention was the mom. Something about her looked damned familiar, but he couldn't put his finger on it. He shrugged it off, returning to the task at hand and remembering that on a truck this old, it was probably under the front of the hood.

"Shit," he said.

"What's happening?" Emerson was suddenly beside him, standing half-buried in the truck.

"Gonna need to teach him how to hot-wire a truck," Birdie told him. "Otherwise, I'm not sure we can get them out alive. Not with what they're planning."

"Can I help?"

Birdie thought about it for a second. Maybe the two of them working together could get it done. He thought through the plan of action in his head, then let Emerson know what he needed to do. When the kid understood, Birdie headed back into the RV where Kiffer had disappeared again. Time for Plan B.

CHAPTER SIXTY-ONE

Inside the hospital, the three people headed down to the level. They could have moved faster if they'd split up, but that was out of the question now. And part of the reason they'd asked for the ghosts' help.

The plan was simple. On each floor, they were going to prepare areas of flammable materials. Prepare, but not light. They didn't want to make that move until the time was right. They strategically placed fire sources on each floor to increase the chances of a blaze, hoping the entity could not handle them all simultaneously.

But if it could, that was where the second part of the plan came in. While the strongest ghosts, the ones capable of doing more than just shuffling papers along the floor or creating breezes, were going to help ignite the flames, the other ghosts were going to raise hell. Not literally, of course, as that would kind of defeat the purpose. But they were tasked with keeping the flames going, no matter what. Normally this wasn't something they'd be able to accomplish, given that they fed on energy, but Charlie had reassured them it wouldn't be a problem. She'd provide them all the food they needed, and in return, they'd provide the supernatural edge to the fire that would render the asbestos useless.

Jacques wasn't sure how she was planning on doing that without feeding the entity as well, but when he'd broached the subject, she'd told him firmly, "Trust me." That was the only thing she'd said about the matter.

The next floor had ugly cloth dividers they removed, and

they also took old bed sheets from closets and beds, piling them up in each ward. It wasn't until Jacques was tearing in half the book of matches to split between them that he realized they had another problem. The matches, which Jacques had fished out of the bottom of one of his cargo pockets, had gotten damp, if not outright wet at some point. When he tried to light one, hoping for once luck would be on their side, there was no reaction. The head of the match just left a discolored smear against the striking strip.

"Goddammit," Jacques cursed, flinging the pile of matches. They couldn't catch a fucking break. There were four floors at Union Grace, and they'd given their only working lighter to the ghost on the top floor. There was no way in hell they were going to pull this off. Not unless they split up. And if they split up, he knew not all of them would make it out alive.

He wasn't going to lose any more people. He had to think.

Mac started rifling through her own pockets, looking for anything they could use. Charlie slipped off her backpack and started digging through it again.

His eyes fell on the neon emergency ghost kit Mac had slung over one shoulder. He frowned and took his own off, sitting it on a bed and pulling it open, while the older female ghost he'd noticed during their meeting hovered over his shoulder. Had he packed anything in there that they could use? The kits were basic. Items meant to give them a chance to escape. Nothing meant for standing their ground. And there was that whole ghosts-feeding-on-energy thing. He hadn't seen the point of bringing candles when they could just be snuffed out.

One by one, he yanked items out of the bag, laying them on the bed. Salt. Iron fillings. Holy water. Two crucifixes. Glow sticks because the misty fuckers could put out every other type of light, but they couldn't screw with those.

Desperation going, he kept rooting around in the bag. Anise oil in a small perfume bottle. A small music box that played Hallelujah. He'd gotten four of them online for cheap because why the hell not? Holy music was supposed to repel spirits.

His hand closed around one last object in the bag. It was wide enough he had to turn it around to get it out of the bag. Silver flares. That one had been one he'd debated on, but they said silver repelled evil. Unfortunately, silver flares weren't something they could use indoors without risking a fire, so he'd forgotten about them. There were three bundled together. Jacques smiled. "Thank you, anxiety."

Charlie and Mac froze, staring at him. He held up the gray sticks. "Flares."

"Boss man," Mac breathed. "I will never give you hell for your Mama Bearing ever again." She slid her bag off and started rummaging for her own flares.

Jacques ripped off the perforated plastic holding the sticks together. "Holding you to that. Prep 'em so that all they have to do is strike it."

Once they had all six flares ready, he mimed the motions to the old woman. She rolled her eyes and mouthed something. He figured there was nothing lost by not hearing whatever she'd said to him. They moved on.

It didn't take long for them to hit the ground floor. There, it was a little more interesting to find flammable materials. However, rancid oil and old napkins got the cafeteria set, and they scavenged more cloth partitions for the emergency room and other areas.

When it came time to go down into the basement, all three of them hesitated. The first floor had been bad enough, but they knew now the entity had set up its primary shop down there.

"I'll do it," Jacques said, heart racing. "I'm not risking

either of you. You stay up here. I'll be back in a couple of minutes."

Charlie grabbed his arm before he could move. "I'll do it," she told him. "I'm safer, and you know it."

Her words brought a sense of deja vu, overlaying the present with memories of the past. This time he couldn't agree with her, though. "This thing's been after you since it woke up," he said. "It wants you, and you know it."

"It won't get me," she said, but there was uncertainty in her eyes. And she was tired, he could tell. She swayed on her feet, with purple smudges beneath her eyes. Everything was taking its toll on her. "I'll poof it if it gets close."

"Charlie," he put his hand on hers. "You need to save your strength for the fires."

"I can do it," she said fiercely.

"But you don't have to." Ana, who hadn't shown herself since the chapel, appeared by the two of them. "I'll take care of it."

"No." Jacques shook his head, the sight of his older sister's form causing a mixture of grief, relief, and determination to swirl inside him. He was so damned glad the entity hadn't gotten to her yet and be damned if he'd lose her all over again now. "If you go down there, it's going to catch you. You understand? It will kill you. Your spirit."

"I'll be okay," Ana soothed him. "I'm not a ghost that was made here. He doesn't have that sort of control over me. He can trap me, but he can't destroy me."

Charlie started to say something, eyes dark and pained, but Ana shot her a sharp look. She closed her mouth, then gave Ana a nod. Then she said, "Ana has more of a chance down there than any of us do. If anyone can do it, it's her."

Jacques knew something wasn't being said, but the two women presented a united, immovable front. He looked at

Ana. "Be safe," he said. "Please. Please be safe. I can't lose you."

"I love you, Squirt," she said, leaning in to place a ghostly kiss on his cheek. Then she plucked one flare from his unresisting hands and headed down into the basement, fading from view before she'd even disappeared into the stairwell.

Charlie closed her eyes. Mac came over to stand beside her, slipping a supportive arm around her waist. Jacques moved to her other side, wrapping an arm around her shoulders. They stood together, anticipation rising with the extending silence, until Charlie abruptly said, "It's time."

There was a moment where Jacques felt like he couldn't breathe, the air growing incredibly thick around them. Then power burst out of Charlie again, and she sagged in their arms. They caught her, and Jacques scooped her up in his arms, relieved to see she was dazed, but not quite unconscious.

"Move," he ordered Mac. Together, they moved to the first of the two piles they'd decided to light for themselves. Mac twisted the cap off the flare, holding it away from her as a shower of sparks shot from the end. She held it long enough to make sure it was going properly before tossing it on the pile, which instantly caught alight.

It took them less than two minutes to do the same to the pile in the Emergency Room. Then they were heading back to the area near the receptionist's desk as smoke filled the space. Jacques hoped they'd be safer for a little longer there, away from flames and in an open space.

"Come on, Bird," he whispered as he sank to his knees with Charlie still cradled in his arms, Mac beside him.

CHAPTER SIXTY-TWO

"Get out of the way, Banshee. I'm coming through the front doors." Kiffer's voice was thick with static, but clear. It stunned all of them for a second. The wool clouding Charlie's mind was just starting to fade, so she was still processing what she heard as Mac and Jacques hauled her to her feet.

"Come on," Mac told her, wrapping an arm around her waist. Together, the three of them moved off to the side, hunkering down in the doorway to the long-term nursing care wing. It was on the opposite side of the lobby from the emergency room. Spirits, some suggestions of forms while others were clearly outlined, circled around them. Smoke swirled outside the perimeter they formed but did not touch the three inside.

"What the hell is he—" Jacques didn't have time to finish asking the question before the sound of metal ramming glass filled the air.

Mac draped herself over Charlie, covering her head and neck with one arm. Charlie tucked her face against Mac's chest while Jacques joined in the pile, protecting Mac's back with his front.

Oxygen from outside entered the locked-down building and made the fires around the three people bloom with fierce heat. They got to their feet and looked at what remained of the glass doors. Charlie's truck had outright destroyed them, and they could see daylight around the mangled frames.

Inside the truck, slumped over the steering wheel, Kiffer started to stir.

Charlie felt a brief pang at the damage to her truck, seeing the smoke rising from its engine compartment. But a truck could be replaced. Jacques and Mac could not.

She grinned at Mac. The blonde grinned back, then wrapped one arm around Charlie's waist and pulled her close. Charlie had just enough time to take a breath before Mac's lips were on hers. She hugged the woman and kissed her back until Jacques interrupted and suggested they wait until they were out of the burning building.

"Spoilsport," Mac muttered against Charlie's lips before pulling back.

Mind a little clearer thanks to the surge of hormones Mac delivered, Charlie let the blonde drag her over to the truck. She rested against the fender while Jacques and Mac got a clearly concussed Kiffer free of the truck. She looked around the lobby, the hair on the back of her neck standing up. The flames doing their best to devour the room should have been spurred by the influx of oxygen from outside, she thought. But that's not what she saw. Instead, the flames were beginning to die down, shrinking beneath an invisible blanket determined to smother them. A pillar that, seconds ago, had been fully engulfed was now only halfway consumed. Charlie could swear the smoke didn't look as dense as it had, either.

It wasn't enough, she understood then. They might be able to escape, but the entity would still live. They'd hurt it maybe, but the fires wouldn't be the killing blow they'd hoped. They wouldn't be able to destroy Union Grace and the entity that controlled it this way.

And it was watching them, she realized as her eyes caught on a slim figure slowly strolling toward them from the stairwell near the cafeteria. A woman, short and curvy, with long blonde hair and blue eyes. One Charlie memorized from the picture she carried in her truck.

For a moment, just a split second, Charlie considered it could actually be her mother. Then she told herself to stop being a dumb ass. Her mother wouldn't be doing a villain's swagger up the hall to them, and the entity had already tried this trick once. It was confident in its victory. That the group had done everything they could, but it had still come out on top. Now it was just toying with them.

"You die and for all we know, whatever sort of paranormal nuclear reactor you have in you might go into meltdown." Jacques' words flashed through her head, sparking a defiant plan.

Charlie turned to the Banshee team just as Kiffer's feet touched the tile floor. "Let's go," she said, gesturing at the doorway. "Let's get the fuck out of here!"

A flaming ceiling tile smacked down next to Mac. Charlie kicked it out of the way before the flames could catch Mac's clothing.

The truck took up most of the space of the doorway, but there was a small opening a couple of feet across on one side. They could wedge themselves through.

Jacques told the blonde to go first. Once she wiggled through the opening, they worked together to get Kiffer through the space. Charlie urged them on as much as she could, feeling the steady approach of the figure closing in behind her. She had to get them out. Had to make sure they were safe.

Jacques tried to get her to go before him, but she shoved him into the opening, telling him, "Stop being a gentleman and get the fuck out."

When he was through, he turned and held out a hand to her. "Come on," he urged as another tile hit the ground next to her. "Let's go."

For a moment, Charlie considered it. But only for a

moment. She'd been running since she was a teen. From her ability. From herself. She was afraid that if she left Union Grace, she would continue to run from it, because she'd learned how to wield it, but not how to stop it. She'd never not be a danger to others.

At least here she could do some good with it. She could make sure the entity didn't get a chance to hurt anyone else. Maybe she could even save the other spirits inside. Her power hadn't hurt them before.

Charlie looked over Jacques' shoulder at Mac. "Keep him safe," she called. Mac looked confused but nodded.

"Charlie? What the hell? Get out here!" Jacques started to come back in through the doorway to get her, but Mac wrapped her arms around him and hauled him backward. While Mac did that, Charlie saw Birdie's still solid looking form saying something to Kiffer. The other man's face registered confusion and then acceptance. Kiffer nodded once, and then Birdie came in to join her.

Charlie raised her eyebrows as he came to stand beside her. "Bad idea."

"Maybe," the ever-stoic man said. "But you have your job, and I have mine. If you fail, I'm going to make sure the sonuvabitch who killed me won't hurt anyone ever again. If you don't, then I'm gonna give his ass a personal escort to hell."

"How do you know what I'm planning to do?"

He rolled his eyes, and said, "You got this." Then he strode off deeper into the hospital, completely ignoring the entity that was approaching the receptionist's desk.

"Why didn't you leave with them?" it asked. The tone was one of worry, but there was nothing but calculation in the ice blue eyes.

Charlie shook her head as she walked toward it, studying the apparition. It looked so real. Almost real enough to touch, if she ignored the way portions of it wavered, going translucent for a heartbeat. Not quite a fully physical manifestation. Not yet.

"I couldn't leave you, Momma," she said. She cast a fearful glance at the fire around them. She wondered if she was laying it on too thick. Acting had never been her strong suit. But she had to try. "I wanted to be with you. But I'm scared."

"Aww, baby," the blonde woman opened her arms, smiling. "It'll be okay. Come here. I've got you."

The words hurt. She knew what the demon was doing, that it was playing to that child-like part of her. She knew it was bullshit, and yet it still hurt. Charlie had dreamed for years of what it would be like to feel her mother hugging her once again, to hear her mother's voice. This blatant mockery used against her made it all the worse.

Charlie accepted that pain as she stepped into the imposter's embrace. She allowed herself a momentary second of imagination that the person she hugged was her mother. She closed her eyes, resting her head on the woman's shoulder, and pulled at the power deep inside her.

She was tired. Flat out exhausted, but it was a physical exhaustion. Her power was there, waiting, and it responded eagerly to her call. Bright and so white it was almost blue, vibrating with energy. Gorgeous now that she had no reason to fear it.

She concentrated on it, on the beauty of what she was taking a moment to fully see and accept for the first time, as the entity plunged a scalpel inside her. Used the sharp pain to open the floodgates wider. It wanted her power? Fine. It could have all of it.

Charlie stumbled as the next stab of the blade punctured her diaphragm, starting to fall, but the entity didn't let her. Instead, it steadied her, held her up with an iron grip on her shoulder, beaming.

"You should have run while you had the chance," it told her, blue eyes going inky black. It drew the scalpel back for a thrust Charlie knew would penetrate her heart.

"That's my line," she gasped as the blade plunged forward, sliding between her ribs and burying itself deep inside the muscle of her heart. There wasn't much pain, mostly a weird flutter in her chest as her heart tried to beat. Otherwise, her body was awash with the tingling sensation that grew exponentially stronger.

Jacques had been right.

As Charlie fell to the floor, right before she went nuclear, she had just enough time to register the other's dawning awareness that it had just fucked up. She smiled as her world became nothing but brilliant white light.

CHAPTER SIXTY-THREE

Six hours later, Union Grace still burned.

Jacques, Kiffer, and Mac sat together in their camping chairs, watching the fire. Their cell phones all worked now, but none of them had any desire to call for help. Not yet. Not until the hospital was so far gone that they were sure it—or the demon inhabiting it—couldn't come back from it.

Jacques still wasn't sure what happened after he'd gotten out of the building. He remembered urging Charlie to hurry up and her being weird about it. But then everything blurred out. When he'd come back to awareness a couple minutes later, it was just in time for all of them to get knocked on their ass by an explosion from within the building. One leaving visible cracks all over the stone exterior.

He'd screamed for Charlie, but Mac and Kiffer wrapped their arms around him and held on for dear life. They kept holding until he stopped struggling. Until his screams turned to tears. And then they'd joined him in that grief, sharing it with him. Only the sight of bright white wisps seeping out of the building's cracks, floating up a few feet before blinking out of existence provided any comfort. They all understood what they were looking at. Union Grace had lost its hold on the ghosts within.

There'd been no sign of Birdie, Ana, and Emerson after the explosion. Jacques could only hope they were amongst the spirits who were moving onto the afterlife they all deserved. His heart hurt, but he clung to the idea that they were finally at peace.

He prayed Charlie was, too.

CHARLIE HAWKINS STOOD on the grounds outside Union Grace, watching the Banshee Investigations team react as the hospital's structural supports finally gave out and the building levels came crashing down on each other. As they cheered, she looked at the teen standing beside her and squeezed his hand. "Did I mention I missed you?"

She could see herself in his eyes now, short and mostly lacking in curves. Like she had been when life had been good to her.

"Yeah, but you can keep on," Emerson De Molyneux said. "Glad to have you back, Chuck."

Charlie narrowed her eyes. "Do not call me that." He knew she hated to be called that.

"Or what?" Emerson let loose of her hand and stepped carefully backward. "Whatcha gonna do about it, Chuck?"

She lunged at him, but he wasn't there. He was already running, feet barely touching the grass. "Get back here! And no fair using super speed. I don't know how to do that yet!" She could run like normal, but normal wasn't nearly fast enough to catch him.

"Last one to the RV is a rotten egg," Emerson called.

"We'll mess their equipment up!"

Emerson halted at the door to the RV, watching her catch up to him. When she halted, gasping for air she no longer needed, he said, quite seriously, "Look, Chuck—"

She balled her hand into a fist and shook it at him.

He grinned, placed a hand over his heart. "It is a sibling's most solemn duty to mess up their other sibling's stuff."

"If we make him lose all his footage, he's gonna murder us," she told him, but she was already starting to giggle.

"Yeah? How? Not a necromancer, last time I checked."

She considered this for a second. "Fair point!" She threw herself at Emerson as she spoke. He caught her and the two tumbled to the floor of the RV as the equipment on the surrounding racks went haywire.

"What the hell?" Jacques' voice boomed, coming to the doorway of the RV. He looked confused, and maybe a little hopeful. "What the hell just happened?"

Knowing full well he couldn't see or hear them, Charlie told him, "Emerson did it." There was weird, staticky sound to her voice, and it took her a second to realize it was echoing through the spirit boxes. All of them. Even though she was pretty sure they didn't keep them turned on when they were put away.

Jacques went still as a statue, paling out. "...Charlie? Are you here?"

Charlie and Emerson looked at each other with wide eyes. Definitely an unexpected development. Emerson's full lips pulled back in a mischievous grin. Not knowing what he was planning, Charlie shook her head and tried to place a hand over his mouth.

He smoothly avoided it, grabbing her hand and trapping it against his chest. "Charlie's not here right now," he said, voice booming from the spirit boxes. "Leave a message after the beep. BEEP."

"Emerson? What the hell are you doing to my equipment?" Jacques' tone shifted from tentative hope to full-on annoyed younger brother.

The two teens clutched each other and howled with laughter.

END

ALSO BY JOURNEY SLOANE

If you enjoyed Surviving Union Grace, you should check these out!

- **"The Breeding Habits of Dragons"** — *Dragonesque*
- **"Ocean Games"** — *Illustrated Worlds Magazine*
- **"A Sister for Christmas"** — *HumourMe Magazine*

ABOUT THE AUTHOR

Journey Sloane is a writer of science fiction and horror with occasional dabbles of romance. Blurring lines and twisting tropes make them the happiest.

They live with their teenager, their two dogs, and their husband (in approximately that order of importance) and are one of those weird few who tried social media for several years and then went, "Nah, I'm good, thanks."

They have been published in Dragonesque, Humor Me Magazine, Illustrated Worlds, and Dark Stars, amongst others.

Fun fact: Surviving Union Grace is the result of a challenge to try to write inside the lines for the first time.

ALSO AVAILABLE FROM NIGHTMARE PRESS!

JENNY'S SPOOKY LITTLE TALES: VOL. 3

The Frightening Floyds have been researching and writing about the paranormal and all things strange and unusual for ten years. To celebrate, Jenny recently compiled ten of her favorite stories from the many books she has written with her husband Jacob, which became Jenny's Spooky Little Tales: Vol. 1. After that, she found ten more stories she really enjoyed, and that became Jenny's Spooky Little Tales: Vol. 2.

Now, she has compiled ten more for Jenny's Spooky Little Tales: Vol. 3. In this collection, you'll find more ghosts, Louisville's leaping alien, the wandering spirit of Walt Disney, two of history's most famous bombshells, an elusive black cat, and even stories from Jenny's memoirs. We hope you enjoy Jenny's Spooky Little Tales: Vol. 3.

www.ingramcontent.com/pod-product-compliance
Lightning Source LLC
La Vergne TN
LVHW091108080826
845145LV00008B/1847

* 9 7 8 1 6 4 9 0 5 0 4 5 8 *